THE PURITANS

The Moorhouse family have risen from the obscurity of an Ayrshire farm to a position of great prosperity in Victorian Glasgow. They are finally 'somebodies', which just makes Bel even more distressed by the behaviour of Phoebe and Henry – they don't seem to understand propriety. Phoebe's beginnings were as the half-sister of the Moorhouses, the daughter of a Highland tinker. She has grown up into a beautiful and elusive creature of the world, and is drawn away from Glasgow. Destiny sweeps her and her husband to Vienna, the romantic and enchanting capital of the Hapsburgs in its heyday of the 1880s...

THE PURITANS

THE PURITANS

by

Guy McCrone

Magna Large Print Books
Long Preston, North Yorkshire,
BD23 4ND, England.

British Library Cataloguing in Publication Data.

McCrone, Guy
   The puritans.

   A catalogue record of this book is
   available from the British Library

   ISBN   978-0-7505-3094-1

First published in Great Britain in 1947

Copyright © 1993 Guy McCrone

Cover illustration © Jill Battaglia/Arcangel Images

The right of Guy McCrone to be identified as the author of this work has been asserted by him in accordance with the Copyright, Designs and Patents Act, 1988

Published in Large Print 2010 by arrangement with Black & White Publishing Ltd.

Magna Large Print is an imprint of Library Magna Books Ltd.

Printed and bound in Great Britain by
T.J. (International) Ltd., Cornwall, PL28 8RW

Chapter One

'What do ye mean, Hayburn?'

There was no reply.

Had Henry Hayburn understood people as well as he understood machines, he would now have realised that his employer was very angry.

Not that the chairman showed it. He took his time. He straightened the large pad of fresh blotting-paper that lay in front of him. He set his pen-tray exactly symmetrical with it. He took up the holders to see that fresh pen-nibs had been put into them this morning. He flicked open the lid of his inkwell to make sure that there was the proper amount of ink. He pushed his letter-basket away from him as though to give himself space. Having done these things, he rested his elbows on either arm of his revolving office chair, brought the tips of his fingers together, looked for a moment through the window at a yard labourer who was wheeling a barrowful of smoking, burnt-out ash to the slag-heap; then, turning his eyes again to the young man on the other side of his desk, watched him without speaking.

The older hands in the office would have

understood the signs. When the chairman did these things, something was coming. It was a long-learnt trick of his, this arranging of everything around him. Thus only could he master himself; avoid saying what was rash or ill-advised. He looked at young Henry Hayburn steadily. That was a trick, too. The chairman knew that his personality was strong; that his gaze could be disconcerting.

The young man stood, ungainly and confused, his hands behind his back, looking, in spite of his beard, like an unrepentant schoolboy. A dark, untidy strand of hair fell on his brow, and his snub, sulky face was crimson. But there was no sign of yielding in the moody eyes that returned the domineering, practised stare of his employer.

The old man had had enough. Hayburn was refusing to take orders. At last the chairman spoke.

'Ye mean to tell me that ye're not going to do what ye're told in this office?' His voice was quietly controlled.

'Not when I know it's wrong, sir.'

'How do ye know it's wrong, Hayburn?'

'I worked it out for myself last night.'

The chairman parted his hands and trifled once more with the things on the desk in front of him. 'How old are ye, Hayburn?'

'Twenty-four, sir.'

'Well, I'm nearer seventy-four. And I don't

8

need to be told what's right and what's wrong by boys. It's cocksureness that's your trouble. How long have ye been here?'

'About six months, sir.'

'I've been here nearly sixty years.'

Again there was silence, and again, after a time, the chairman broke it.

'Well? Are ye going on with that job, Hayburn?'

'No.'

The old man jumped up. It was a long time since his authority had been flouted like this. 'Get your money from the cashier and get out of here!' He spoke through shut teeth. He turned away from Henry, striking his hands together behind his back, striding to the window, and gazing out fixedly.

Henry went. Presently, the chairman was surprised to find himself trembling.

At his age it wasn't good to allow himself to get so angry. He came back to his chair and sat down heavily.

'Impertinence!' he muttered to himself. But, as he formed the word, he knew it wasn't quite that with young Hayburn. There had been a clash of wills, and he had not succeeded in making the young man's will yield to his own. No. Young Hayburn might be headstrong and foolish. But this was not common impertinence. He was brilliant, and his brilliance, untempered by experience, made the boy arrogant.

But, if only for his health's sake, he must banish his anger. And he must make his peace with the son of his dead friend, Robert Hayburn.

He bent forward and banged the brass bell on his table. 'Is Hayburn there?'

Henry came back into the chairman's private room. He carried his hat.

The old man held out his hand. 'Ye're the son of a very old friend, Henry,' he said, using the young man's first name again now that he had ceased to be an employee. 'It would be a bad business for us if we didna part friends.'

There was a childish, almost appealing look in Henry's face as he took his hand, mumbling: 'Thank you, sir.'

'I thought I was doing you a good turn taking you in here. I thought that maybe–' The chairman had meant to say things about taking Henry's father's place; about helping Henry back to prosperity. But he realised in time that anything he might say would have an air of falseness to this strange young man with his strong opinions. There was nothing to do, then, but shake the hand that Henry gave him, wish him well, and repeat his hope that what had passed would make no difference to their friendship.

Henry stammered assurances. But as he turned and went out, each of them knew that they had merely thrown crumbs to appearances; that their ideas were flatly opposed; that there could never be any question of Henry's remaining in the employ of the established and unprogressive firm of which this old man was the chairman.

Chapter Two

Bel Moorhouse sat on the rocks, awaiting the arrival of her husband on the weekend steamer. From where she sat near the new-built pier, Brodick Bay stretched away from her in a crescent of summer loveliness. The sweep of golden sand. The little Highland village. The green woods. Above them the moors and hills, turning purple, here and there, with the first of the bell heather. And, assembling all this, giving shape to the picture, the elegant cone of Goatfell, basking up there across the bay in the July sunshine.

But Bel was not particularly in tune with all this beauty, as she sat, too carefully dressed for this, the least conventional of islands, absently digging the point of her parasol into a crevice of the rock. From time to time she looked up from her thoughts to assess the size of the squat black dot out there on the diamond horizon. The dot was her husband's steamer as it paddled its way across the breezy, sunlit Firth on its Saturday afternoon run to the Island of Arran.

No. It was all very well. Brodick was beautiful, of course, and the children liked running wild. But there were limits. After all, the Moorhouse family were turning into somebodies, and would have to live accordingly. Exactly a week ago, they had all spent the day at Duntrafford. Arthur's brother Mungo, by virtue of his marriage to its heiress, was, however simple his ways might seem, a man of substance. And David, Arthur's younger brother, had married another young woman of wealth. David was no countryman. He had poise to unite to the fortune his marriage had brought him. Bel had no doubt that he and his wife, Grace, would fly high before they had finished.

She did not suffer from any narrow jealousy, but she had no intention of being left behind. Were Mungo's and David's children to be allowed to grow up looking down their noses at Arthur's children? Not so long as the mother of Arthur's children had any say in the matter.

In the concentration of her thoughts, Bel dug her parasol into the crevice of the rock with so much force that when she drew it out again, she found, to her irritation, that the point had lost its metal ferrule. She turned it round, examined it ruefully, then laid it down by her side.

12

Out on the sparkling horizon the dot was beginning to increase in size. Bel experienced a quick, compensating emotion of pleasure that soon her husband would be with her. She leant forward and plucked a little posy of sea-pinks that were growing primly out of a compact cushion of green, wedged among the stones beside her. Neat-handed in everything, she began to shape these into a formal little bouquet which, perhaps, she would tie up with grass and give to her six-year-old daughter Isabel. Down there just beneath her, out of the wind, a glassy sea was rising and falling, breathing among the rocks. Looking into it, she could glimpse a waving garden of sea-weed, and, now and then, the silver belly of a fish.

Bel continued with Isabel's posy, thinking. Was it wrong to have social ambition for one's children. She could not think so. It was someone like Sophia Butter, who was inept with the mere mechanisms of life – remembering to pay the butcher and baker, inducing kettles to boil and pots to stew – who would tell you, piously, that her only ambition for her children was to have them become good and wholesome members of society. Bel could see no reason why riches and privilege should not be added to goodness and wholesomeness.

She was glad that Sophia and her family

had not taken a house in Brodick this summer. Their extreme homeliness, and the fact that Sophia was forever borrowing things she had forgotten to bring, would have annoyed her. Mary McNairn and her family were bad enough. But if, as relatives, they were without distinction, at least they were not without competence in conducting their lives. You could always reckon upon Mary providing her share of cosy, if pedestrian, hospitality.

This very afternoon, for instance, she had taken the whole of Bel's family to picnic and bathe in Glen Rosa. Phœbe, little Arthur and the two McNairn boys had had to walk; while Tom and Isabel, being younger, had gone with their Aunt Mary, the little twin cousins, a nursemaid, and much good food, in a farmer's wagonette. Bel sighed a little at the thought of Mary's picnic.

A little breeze had sprung up, rippling the plume in Bel's straw hat, and setting her wondering if strands of her fine, fair hair had come loose, thus making her untidy to meet her husband. Out in the sea the black dot had transformed itself into a midget paddle-steamer with a wisp of smoke blowing from its tiny funnel; and with little flashes of white showing, now and then, as the bow and the paddles encountered the waves that must be running out there beyond the bay. Bel turned towards the pier. People were beginning to move down to its end, for at Brodick the arrival of the steamer was ever an event of importance. Waiting at the gates of the pier were one or two farmers' traps and a cart. She stood up, shook the grass from the folds of her dress, made sure that it lay smooth on her waist and hips, adjusted her hat and hair as best she could, and picked up the damaged parasol. As she finished doing this, she was surprised to hear Mary McNairn calling her.

II

'Bel! Bel dear! Hullo!' Mary's flat voice was doing it's best to make itself heard.

Bel gave Mary a little wave of surprised recognition, as they advanced to meet each other across the natural lawn of short sea-grass which lay between the shore road and the rocks. How matronly Mary was becoming, Bel could not help thinking, as she took in her sister-in-law's plump figure, her too easily fitting black dress, the coloured shawl on her shoulders, and her flapping straw hat. After all, Mary was not yet forty; and Bel did not like to feel that her contemporaries were beginning to look old.

'I thought I would find you here,' Mary said as they wandered back for a moment to where Bel had been sitting.

15

'But how did you manage to come, Mary? I thought you were with the picnic in Glen Rosa.'

Mary explained that a friendly crofter had stopped his little cart to ask after the family. She had begged him for a lift. 'You see, I was worrying about George. I felt I wanted to come to meet him.'

'George?' Bel turned to her sister-in-law.

'Yes. He's not quite well. I've been worrying dreadfully.'

Bel looked at Mary, and received what almost amounted to a shock. For a moment a quick look of terror had risen to the surface of her plump complacence, then died away again as she took control of herself.

'But you haven't told me anything about this, Mary. George isn't really ill, is he?'

'I don't know. I hope not. He was to be examined this week. There's the steamer coming in. We'd better go.' Mary did not seem to want to speak of George's threatened illness further.

Bel followed her, wondering. The McNairns had always been so smug. Hopes, fears and tremulous uncertainties were things you simply couldn't connect with the McNairns. They weren't quite human. That they could have any possible spark of passion for each other, in their squat, well-fed bodies, was the last thing that would ever occur to anyone about George and Mary. But now,

16

surprisingly, Bel had caught a glimpse. People could love each other, then, even if they were fat and self-centred.

The steamer was in full view now. In a moment or two she would be slowing down. They could see the Saturday evening crowd from Glasgow leaning over her railings, eager to catch their first, close glimpse of the beloved island.

Bel took out the necessary coppers to pay for their admittance through the wicket gate of the pier, and they continued down its short length, preparing to meet their men-folk.

'Is anyone coming besides Arthur?' Mary asked presently.

'Henry Hayburn.'

'Did Phœbe know he was coming by this boat?'

'I don't know, Mary – yes, she must have known.'

'It's queer she didn't want to come down with me to meet him. There was room in the cart,' Mary said.

'I've never the least idea what's going on between these two. They don't seem to me to behave like an engaged couple.'

Now the *Ivanhoe* was in the bay, swinging round in order to take the pier at a proper angle. Daring spirits were out in rowing-boats, waving in the gaiety of their holiday mood to any passengers on board that would bother to wave back to them; waiting to row into the white foam that the steamer's paddles would presently leave in her wake.

'Do you think their marriage will ever come off?' Mary asked as they stood waiting.

Bel shook her head thoughtfully and shrugged.

'Do you think he's good enough for Phœbe?'

The picture of Phœbe's radiance, as she marshalled the children to take them off to the picnic today, came to Bel. A beautiful creature; and only nineteen. Why should she waste her loveliness on this graceless, talkative young man? And she didn't even seem to care much about him. If Henry still had his father's fortune, then, of course, it would have been different. But now he had nothing. He was, so far as Bel knew, a mere employee. And, as she had just been reminding herself as she sat there on the rocks, the Moorhouse family were turning into somebodies.

'No, Mary. I don't think Henry Hayburn is good enough for Phœbe,' she said at last. 'People say he's very clever, of course,' she added, her eyes still on the incoming steamer.

'It's time he showed some of it,' Mary's flat voice said beside her.

'That's what I say.'

'I don't think you should worry, Bel. If she

hasn't even bothered to come down to meet the man she is supposed to be engaged to, the affair won't last long.'

The *Ivanhoe* had come alongside now. There were the ringings of bells and the thrashing of paddles as she manoeuvred into position. Coils of slender pilot rope were thrown up from the deck, and the heavy hawsers to which they were attached were dragged up by powerful Highland hands that seized the giant loops and slid them over the stanchions of the pier.

Wives waved to husbands; hosts to week-end guests. There was shouting in Lowland Scots and Arran Gaelic. A rattling of gang-ways. Those who were coming off stood waiting on the deck, in conventional City clothes, holding handbags and overcoats, and bringing with them a breath of the town from which they were escaping. The horn was sounded, emitting a jet of pure white steam which rose for a moment to make a contrast with the cloud of black smoke issuing from the funnel; then was lost, as together, black and white, the smoke was blown down the wind. There was tumult, laughter and the bumping of luggage; and as a fitting back-ground, a German band that Bel recognised as one that played in the streets of Hillhead at other times of the year, kept pumping out the notes of the 'Blue Danube' waltz from a sheltered corner of the deck.

III

'There they are!' Mary had spied the three men among the crowd that waited while the gangway, which had now been slid across, was adjusted to its proper position on the paddle-box.

Arthur was looking up at Bel, a smile on his lean, handsome face. As her eyes caught his, he raised a hand in a friendly salute. Bel was filled, for a moment, with a feeling of keen pleasure. After a day or two of separation, the sight of Arthur meant protection, permanence and the completion of herself.

Baillie George McNairn was standing, stout and apparently unemotional, looking very much as usual, Bel thought. He, too, allowed a glint of recognition to rise up to them from his plump face.

'I hope George is all right,' Mary was saying beside her.

'I'm sure he is, dear. I wouldn't worry if I were you.' And then, to change the subject, perhaps, Bel added: 'What strange clothes Henry Hayburn seems to be wearing.'

Henry was wearing his suit of large, trellis checks, and the cloth cap of the same stuff, which it was his pleasure to affect when he came into the country. It gave him an odd, buttoned-up appearance, that seemed to accentuate the lanky gracelessess of his body. As though he knew his name was being mentioned, he suddenly turned in the direction of Bel and Mary, and his plain, boyish face was lit up in a quick smile.

Bel felt a stab of compunction. There was, after all, something disarming about Henry. She caught herself feeling annoyed with Phœbe that she had not come back from the picnic in time to meet him.

Henry wriggled his way through the waiting crowd to the side of the steamer, and shouted a friendly 'Hullo' to the ladies above him. Bel wondered if the absence of Phœbe had even occurred to this strange young man.

'Hullo, Henry!' she called back to him. 'They seem to be taking a long time to let you off.'

'Yes. Some of the hands are helping over there.' Henry cast his eyes along the side of the boat.

Bel's eyes followed them. 'Somebody getting a new cart?' she asked.

A gangway of planks was being laid at another part. Half a dozen deck-hands were standing ready to drag across them a brand-new farm-cart, which had been brought from the mainland. The cart looked like a giant toy, Bel could not help thinking. It was new painted, bright red and green, and the metal parts were shining.

'There we are now!' Henry wriggled back to his place beside Arthur and George.

The passengers, struggling with their belongings, had begun to come, one at a time, up the gangway. Presently the two husbands came, carrying neat weekend gladstone bags, and followed by Henry carrying a small and shabby carpet one. The elder men bestowed the responsible, conjugal kisses that husbands bestow upon wives in public, while Henry gave the ladies a hearty handshake, then began looking about him anxiously.

Again Bel felt a pang. 'I'm sorry Phœbe's been kept at a picnic, Henry. But she ought to be back by the time we get home.'

Henry merely said 'Oh,' and went on looking about him. 'I've brought my ordinary with me,' he said, using the customary name for the penny-farthing bicycle of the period, and adding: 'I suppose they'll bring it with the rest of the luggage after they get the cart off. Just go after Mary and George, and I'll follow you. Good heavens! Look what's coming!'

The main gate at the end of the pier had been thrown open, and a giant Clydesdale horse was being led towards them by a brown-skinned Highland lad with bare feet. The boy was grinning broadly as he came.

'It must have come down to take away the cart,' Arthur said, looking towards the animal.

'But look who's on its back!' Henry was laughing and waving wildly.

No, Bel couldn't think this funny! There was her husband's sister Phœbe, and her own son Arthur, perched high on the great creature's back, coming down the pier in front of all the people! Was Phœbe mad? Had she forgotten the meaning of the word propriety? For a young lady in her position to be sitting up there, hatless and dishevelled, making an exhibition of herself, was something of which Bel could not approve! And little Arthur was only eight, and might fall off and be seriously hurt! Indeed, if the horse started suddenly, they might both be thrown from the pier into the water.

'Arthur, tell them to come down at once! This is disgraceful! Mary, speak to Phœbe at once! She's your sister.'

'Come down, Phœbe,' Mary called placidly, looking up. George had had time to tell her that his doctor's report was good, and Mary could not feel angry, now, with anybody. And as Henry and Arthur laid down their bags and ran forward to help them to descend, Mary added: 'Her mother was a Highland tinker. She looked very like her sitting up there.'

But Bel was in no mood for family history or romantic likenesses. Besides, if anyone in the family had low connections, it was time they were forgetting them. When at last they stood before her she merely said: 'Phœbe and Arthur, I'm very disappointed with you,' then marched off down the pier on her husband's arm.

'Well-put-together young woman, Phœbe is, now,' George remarked to Mary as they followed after.

'Time she was learning sense. Bel was quite right to be angry!' Mary said. Now that she had George's assurance that his health would allow their smooth life to continue as usual, she did not in the least see why the baillie should be encouraged in his altogether too easily aroused interest in the slenderness of waists and the shapeliness of feet. The small eyes in George's fat face were over quick, Mary knew, when it came to feminine perfection. 'Like Henry the Eighth's,' she had said to herself angrily on a more dangerous occasion.

As the two married couples made their way along the shore road towards their rented houses, leaving the young people to their own devices, they were startled by a bicycle bell, and shouts of 'Get out of the way!' They turned to find Henry, perched on his penny-farthing bicycle, steering with one hand and carrying his carpet-bag in the other. He was going as slowly as possible so that Phœbe and Arthur could pant along beside him. He nearly fell off through trying to wave his handbag at the others as he passed them.

'Phœbe came down to meet Henry, after all,' Mary said to Bel when the three had passed on in front.

Bel merely said 'Yes.' But now she was fixed in her resolve. These free-and-easy Arran holidays must come to an end. Nothing was to be gained from this ridiculous unconventionality. Next summer the family would find themselves in some resort where convention must be observed.

Chapter Three

Mrs. Barrowfield was one of those women who don't need to look at their knitting. Her hands seemed to be leading a busy life of their own as they fashioned stockings for her elder grandson. The rest of her was at peace, as she sat in a wicker chair in the little front garden of the farmhouse her daughter had rented for July and August.

Though it may seem strange on a Scottish island, Mrs. Barrowfield was sitting under a palm-tree. Strange, but not impossible, for, as the shores of Arran are washed by the waters of the Gulf Stream, and the mountains catch the rains and winds from the warm south-west, frost is no great menace.

It was a little unkempt garden, with an odd flower or two springing up, rather from among the uncut grass, than from any discernible plot. But it was surrounded by a low hedge of fuchsia now in full bloom, and the view from it swept the beauty of the bay.

The late afternoon sunshine caused the old lady to contract her almost masculine features now and then. A starched cap, spotlessly white, was set upon her grey curls, and her best shawl was on her shoulders. It was only right that she should receive her son-in-law with proper dignity.

Although she could not see the pier from here, she had heard the beat of the steamer's paddles, caught odd, drifting music, and seen black smoke blow down the wind. Bel would be coming back with Arthur; and, by the way, there would be that queer Hayburn boy. She had almost forgotten him. She didn't quite know what to think about Henry. But Phœbe had engaged herself to him, and Mrs. Barrowfield liked Phœbe. It was too bad that he had lost all his money. Or perhaps not – at his age?

But her hopes and fears for Phœbe and her future were presently interrupted. A piping voice said: 'Hullo, Granny,' and her granddaughter Isabel opened the little garden gate and came in, leading her younger brother Thomas by the hand.

As grandmothers will, Mrs. Barrowfield

found herself re-examining her descendants with critical affection. She was pleased to note that, in so far as six can be the image of thirty-three, Isabel was the image of Bel. Little Thomas, a gentle little boy of four, reminded her more of David Moorhouse than of his father.

'Well, bairns? Have ye had a nice picnic? Come here to me, Isabel.' The child went. 'Ye've got hair like yer mother.' Her grandmother took the round crook comb from the child's fair hair, combed it a little, then pushed it back into place over the front of her head. Having smoothed down her little, braided serge dress, and adjusted her pinafore, she said: 'There now. Tell me what you saw.'

'Glen Rosa,' little Thomas said, looking at his grandmother solemnly.

'Tell Granny who spoke to you in Glen Rosa,' Isabel said, prompting.

'A Duke.' Thomas did not approve of wasting syllables.

'A Duke? The Duke of Hamilton?'

Isabel filled in the details breathlessly. A gentleman on horseback had spoken to Aunt Phœbe, Thomas and herself, as they were fetching milk for the picnic. He had been talking to the farmer's wife, and had bent down to ask them if they were visitors from Glasgow, how they were enjoying their holiday in Arran, and if their father and mother were well and enjoying Arran too? Aunt Phœbe had said they were all enjoying themselves very much. And Isabel, and even little Thomas, had said: 'Thank you, sir.'

'Where were the rest?' Mrs. Barrowfield asked.

'Getting sticks for the fire,' Isabel said. 'He didn't see them.'

The old lady purred as she took up her knitting again. She was, of course, a staunch partisan of her own grandchildren. That the landowner, using the kindly formula of greeting he was known to keep for summer visitors to his island, had greeted Bel's children, and not Mary McNairn's, couldn't fail to give her satisfaction.

Presently, Sarah the housemaid, rather less starched than at Grosvenor Terrace, but still strangely impeccable for these rustic surroundings, appeared at the farmhouse door and led the children away.

But Mrs. Barrowfield was not to be left in peace. For now there was a rattling at the gate, the sound of voices, and Phœbe, Henry Hayburn and her elder grandson came in. They were flushed and hot from coming up the hill. Phœbe, dishevelled and glowing, was in one of her moods. Her queer-set eyes were smouldering. Giving the old lady the merest recognition without bothering to smile, she passed on into the house. Henry, having successfully pushed his ungainly bicycle into the garden, came forward and gave Mrs. Barrowfield his hand.

He saw the enquiry in her eyes as they followed Phœbe. 'She's fallen out with Bel,' he said by way of explanation.

'Dear me, Henry. What about?'

'Aunt Phœbe and I rode down from Glen Rosa to the pier on one of the cart-horses, and mother was very angry. She said it was no way for a lady to behave,' Arthur chimed in pertly.

His grandmother looked about her placidly, her fingers continuing independently with her work. 'Yer mother's getting very genteel,' she said at length. And added: 'When I was yer Aunt Phœbe's age, I often had rides on cart-horses.'

II

When Henry had passed into the house, Mrs. Barrowfield was left once more by herself in the garden. She smiled a little. Her beloved, beautiful and successful daughter Bel was inclined to be pompous these days; to keep remembering what she was pleased to call her position. And, as the years went on, and the tide of prosperity rose round her, Bel, her mother was afraid, would become more and more so. The old woman thought of Bel's father. The lamented Doctor

Barrowfield had been a very self-important sort of man. But she had loved him. And she could not love their daughter any the less, when she showed herself like him.

Still, it was comic, Mrs. Barrowfield could not help thinking, how, every now and then, something happened to shatter Bel's sense of propriety. And usually it was Phœbe who was responsible for the shattering. Queer how she, Bel's mother, always found herself siding with Phœbe and not with her own daughter. She wondered why. But here were Bel and Arthur coming up the hill.

Bel merrily made a sign of greeting to her mother, asked if the others had arrived, announced her intention of seeing to things, and passed into the house. Arthur dropped his bag and packages on the grass beside his mother-in-law, and bent down to kiss her.

The old woman patted his shoulder. Ten years of affection, begun as a duty, had ended in a relationship which was close, unforced and warm.

'Ye'll be tired?' she said as her son-in-law stood, hat in hand, looking at the beauty about him.

'It was warm coming up here,' he said, still looking into the distance. 'Where are the bairns?' he asked at last, turning.

'Getting their faces washed. Sit down and rest yourself.'

Arthur picked up an empty wicker chair

that his wife had been occupying earlier in the afternoon, and sat himself down beside Mrs. Barrowfield. For a few moments he would rest and let Arran sink into him.

The smell of the sea, of the farmyard, of the tangle of moss-roses growing wild in a corner of the garden; the smell of bog myrtle and heather borne on the breeze from the hills above them. A golden quality was coming into the early evening light. The sun, striking lower, had begun to clothe the mountain across the bay in warmer tones; and, lighting it from one side, was throwing boulders, craggy outcrops and the sunken bed of a stream into black relief. The little herd of cows belonging to the farm were lowing as they passed the garden gate, driven in by the farm-girl to the evening milking.

Arthur continued to look about him, sighed with satisfaction and said: 'This is fine!'

Mrs. Barrowfield's needles clicked with satisfaction. She liked having a man to herself. Doubly so, if the man were Arthur. 'What's all this about Bel and Phœbe?' she asked presently, dropping her voice that it should not reach the open windows.

Arthur gave his version of the story of Phœbe and the carthorse. He was inclined to agree that Bel had made too much of it. 'But that's not what's bothering Bel now,' he went on. 'Ye see,' he said, dropping his voice still further, 'last week Henry Hayburn got the sack.'

'The sack! From his work?'

'He was sent away.'

Mrs. Barrowfield laid down her knitting, rested her hands on her lap and turned to Arthur. 'Did Henry tell ye this, Arthur?'

'Yes. On the steamer coming across.'

'And was he not ashamed to tell ye?'

Arthur considered for a moment. 'No,' he said. 'He was quite joco.'

'He looked joco when he came in here a minute since. He didna look up nor down.' She thought for a moment, then asked: 'And what does he think he's going to get married on?'

Arthur shook his head. In Moorhouse circles it was unheard of to be dismissed from one's work.

'What does Bel say?' the old lady asked presently.

'She's not very pleased.'

But now Bel reappeared herself, to make a third in this whispered colloquy, and to express her own displeasure.

'The plain fact is,' she said, sitting on the grass between their chairs, that she need not raise her voice, 'the sooner Phœbe and Henry decide to give up their engagement the better. I don't believe either one or the other of them knows what the word responsibility means! I don't believe they're even in love with each other! Like grown-up people, I

32

mean. I think Phœbe was just sorry for Henry, when she promised to marry him last autumn. I remember how queer she was on the night it happened.' Despite her indignation, Bel, turning to gaze out to sea, let memory take hold of her. Yes, on that night Phœbe had been very strange.

'But can anybody make them break it?' her mother asked, bringing her back.

Bel shrugged. 'Well?' she demanded in a whisper which was hot with desperation. 'What is it to be? He's crazy and she's crazy! And the one encourages the other!'

'I've always been told he was clever,' her mother said.

'And is he to keep her waiting, while he goes on being clever? I don't think being sent away is at all clever! And all the time she'll be getting older! And maybe at the end they'll find they don't want each other! This kind of thing may go on wasting the girl's life for years!'

Mrs. Barrowfield laid a hand on Bel. 'Don't excite yerself, my dear. Don't excite yerself! They're good bairns. Both of them.' She turned to Arthur. 'Did he tell you what he was sent away for?'

'Some job he refused to do.'

'Refused?'

'In his opinion the calculations werena right, or something.'

Bel, who had been dabbing her eyes, sat

33

up and demanded fiercely, 'What right has he to have an opinion?' She stared indignantly before her and added: 'And then he arrives down here with his bicycle, and behaves like a clown!'

Nobody answered this. They sat in silence looking at the view before them. The light on Goatfell had become still more golden. The wind was quite down. Smoke from the chimneys of thatched cottages was rising up perpendicularly against the dark woods. They could hear hens cackling in the yard behind the house as the farmer's wife called them to be fed. Boys with a dog, far away on the sands, were throwing sticks into the water. In the stillness, they could catch, even at this distance, the animal's excited barking. Far out on the horizon a ship was moving.

Mrs. Barrowfield took up her knitting. Once again she found herself siding with the young people against her daughter. If Henry and Phœbe had the spirit to be crazy and to behave like clowns, perhaps, after all, it might be no bad thing. There was more to this story than had yet been told her. Bare facts were not enough. She would make an opportunity to question Henry, herself.

Little Isabel came out of the house to greet her father and tell them their meal was ready.

III

The face of the old minister, people said, resembled nothing so much as the face of an eagle; a pleasant eagle, most likely, if you met him out walking on any other day but Sunday. Now, however, there was no pleasantness in it. He had a flock to save, and that, if anything could be, was a matter for deadly earnest. He paused, transfixing for a long instant a worshipper who had dared to cough. Then, taking in all the ladies of the congregation with a sweeping glance, he delivered one of the broadsides for which he was famous. 'And as for you, with your flowers waggin' in your bonnets. They'll no' be lasting long where you are going! They will all be burnt up!'

Arthur the Second looked up nervously. The poppies, cornflower and wheat-ears surrounding the crown of his Aunt Phœbe's straw hat would not stand a chance, he was afraid. And the curling lime-green ostrich plume which, along with the lime-green veil, drooped so elegantly at the back of his mother's fair and shining head would be inflammable too, he feared. Probably his granny, with her tight little black bonnet, would do better. The licking flames would find less to catch hold of.

He was surprised how calmly they were

taking it. His mother and his Granny had not moved a muscle. For a moment he wondered if his Aunt Phœbe's eyes had begun to dance, but a second look found them cast down and prim as ever. His father and Mr. Hayburn did not seem to be unduly troubled either. So perhaps it was all right. Perhaps this Arran minister, with his strange Highland accent, did not mean everything he said. Besides, anyone so calm and radiant as his mother, or so friendly and indulgent as his Aunt Phœbe, were far too nice to have the trimmings burnt off their hats.

Arthur's mind sought refuge in the basket of strawberries his father had brought with him from the Glasgow fruit market yesterday evening, and the bowl of thick farm cream that was to accompany them to the midday dinner-table, when the family had arrived back in church.

The sun streamed through the plain glass windows of the little, unadorned church. Dust particles, floating through its slanting rays, turned for a moment to silver, then were lost again against the shadows. Outside, a corncrake was sounding his ratchet among the green corn. Somewhere a bee was buzzing. Now they were all standing up to sing the last hymn, trying to catch the tune from the slow, toneless voice of the precentor. Now the service was over and they were standing outside the little church, talking with acquaintances, and basking in the July glory about them.

As the church was some way out of Brodick, Arthur Moorhouse had borrowed his landlord's gig, and now was gone to fetch it at the nearby farm where it had been left. Although at Grosvenor Terrace his wife had a carriage of her own and a coachman to attend her, this Arran unconventionality was pleasant to Arthur. Like many another countryman who had found fortune and formality in the City, he liked to remember at times that he himself was a farmer's son and could harness a horse to a gig and drive it with the best of them. It was, perhaps, one of the greatest charms of Arran that it allowed the striving and successful to give up the struggle for a time, to touch back to their own simple beginnings.

The gig had been overloaded during their coming. Henry announced his intention of walking back. Bel promised to delay their meal for half an hour. Phœbe declared she would join him.

The weekend had not, so far, gone particularly well for this temperamental couple. They set out in the direction of home, saying nothing, pleased to be alone together. Henry seemed as disinclined for talk as she was, so Phœbe left him in peace. The Arthur Moorhouse atmosphere had been noticeably chilly. The clash of Phœbe's high spirits with Bel's propriety had only been the beginning of it. When it was known that Henry had been forced to relinquish an excellent business opportunity, specially made for him, merely because he, Henry, had chosen to set what looked like nothing more than his own wilfulness against greater experience, then the temperature had dropped steeply.

It is not pleasant to feel oneself regarded as the single failure in a family of successes. And it was just this feeling that was beginning to penetrate. Yet, rightly or wrongly, Henry felt confident that success was in him. He knew he was quick, educated and diligent. If, outwardly, he seemed undisciplined, it was merely because he could only acknowledge a sharp, unforgiving inner discipline. But, for the success-mongering Moorhouses, this, it would seem, was not enough. But how could he make them understand?

Life, until the collapse of last autumn, had been handed to Henry to play with. A dangerous toy. But he was one of those young men an assured fortune would not have spoilt. He would merely have put what he needed of it to the uses of his calling. And, unlike his own brother Stephen, have continued on his way, quite heedless of the privileges that money might have bought him.

He had been awakened early this morning with the crowing of cocks, the cackle of

laying hens, and the other, pleasant farmyard noises. He had lain across the hills and
valleys of his lumpy Arran bed, staring at the
crude, faded roses of his wallpaper, thinking.

Last night, made tactless, perhaps, by her
smouldering annoyance, Bel had talked
much about the doings of the family. David
and Grace were now taking over Aucheneame. Mrs. Dermott had determined to
come into Kelvinside, buy a suitable house,
and devote herself to her committees. Her
daughter and son-in-law were planning to
extend the garden and build on a nursery
wing to the house. Mungo Ruanthorpe-
Moorhouse had bought a tiny and very
valuable Shetland pony against the time
when his son should be able to sit on its
back. The baby's grandfather, Sir Charles,
Bel understood, had already transferred a
substantial block of Consols to his grandson's name. Every word she uttered seemed
so pointedly to refer to the success of the
others, and their power to spend lavishly,
that even Henry's indifference had begun to
do more than wonder if her talk were
deliberately aimed.

IV

The couple walked briskly along in the

sunlight. It was strange that lovers should have so little to say to each other. But these were strange lovers and they were well accustomed to long silences together.

Henry was dismayed and puzzled. He had never been pressed about his doings in the old days. Indeed, his mother had not wanted him to take up any work seriously. She had wanted Stephen and himself to occupy their time being gentlemen. That was ridiculous, of course. Still, the scramble for fortune and position had never, until now, seemed a necessity to him.

All about them were fields of growing corn, studded here and there with poppies; fields of fresh-cut hay, of rich green pasture. Down on the right the sparkling sea. And in the distance in front of them the peak of Goatfell and the rugged splendour of the castles. White butterflies were dancing among the seeding grasses, the harebells and the dandelions by the roadside.

What did Phœbe think about it, he wondered? In his life there was Phœbe, and, far behind her, everybody else. And yet there was not much love-making between this odd couple. In times of normal happiness they fed on each other's eagerness like two schoolchildren. If there was passion, it flowed deep, almost beyond the consciousness of either. Bel had often said of them that neither was quite adult. In one sense she was right.

'Your folks don't like me, Phœbe,' he said suddenly.

She was accustomed to his breaking in like this. She took a moment to take in his words. 'They don't like me either,' she said. 'After last night Bel thinks I don't know how to behave myself like a lady.' Her face darkened for a moment. Then she laughed. 'She'll get over it.'

Henry plucked at a long grass that sprouted by the wayside, and sucked its tender end, reflecting. 'She'll get over anything you do. But I'm different. I'm just a stranger,' he added, using the last word in its Scotch sense, meaning someone who is not a relation.

'How can you be a stranger, if you are going to marry me?'

'I'm not sure that she wants you to marry me.'

'Nobody's asking her what she wants.'

'They don't think I'm good enough for you.'

'Good enough, Henry! A Hayburn not good enough for me!'

'It would have been all right last year, when mother was alive and we had our money.'

'That's rubbish. What difference does that make?' Yet even Phœbe knew there was a difference. She could not be unconscious of it. She knew the Moorhouse yardstick. The

41

thought roused a feeling of rebellion.

'It's sensible enough,' Henry went on, almost as though he were thinking aloud. 'After all, we can't be married till I can earn a living.'

'You know perfectly well I can wait.'

'Do you want to wait, Phœbe?'

'Not for ever.' She turned to look at him. Their eyes met.

For an instant Phœbe caught a glimpse of the sudden, almost pitiful defencelessness that could weave itself so strangely into the texture of Henry's indifference. And the quick of her sympathy was cut almost as it had been cut on that night of his despair; the night upon which she had promised to become his wife.

She gave him her hand.

V

Mrs. Barrowfield spent August at home. This happened every summer. Bel always pressed her mother to stay with them for as long as they should be by the sea, but much as she liked her daughter and her grandchildren, the old lady felt that a month of improvised comfort, of smoking peat-fires, of Arran downpours, of cramped rooms, was as much as she had any taste for. She began to long for the ordered quiet of her own flat in Monteith Row.

Besides, town was not unattractive to her in August. Most people were away, and such social obligations as the remainder of the year laid upon her did not exist. Her son-in-law, Arthur, who always had his holiday at the fair in July, and was, in consequence, left to himself in August, came frequently to see her. David Moorhouse, before his marriage, had often visited her at this time too. She liked these masculine attentions. It amused Bel to tease her mother about her August 'young men'. This year David's bachelor life had, of course, come to an end. But now it would seem that Henry Hayburn was beginning to take his place.

She had invited him to visit her when they were together in Brodick, and Henry, sensing sympathy at the core of Mrs. Barrowfield's downrightness, had come. A sudden, lively friendship had sprung up between them. The strange, erratic young man had taken to dropping in of an evening. She enjoyed his excitable, self-revealing talk, his regardlessness of convention, his quick confidence in herself. She realised his great loneliness; the loneliness of someone young and eager who has not yet found his place in the scheme of things. She was flattered that he should come to her, an old woman, for understanding and support.

It is not to be wondered at, therefore, that

Mrs. Barrowfield had become Henry's partisan. He had explained to her, with much technical and quite incomprehensible detail, just why he had to leave his last employment. Loyally, she declared that she quite saw, and was convinced that there was nothing else for him to do. She believed that there were great potentialities in Henry. Either for good or ill. His ardour would either make or break him. If he were headed in the right direction, then he would do great things.

He told her about Phœbe: how Phœbe was everything to him. But Mrs. Barrowfield sometimes wondered. Phœbe was so much a bird of the storm herself. How would these two unstable creatures fare together?

This summer of 1879 was long and dragging for the young man. World trade continued in the doldrums. Henry could suddenly appear at Monteith Row and declare that he was finished with Scotland; that nothing was any good; that he had determined to emigrate. Thousands were going to the New World. Why shouldn't he? Mrs. Barrowfield's experience knew not to take these outbursts at their face value. He had merely come to draw strength from her sympathy, to let off steam.

Usually he found her in an arm-chair by the open window, busy with her work. She would command him to sit down, order tea to be brought, and listen while he talked himself out. With a brisk, cheerful tact she would counsel patience. She would strive to renew his faith in himself; to remind him of his abilities. The right employment would presently present itself. It was merely a question of time. What about Phœbe, if he chose to emigrate? Did he imagine for one moment that her brothers would allow her to follow him into the wilderness?

Sooner or later peace would descend. If it were evening, there would be birds chirping in the trees outside the window. Beyond, couples could be seen in the distance, wandering across the wide, cool expanses of Glasgow Green. Presently the lamplighter would come, and the branches near the lamps he had lighted would take on the vivid look of painted scenery. In later August the gossamer mists of approaching autumn would rise from the distant Clyde and wreathe their wisps across the darkening Green. There would be the tap of an occasional step on the pavement beneath them; the voices of children playing in the gloaming; the sounds of far-off laughter.

And now Henry's talk would be changed from shrill expostulation to comfortable commonplace, while the old woman sat sewing, saying nothing. But she would smile in secret, tell herself that young people needed their elders sometimes, and assure herself that once more she had given back to her young friend the strength to continue with the highly arduous occupation of being young, impatient and eager.

Chapter Four

Mungo Ruanthorpe-Moorhouse was a miracle of good temper – or so, at least, his parents-in-law, Sir Charles Ruanthorpe and his lady, were constantly heard to declare. But on this fine September morning it was taking Mungo all his time.

The harvest was in full swing, and Mungo was busy. Arrangements of all kinds had to be made at the Laigh Farm. And, in addition, as a progressive farmer, he had purchased one of the new combined reaping and binding machines, that not only cut the corn, but actually, as it went along, forced it into sheaves, tied it with hemp string, and cast it to one side ready to be set up in 'stooks'. Everything needed his attention, especially the new reaper and binder: for if this turned out to be a failure, he would be confronted by the unpleasant fact that he had been wasting good money. In addition, he knew that his fellow farmers would smile, and, in their blunt country fashion, inform him that they could have told him from the beginning that these newfangled, mechanical devices were never any good.

Now, as he stood among his cornfields, in the yellow sunshine of this Ayrshire September morning, a messenger came from Duntrafford bearing a letter in Sir Charles's hand. Mungo opened the letter apprehensively. Had something gone wrong? Was someone ill? Margaret? Or his three-months-old son? He was not accustomed to having messages sent to him thus while he was in the fields.

But the letter, disdaining apology or explanation, informed Sir Charles's son-in-law that Sir Charles was sending a foreign gentleman to see the working of the automatic reaper and binder, and would Mungo be so good as to show everything and explain everything the gentleman wanted to know. He would perhaps ask young Henry Hayburn, who happened to be staying along with Phœbe at the Dower House, to bring the gentleman over some time this afternoon while harvesting was in progress. The stranger was an Austrian banker and had connections with Sir Charles's stockbrokers in London.

The stable-boy, who had ridden across with the letter, saw Mr. Moorhouse crush it roughly in his hand and thrust it deep into his trouser-pocket. But he could not see how

Mr. Moorhouse had to crush as roughly his quick annoyance at this needless interruption. What possible right had a banker, of all people, to come wasting a busy farmer's time? What interest could this binder be to a foreigner? Margaret's father was country bred. He should have known better. But he was eighty years old and very petted.

Mungo Moorhouse, however, was by nature restrained and moderate. 'Ye can tell them it's all right for the afternoon,' he said none too graciously; and the stable-boy rode off to deliver the message.

II

It will never be known whether Sir Charles had bidden Henry Hayburn to lunch with the intention of finding employment for him. It is not improbable. For, as Mungo's sister Phœbe showed no sign of giving Henry up, his lack of employment had become a family problem. Besides, there was something about Henry's spirit and quickness that appealed to the old man. A command had come to the Dower House. Henry was required by Sir Charles to come across and meet an Austrian gentleman.

Who was he? Margaret Ruanthorpe-Moorhouse did not know. Was Phœbe expected along with Henry? They did not say so. Henry went alone.

He found the old laird of Duntrafford and Lady Ruanthorpe in the great drawing-room of the house. Although the autumn sunshine was pouring through the festooned lace curtains of the long windows, filling the pleasantly rich and padded room with warmth as well as light, a bright fire was burning. Margaret's parents sat on great chairs on either side of it. Sir Charles's old house spaniels lay on the rug. At his elbow was a decanter of sherry. There were Michaelmas daisies, late roses, and yellow beech leaves. A country room that could belong only to subjects of the Queen.

But now, at once, a different note was struck. The rather swarthy gentleman who was being presented to Henry did not belong to this picture.

Sir Charles was doing the honours. 'Come along, Hayburn. Glad to see you. I see you didn't bring Phœbe.' Whether Sir Charles was pleased or sorry about his, Henry could not discover, as he gave his hand to his hostess, then to the old man, who went on talking: 'By the way, how is my grandson, Hayburn? I haven't seen him for two days. I must go round after tea.'

Lady Ruanthorpe expostulated. 'Really, Charles! How can you expect Henry to take an interest in a baby?'

'I don't see why not.'

'Hadn't you better stop arguing, and introduce Henry to Mr. Hirsch.'

Henry gave Mr. Maximilian Hirsch of Vienna his hand, noting the while, in his not very far-travelled mind, that Mr. Hirsch looked like a piano-tuner. But if Henry's parochiality could only think of a piano-tuner, his common sense quickly told him that the stranger, with his bowing and smiling, his shock of black hair, and his bushy side-whiskers, cut in accordance with the fashion set by his Emperor, was much more a man of the world than he was himself.

Mr. Hirsch spoke English with an accent, but almost without fault. He knew London intimately, he said, and had many business interests and friends there. His chief occupation was banking, but it was banking in the Continental sense, which meant that he was not excluded from the practical direction of several manufacturing ventures. He was always, he said, on the outlook for new ideas to exploit. He had been sent to Glasgow by a friend in London to obtain information that would be of use to him in connection with steam river-craft on the Danube.

As Henry was sipping his sherry, he began to regard the foreigner with awe. This man had been received by the heads of many famous Glasgow firms. He talked with intelligence, much more intelligence than old Sir Charles, who was obviously bored, and impatient for his lunch.

The young man became interested. Had Mr. Hirsch seen this at such a shipyard? Had Mr. Hirsch seen that at such another engine shop? Henry's eyes kindled and his tongue wagged. He did not know that he was revealing himself. That this intelligent cosmopolitan had come to seek after such a one as himself.

Sir Charles had become more and more testy. He did not like torrents of talk he could not understand; could not even hear properly. He grunted. He offered more sherry. He demanded of his wife when she had told Campbell to announce lunch. He adjusted his stock. He dragged his gold watch out of its spacious pocket in his waist-coat, and snapped it open and snapped it shut.

The visitor stopped, smiling. 'But we are talking too much Mr.–? I do not think that I heard your name?'

'Hayburn.' Henry, brought to earth, looked about him a little abashed.

Mr. Hirsch said the name after him. 'Hayburn?'

Henry repeated it.

For a moment the stranger seemed to be seeking about in his mind. 'Hayburn,' he said presently, and added: 'It is strange that I should know your name.' He stopped again, then exclaimed: 'Ah! Robert Hayburn of Glasgow! A famous engineer. I have heard of him many times.' And suddenly: 'Your father?'

'He was. My father died some years ago.'

'But you are in his famous Company, of course?'

Lady Ruanthorpe, gruff and old though she might be, felt that here was a situation with which she had better deal. She saw the blush on the young man's face.

She interposed with resolution. 'You know, Mr. Hirsch, I think it would be such a good thing if Henry drove you over to see my son-in-law's reaping machine this afternoon. I feel you have got all sorts of things to talk about.' And then with relief: 'Oh, there you are, Campbell. Thank you. Come along, everybody. I expect you're all starving.'

And Mr. Hirsch could not at all understand why the old woman had thus cut into his conversation. Like every other Continental, he found himself marvelling at the bad manners of the Islanders.

III

Maximilian Hirsch, urbane, highly civilised and intellectually curious, was enjoying this, his first visit to Scotland. This northern land was so different, its customs so apart. When

52

he got himself home again to his comfortable and expensive first-floor apartments in the Inner City of Vienna, with its windows overlooking the Minoriten Church, he would have something to tell his friends of the strange, rigid ways of life, and the sombrely prosperous town, where he had just been spending his Sunday. The outward appearance of the London Sunday was sober enough. But, after all, London was a great, cosmopolitan city. There was plenty of amusement to be found by a sophisticated foreigner who knew where to look for it.

But yesterday, Glasgow had been quite dead. He had walked out from his hotel to look at the City, as it lay, quiet and resting, in the September sunshine. The sound of church bells. The earnest Protestants hurrying to church. Heavily bearded, black-coated men raising their tall hats and smiling seriously in greeting, as, together with their wives, their sons and their daughters, they hurried to foregather in tasteless yellow pine vestibules and passed on out of sight into their austere places of worship.

And yet they seemed a prosperous, well-fed people, and their faces, on the whole, appeared contented, even complacent. But what did they do to amuse themselves, to exercise their intellects, to feed their minds, on this, their day of freedom? Even the workpeople – those of them who could be seen about – seemed not to expect amusement. They roamed the traffickless thoroughfares, or stood at street corners in knots, gossiping.

He came from a city where amusement was deemed a necessary food for the spirit. He could see no attempt at light-heartedness here. At home, on an early September Sunday morning, the workpeople would be streaming to the open spaces of the Prater, Vienna's popular and fashionable park. Or the young and enterprising would be crowding the horse-trams and singing without self-consciousness to the accompaniment of trotting hoofs and tinkling bells, as they rode towards the suburbs to spend their day eating and dancing in the gardens of one of the many restaurants, or wandering happily in the Vienna Woods.

And the fashionable world – or such of it as had already come back from the country – would have its ceremonial carriage parade in the afternoon in the Prater, and later make its appearance at the opera or in the theatres.

In Glasgow, throughout the afternoon there was nothing, it seemed, but stagnation, and in the evening another dose of church.

But they were not uninteresting, these people; so long as one were not condemned to spend one's life among them. In his busi-

ness interviews he had met much forcefulness of character, much agility of mind. He
had found them resourceful, eager and
shrewd, beneath what seemed to be a
universal pose of slow-wittedness and pompous courtesy. A baffling species, even for a
fine-taster of peoples and places like himself.

He was glad Lady Ruanthorpe had given
him this young man to drive out with. He
was of the species, but divergent from it. For
young Mr. Hayburn was without pompous-
ness. He was boyish, quick and candid. And,
it would seem, far from stupid. Yes, Henry
might be of use.

He sat up on the high seat of the Duntrafford gig, looking about him, as his companion drove in the narrow Ayrshire farm
roads; between beech hedges, which, here
and there, were beginning to turn from dark
green to yellow; between hawthorns hanging
with crimson berries. He marvelled that
beyond them in the fields the corn was still
waiting to be cut. In his own, more southern
country the oat crop had already been
gathered weeks ago. Here in this northern
land the year's cycle was later. But it was a
beautiful, mellow country, well tended and
eloquent of a healthy peasant life; unspoiled
by the industries that had ruined so much of
the Island.

'Have you seen this reaping and binding
machine, Mr. Hayburn?' he asked his com-

panion presently.

Henry, who was not a practised driver, did not take his eyes from the horse's head. 'No, I haven't,' he said.

'It should save a great deal of labour in the fields. Yes?'

'I suppose it does.'

'It must be a very clever invention. To cut and tie at the same time.'

'Yes.'

'Do you understand the principle?'

'I've never tried.'

'But you are an engineer. I would have thought...'

'Oh, I dare say I would understand it quickly enough, if I had to.'

Strange young man. His answers were almost rude; yet the Austrian could see that they were not so intended.

Suddenly, after successfully negotiating a corner, Henry turned:

'Do *you* understand it?' he asked unexpectedly.

'No. But I'm very interested. I may try to get the patent, and open a factory for reapers in Vienna. You see, in my country, or rather in Hungary, corn-growing is the most important industry. We could make them in Vienna and send them down the Danube.' Mr. Hirsch waited for Henry's comment.

But he only said: 'I don't know whether it's any good or not,' and went on driving.

IV

If this morning Mungo had felt annoyance at the prospect of having to receive a visitor sent by his fussy, self-important father-in-law, the happenings of the early afternoon had done nothing to lessen it. Just after his men had returned to work, the new reaper and binder broke down.

Mungo was a good farmer, but he was a bad, impatient mechanic. Like peasants all the world over, he was inclined to believe that a complicated mechanism has some strange, magic life of its own. That, if it goes wrong, it must be propitiated, rather than painstakingly understood and set aright. The workers stood by waiting, uncomfortable at his displeasure. They were well aware that Mungo was loathing the enforced idleness for which he would have to pay them.

The harvest field was in a state of angry tension when Henry and his companion arrived. Henry called to a man to open the gate of the field to allow him to drive in, then begged him to hold the horse's head. This done, the visitors alighted. Mungo, perfectly aware of their coming, made no sign. He had not wanted to be bothered with Sir Charles's foreigner this morning, still less did he want him now.

Mr. Hirsch had heard that the Scots could be ungracious. He was to get a demonstration of it now. He crossed the expanse of stubble – where the reaping machine had already done its work – hat in hand, ready to greet Sir Charles Ruanthorpe's son-in-law. But Sir Charles Ruanthorpe's son-in-law did not bother to raise himself from his crouched position. He merely presented Sir Charles's visitor with his back.

This rudeness might have been disturbing. But Mr. Hirsch, being a man of many worlds, did not allow it to be so. He had not come here to worry about hurt feelings. He turned to his young companion, and waited. The young man made no attempt to effect an introduction. He was intent upon what Mungo was doing. Presently Henry spoke.

'What's the trouble, Mungo?'

'I wish I could tell ye,' was flung back over Mungo's shoulder.

'Have you been stuck for long?'

'Since dinner-time.'

'Let me have a look.'

Mr. Hirsch was astonished at the change in Henry; his sudden excitement before a mechanical problem. Now he was down on his knees, regardless of his clothes, having pushed Mungo and his assistant aside.

The Austrian did not mind that Mungo, standing up stiffly and slowly from his crouched position, did not bother, even now, to greet him. The sudden animation of this strange boy fascinated him.

'Look, Mungo. A nut has come loose and got lost there. And therefore that thing has come out of its place. Oh, and good lord! Look at that! If you had tried to drive any further you would have smashed the whole machine! For heaven's sake unharness the horses now, before they move and do any damage!'

The young man was in control. The others were doing as he told them. As the horses were led forward out of harm's way, Henry was flinging off his coat and rolling up his sleeves.

'What have you got in your tool-box? Yes, I want that spanner. Oh, and good – there's a spare nut the right size! It'll do for the one that's got lost. Now, what happens here?'

His hands were strong, deft and trained. They seemed to be leading a life of their own; quick, with mechanical understanding. There was education, skill, and a great, urgent talent.

He worked rapidly and with fanatical concentration. For him there were no white clouds in the sky, no golden landscape, no calling moor birds; no field-workers, impatient to get on with their harvesting. His hands, his clothes, his face even, were smeared with grease, as he crawled hither and thither, beneath and around this piece of dead mechanism it was his passion to bring back to life.

At last he rose, oily and grinning. 'There. That should be all right. Put the horses back and try it.' And presently he was running, cheerful and dishevelled, shouting instructions to Mungo in the driving-seat, as the reaper cut its way successfully down the next stretch of standing corn, throwing out at rhythmic intervals the finished sheaves.

When the cavalcade had returned triumphant to the point at which they had started, it suddenly occurred to Henry to introduce Sir Charles's guest. Mungo, more mellow now, regretted that his hands were too dirty to be shaken; but he expressed his pleasure at seeing Mr. Hirsch, and told him he would be pleased to show him his new, and altogether excellent combined reaper and binder.

V

They had, of course, to consult the family. The family came into everything. A strange, foreign gentleman, who went by the name of Maximilian Hirsch, had offered Henry an important post in a new factory in Vienna. If there had been anything for him at home, Henry and Phœbe would not have considered the proposition for a moment.

But there was nothing. The summer had dragged on, nerves had been frayed, and things had looked hopeless. Now there was this man offering a sum which, if Henry took pencil and paper, and turned things called *Gülden* and *Kreutzers* into pounds, shillings and pence, seemed really quite a lot. Quite enough to live on, perhaps even to marry on; if, when Henry got there, he found that Vienna was a place suitable for a properly-brought-up young lady.

Vienna. Round the fireplace of Bel's drawing-room in Grosvenor Terrace they got out Arthur's atlas and peered at the dot on the map. It did not tell them very much. They knew it was the capital of Austria, and appeared to be situated on the Danube, which, according to the waltz, then in high popularity, was beautiful and blue. That was all very well, but were the people on its banks God-fearing and civilised and fit for a Hayburn, and possibly a Moorhouse, to mix with?

They were simple people, these, who gazed at this black dot in the centre of the map of Europe; none of them many generations away from the peasantry. And what education they had, had been gained as an aid to their advancement in the world. They had not yet had time for foreign travel.

Mr. Hirsch had given Henry a week to decide. If he accepted, then he was to travel to London, and thence continue his journey in his company. Henry was unsure of himself. Now he was being asked to cast his moorings and set his course for the unknown. Besides, he did not particularly want to work in a factory for making reaping machines. His interests lay in the heavy industries that ran in the veins of his own city.

But Phœbe kept urging him. Her sense of adventure was kindled. Let him go, she said, get things started, and she would come to him. Or, if that were not allowed by Bel, he would, surely be given time to come home and fetch her. Let him think what fun it would be for them to be alone in a strange, new city, making new friends, finding a new life.

Upon a suggestion of Phœbe's going at once with Henry, Bel put down her foot. No; Phœbe could not possibly go until Henry had found out what sort of place Vienna was, and established a settled and comfortable existence for her. If he could not do without her for a time, then he must stay at home.

But staying at home meant having no work to do, and Henry did not want that. It was very difficult.

What had Sir Charles thought? Sir Charles had thought the offer an excellent one. Just the very thing. He himself had been in Vienna once as a young man. He could not remember the year, but it was before he was married. It must have been a long time ago, because he had gone through Switzerland in a stage coach sort of thing. And Phœbe had better pack her bags and go with Henry, for, if his memory served him right, there were one or two handsome young women in Vienna.

All of which, being in substance reported to Bel, was not particularly reassuring. Sir Charles was very well, and in their burghers' hearts they were proud to be connected with him; but, with some justification, they were none too sure of the oats Sir Charles must once have sown.

During this week of indecision, discussion raged furiously in the Moorhouse family. Stephen, Henry's elder brother, feeling himself confined and prospectless in the offices of Dermott Ships, urged Henry to get away at all costs. Stephen's advice meant much to Henry. David, who had never put forth any effort beyond keeping his place in the procession of prosperity, told Henry from the safety of his pedestal that he seriously thought Vienna would be the making of him. Sophia bustled in to say that William had read that the Viennese were all Roman Catholics and went to the theatre on Sunday; and she would not at all approve if it were Wil or Margy who thought of going. Mary, who happened to be calling on Bel at the same time, felt that home was the best place for all young people, and that she and George had always done very well just staying quietly in Glasgow. Mrs. Dermott wondered what kind of schemes there were for social betterment in Vienna; and hoped Henry would have time to look round and write her about them. And Bel and Arthur, who were the only ones who were genuinely troubled, did not know what to advise, and worried their heads off.

In the end, it was old Mrs. Barrowfield who weighed down the scales in favour of Henry's going. She had learnt much about the young man during the many visits he had paid her in the dog-days of the summer. Anything was better for him than these last two months of unhappy idleness. Frustration and a growing suspicion of his own futility might begin to undermine his splendid eagerness. This offer would stop all that. And it would develop Henry, turn him into a man, to find himself pitched headlong into new responsibilities, new labours, a new world. In some ways he was immature, boyishly dependent on sympathy, lacking in the confidence his abilities seemed to warrant. Nothing could be better for him than that he should go to this strange city to find his feet, learn to depend upon himself, and make his mistakes away from the criticism of those who knew him.

And so it came about that, as an eastward-bound express flew on its way relentlessly through the pale mists of a late September dawn, an odd-looking young man, homesick and dishevelled from the long night journey, peered from the window at the eddying, clay-coloured waters of the River Danube, at the unfamiliar reds and browns of the autumn vinelands, at the odd little wayside stations that rushed past him, all of them painted in the official black and yellow of the Austro-Hungarian Empire.

Chapter Five

Josephine – known among her intimates as Pepi – Klem, only child of Joseph and Martha Klem, of the new-built and very unfashionable Quellengasse in the Favoriten suburb of Vienna, was often described by her good-natured and pleasantly sentimental parents as the light of their lives. But if Pepi was a light in the lives of her adoring parents, she was a light that gave forth sparks. And there had been sparks this Monday morning before her father, a bank clerk, had taken himself off to his duties. Indeed, if her parents had addressed any remark whatever to Pepi during the weekend, sparks had been the result.

Now she was banging about the little flat in the Quellengasse, viciously punching up the feather-beds, and putting them to air at the window, rubbing up the hardwood floor as though it were the face of a prostrate enemy, and wringing washcloths as though they were the necks of her foes. Before this tornado her meek and kind-hearted mother had fled to do the morning shopping, leaving Pepi and her displeasure shut up and alone in the apartment. She knew from experience that her daughter would probably do the housework in half the usual time out of sheer bad temper. And she prayed that when she got back Pepi should have become more calm.

It was Pepi's father who had raised the storm again this morning, over their rolls and coffee, by asking, well, what was he to say to Herr Pommer? Pepi had exploded. Herr Pommer? The Pommer had nothing to do with her. What did he mean, Herr Pommer? He could say what he liked to Herr Pommer. The Pommer did not exist so far as she was concerned.

Her mother had tried to interpose. Pepperl must not talk to the Papa like that. The Papa was thinking of her future. The Papa wanted her to become betrothed to a nice, steady young man, who had a nice steady post in the bank like the Papa himself. And

Herr Pommer was being so steady. The Papa said that in no time at all he would be able to marry her, and install her in nice apartments just like these ones here. And who knew, perhaps in a year or two there would be a dear little baby to take up her interest, when the good Pommer was at the bank?

At this, Pepi, who was not perhaps so innocent as her childish pug nose and her surprised brown eyes might indicate, said the Viennese equivalent of 'Bosh!' and dissolved into tears of fury. She would get something better than the Pommer, with his apologetic cough and his worn, grey-cotton gloves. And if she didn't get that, she would stay as she was! And a nice apartment like this one here? Out in a suburb, within pleasant reach of the meat market, the goods railway station and the gas-works? And even that was too expensive for them. Were they not, even now, trying to rent one of their rooms to a suitable tenant? The Pommer was not yet thirty, and the Papa was fifty-five. When, she asked, would Herr Pommer come to achieve the Papa's magnificent income?

By this time her father had got himself into his short Viennese overcoat, set his soft hat upon his blond, distracted head, opened the door of the flat and fled.

It was after this that the child said something that somewhat alarmed her mother.

Pepi dried her eyes, fixed them, gimlet-like, upon the older woman and said: 'I don't care. I'll go and ask Lisa Fischer to find some work for me to do!'

Even Frau Klem's mildness was shaken. 'You'll what?'

'You know very well I want to be a singer.'

'Not that kind of singer, I hope.'

Lisa, a young second cousin of Herr Klem, had shaken the family dust from her elegant shoes, and taken herself into the chorus of comic opera. But though her relatives had now little opportunity for talk with Lisa, it was obvious to all of them that more than the pay of a lady of the chorus supported her magnificence.

Vienna was an important capital city. But in certain respects it had the gossipy qualities of a market town. In the Inner City, or in the great main carriage-way of the Prater, everybody kept meeting everybody else. Only yesterday afternoon the Klem family had seen a very fashionable Lisa indeed, tricked out with feathers, parasol and gloves, driving in a glittering private phæton beside an officer of the Hungarian Guard, pass over the Aspern Bridge on the way to the Prater. Her older relatives had dropped their eyes discreetly. But a glimmer of recognition had passed between Lisa and her young cousin.

Having gained a sufficiency of composure, Pepi's mother managed to ask: 'Have you any idea what kind of woman Lisa Fischer is?'

'A singer. What else?' Pepi was perfectly aware of the right answer. But she knew her mother, and enjoyed driving her into corners.

Frau Klem rose from the coffee-table troubled. 'Well, if you don't know the answer to that question, I dare say it's just as well,' she said, hedging. 'But let me tell you, my child, any thought you have of following Lisa's example is playing with fire.' And having thus, not quite honestly, quieted her conscience, she put on her hat and went out to buy blood sausage and sour cabbage.

II

Having done everything else in the house that she intended to do, Pepi went back to the open window to take in the feather-beds. As she did so, she stopped to look out. It was a pale, late September morning. A light fog hung over that part of Vienna which could be seen from her window, high up in the Quellengasse. Far on her left she could just make out the slender spire of the Cathedral of Saint Stephen – an insubstantial fretwork ghost, hardly distinguishable in the morning haze above the Inner City. Down there, much nearer and more distinct, were the solid towers of the Imperial Arsenal. And over there, in the distance, beyond the houses of the Landstrasse district, stretched the great expanse of the Prater.

Beneath her the street was depressingly autumnal and silent. What little traffic there was seemed to be strangely hushed. The leaves on the newly planted trees beneath her were limp and colourless. She could hear the barking of a dog, coming from a distance. Having put the feather-beds back, she returned to the window and sighed dispiritedly.

She felt low and frustrated, as only nineteen can. Here she was, young, pretty, a creature of endless potentiality, and all the future was to be allowed to hold for her was Willi Pommer. A tear dropped on the window-sill. Pepi looked at it ruefully. Another splashed beside it. Let them all come! She was no longer angry. Her spirit was gone. She was nothing more now than a poor, tragic child! Let them go on falling until they made a waterfall down the front of the building, splashing first on old Frau Wolfert's window-sill immediately below, and then next into the geraniums of the Linsenmayer's window-boxes before they finally flooded the pavement.

Taken now with this tragic fantasy, Pepi leant a little farther out of the window just to look down to see what exact part of the pavement the waterfall would strike. In doing so, she received a sudden shock. For there on the pavement, immediately beneath, with every appearance of making to ascend, were two young men. She drew in her head abruptly; but almost at once, that she might not be mistaken, she thrust it out again. As she did so, a soiled, grey-cotton hand pointed out the number. Yes, it was the Pommer himself.

It is a strange fact that young women on the point of meeting suitors it is their firm intention to reject should rush to their mirrors before they meet them. But this was what Pepi did. And when, at last, the door of the Klem's flat was opened to Herr Pommer and his companion, they were confronted by a little lady who was the ultimate expression of provocation and offhand charm. Herr Pommer, shabby Viennese bank clerk though he was, bent over Pepi's hand with a reverent elegance that would have done credit to an Esterhazy, a Trauttmannsdorff or a Dietrich-stein, his shock of mouse-coloured hair falling over his brow as he did so.

Was Fräulein Pepi's gracious Mama at home?

Fräulein Pepi regretted.

Because he had brought this English – no, Scottish gentleman, on the suggestion of Fräulein Pepi's honoured Papa. This gentleman was on the outlook for a room in the house of honourable people, where he

71

might be one of the family and practise his German. He had come all the way from Scotland to organise and manage a new factory in the Neubau district. In the meantime, Herr Pommer, pleased to impress upon Pepi his accomplishments, told her somewhat off-handedly that he had given himself up to acting as this gentleman's interpreter, the great Maximilian Hirsch having decreed that he should do so.

Fräulein Pepi permitted herself some show of interest. The gentleman from Scotland was formally presented to her. He was a bony sort of young man with an abrupt handshake, queer English clothes, and no discernible manners. But he had white teeth, a disarming smile and did not look unfriendly. And, putting him at his lowest, at least he was a novelty. So she hastened to say that although she was the only one at home, she was sure it would be all right to show the gentleman the spare room, as he had been sent by the Papa.

She allowed herself to remark, however, that it seemed strange for him to be seeking rooms in the Favoriten district when his work lay in the Neubau. Secretly, Herr Pommer gave Pepi a bad mark for this. Although he hoped to make her his wife, and although she spoke in a tongue that was quite incomprehensible to the stranger, she must learn that in business – even if it only be the letting of a room – one did not as much as breathe of disadvantages at the moment of negotiation. He said nothing, however, but followed her along, with his companion, into the house. Pepi, remarking that her mother was due to appear at any moment, left the front door open.

III

There were endless peculiarities about the young 'Englishman' who had taken a room at the Klems' in the Quellengasse. And one of the chief of these was that he kept insisting – at first by means of Pommer, his interpreter – that there was no English blood in him whatever; that he came from Scotland. Had not the Klems heard of the land of Mary Stuart, of Shakespeare's Macbeth, and of Sir Walter Scott?

Of course they had! Were not Schiller's 'Maria Stuart' and Shakespeare's 'Macbeth' on the repertoire of the Hofburg Theatre? And Walter Scott? Who had not read Walter Scott? In this City of culture even humble people like the Klems must not admit any ignorance.

But indeed this young Islander was a strange, incomprehensible being. Old Frau Kummer, farther down the Quellengasse, had once had an Oriental medical student who had come to Vienna to study under the great Billroth. And dark though his skin had been, and fantastic his garments, he had seemed to adjust himself much more easily to the life of Vienna. He had been gay and erratic. He had spent hours pleasantly wasting his time in suburban cafés, or in the large coffee-houses on the Ring. He had had several private adventures more or less publicly; and had, in other words, behaved in a way that was normal and understandable. But he had paid well, and old Frau Kummer had been fond of him. Although, indeed, she had been compelled to return a niece, who was in Vienna learning millinery, to her home in Pressburg. The Oriental gentleman was taking her for more rides on the switchback in the People's Prater than Frau Kummer considered wise.

There was nothing of this about the Klems' 'Englishman'. Apart from the fact that he paid regularly, he was different in every respect. Yet no one could say that he wasn't an easy lodger. He was almost no trouble. He was the most serious young man the Quellengasse had ever seen. He took morning coffee at an early hour, then set out on one of the new safety bicycles; bicycles with both wheels the same size – in Vienna the best-known make were 'Kangaroos'– to pedal his way across to his factory in the Neubau. Much to the interest of the Favoriten district.

By means of Herr Pommer, he explained that it saved his waiting for the infrequent horse-trams. In the evening he came back for his meal, and thereafter took himself to his own room, where, on certain nights, Herr Pommer came to give him lessons in German.

In his absence, Pepi took much interest in the foreigner's belongings. It was a way of finding out about him. He had begged for a larger table at which to work, and this was now strewn with technical books and drawings, engineer's blueprints, a German grammar, notebooks containing hieroglyphics connected with his work, and German exercises written out for Willi Pommer.

There were two little photographs. One of a rather forbidding old woman in a white cap, to whom he bore some resemblance, and another of a girl about Pepi's own age. Pepi spent much time wondering about this girl. She was stiffly posed, and wore a fur bonnet that was dowdy by Viennese standards, but, in the picture at least, she was beautiful, with eyes that slanted a little in the same way as the eyes of a Tartar gipsy who had once told Pepi's fortune in the Prater. Was he betrothed to this girl? Married to her? Was she his sister? Had not Pepi been hotly determined to keep Willi Pommer at a distance, she would have begged him to find out.

But, as the weeks passed, the barrier of

language began to dissolve. Herr Pommer had reported at once that his pupil was very intelligent, that, in the factory, his quick mind and his practical good sense were combined with a surprising creativeness. Maximilian Hirsch had shown astuteness in employing this young man. Some time in the beginning of the New Year he would have the little factory running. And it was the same with his study of German. Before many weeks Henry was giving directions to the men in the factory. Here and there Pommer would catch him using their own homely, uninflected speech. He told him that this was not German, but that he was in good company, as the Emperor Franz Joseph, too, spoke Viennese. Henry replied he did not mind what he spoke, so long as the men obeyed him.

Pepi's interest in Herr Hayburn grew as his ability to express himself increased. Now he went out of his way to talk to all of them, begging them to set him right when he went wrong; which was continually. There was laughter at this, and friendliness, and the warm-hearted, suburban family began to like the stranger who had come among them.

At this time Pepi Klem was happy. Her ambition to be a singer had, strangely, ceased to trouble her. Although Willi Pommer came continually to work with Herr Hayburn, she managed to keep him at arm's length, and her parents seemed prepared to let things be.

The young foreigner occupied her mind. She helped him with his stumbling German. She corrected his exercises. He was so unlike other young men, that it was possible, somehow, to treat him with camaraderie, like a schoolboy; to scold him and laugh at him; to forget he was a creature of the opposite sex. And yet he seemed to like her; to turn to her ready friendliness when he was lonely. It was not quite without a pang that Pepi learned that Henry was betrothed to the young woman in the photograph; that he intended to marry her whenever it was possible. But everything about him was so strange, so unreal, that Pepi felt she need not quite believe it.

On Sundays, now, when it was fine, the Klems took him sightseeing. To any Viennese, there is nothing so well worth seeing as Vienna. He seemed to enjoy himself, but his enjoyment had an austerity, an odd, Puritan self-consciousness, that would not be shaken off.

At this time the building of the Ring was in progress. The walls and ramparts of the Inner City had been thrown level to make the most spectacular boulevard in Europe – a spacious circle round the inner town, with trees and gardens being planted and many public buildings nearing completion.

Herr Hayburn's interest seemed caught

with all this planning and laying out. What was the purpose of this great building? And that? It was awkward to be made to feel ignorant about these things by a foreigner. Pepi and Frau Klem were not quite sure which was the new town hall, which the new university, which the new parliament buildings, which the new museums. They had sometimes to refer these questions to the Papa.

But why bother about solemn, unimportant things like public buildings, in this, the capital of elegant pleasure?

IV

Now, in less than a week it would be Christmas. Emerging from the overheated atmosphere of the bank, Willi Pommer dug his gloved hands deep into the pockets of his short overcoat and looked apprehensively at the sky. It was the colour of lead. The snow was late this year, but now it looked like coming. A sharp gust of wind from the east blew papers and straw along the street. Piled-up mud, swept to the side, was frozen to solid iron.

Willi turned up the fur collar of his coat and started off up the street. Somewhere a clock struck the quarter before midday. He had not realised the morning was so far gone. He had been given a note from Maximilian Hirsch to deliver to Mr. Hayburn at the factory in the Neubau, but he decided he would have a walk to rid his lungs of the stifling air of the bank, have lunch somewhere, and deliver the message thereafter. That would be time enough. He was in no hurry to see Mr. Hayburn this morning.

Willi Pommer was depressed, and Mr. Hayburn had much to do with his depression. When the Scotsman had come at first, everything had looked so promising. The study Pommer had made of English had, at last, turned to his advantage. On his return from London, Maximilian Hirsch had enquired among the clerks if any of them knew English well enough to act as interpreter for a young Scotsman who had come to Vienna. Willi had offered himself. It had given him a sudden importance in the eyes of his fellow clerks; it had also allowed him much greater freedom; for, of necessity, his time as an interpreter must be irregular. He had attached himself to this young man from Scotland with an interest almost amounting to passion. In every way he was so different; so incomprehensible, yet so fresh; so far removed from the humdrum of other young men in Vienna, with their favourite cafés, where they sat for hours playing tarock or dominoes, their adventures that were so commonplace that they were scarcely adventures at all, their talk of horse-racing in the Freudenau.

His new duties had made him feel a being set apart; had raised him up into that world of intellect which counts so much with the Viennese. Had he not been such a styleless creature, Willi would have begun to give himself airs.

As he walked from the Bankgasse towards the Franzensring, he came on the staging and partially built walls of what was destined to be the new Imperial Theatre. The intense cold had brought work to a standstill. Scaffolding and stonework alike were rimed with frost. Smoke was rising from the braziers of the crouching watchmen. An itinerant Slovenian peasant in a shaggy sheepskin coat was trying to sell roast chestnuts from his little, wheeled charcoal oven.

Yes. And the culmination of his good luck had come when Mr. Hayburn, tiring of his hotel - or its cost – had begged him to find rooms. Or luck at first it had seemed. Willi's senior at the bank, Joseph Klem, had always been his friend. So much so, indeed, that Joseph and Martha Klem had smiled upon his application for the hand of their daughter. With his pupil settled in the Klem household the advantage to everyone would be great indeed. The foreigner, who seemed quite overwhelmingly respectable for so young a man, would have pleasant lodgings.

The good Frau Klem would receive a welcome addition to her housekeeping money. And he, Pommer, in his capacity of English tutor and interpreter, would of necessity be constantly received in the flat, and thus be able to press his suit with the desirable but rather too high-spirited Pepi.

But as the autumn moved into winter, things had not seemed to get better. Mr. Hayburn's apparent boyishness, his immaturity, seemed to appeal to the young woman. Were they genuine? Or was this yet another example of Albion's perfidy? They had struck up a great friendship, it seemed. She was forever helping him with his German; trying to tease the solemnity out of him.

Slow, single feathers of snow were falling out of the sky as Willi Pommer turned from the Franzensring into the Burgring. By the afternoon, Vienna would wear her winter mantle. Over there, before him in the distance, a company of the Imperial Guard had swept through the Burgtor, their splendid, nervous horses dancing in the sharp cold as they crossed the wide expanse of the Ring on their way to the Imperial stables. It must be after twelve. The Palace Guard was changed.

Somehow the sight of them gave Willi confidence. Pepi was young and wilful. But she was a lovely, gay little creature. Things must take a favourable turn soon.

Deep in this thought, Willi did not notice that a long, striding figure enveloped in a rough Inverness cape was coming towards him. Henry Hayburn hailed him with a shout: 'Hullo, Pommer.'

Willi jumped. The Hayburn was the last person he had expected just then. He was annoyed to find himself returning Henry's greeting almost with an air of guilt.

But Mr. Hayburn certainly noticed nothing. He was radiant, friendly and bursting with news. 'Do you know where I've been?' he demanded gaily, taking the Austrian's arm.

'Where, Mr. Hayburn?'

'I've been down in town arranging my ticket. I've been given leave to go home at Christmas. I'm getting married. I'm going to surprise them.'

'Ach! But I did not know you had...'

'Yes, well, I have. And I am going to bring her back with me. Come and have lunch.'

Herr Pommer was led away expressing congratulations that came from his heart.

Chapter Six

Bel Moorhouse was enjoying herself as an invalid might enjoy convalescence. It was no unpleasant thing to feel that the battle was over, just for the moment; that there need be no more gathering of her forces, no more steeling of the nerves.

Bel had given the customary family Christmas party at Grosvenor Terrace two days ago, and it had been a tiring business. Her sense of hospitality, her sense of importance, her vanity and her kindness of heart had joined themselves together and forced her to ask everybody. And so, in addition to the usual McNairn and Butter families, there had been Mungo and Margaret, and David and Grace; and as Grace's mother, Mrs. Dermott, could not be left solitary, she, too, had received an invitation.

But now, on Saturday evening two days later, Bel's troubles were behind her. The house, except for the still hanging Christmas decorations, showed no trace of the recent upheaval. Exhausted maids had been placated, and she, herself, could rest. She sat by a blazing fire in the pleasant drawing-room of Grosvenor Terrace, her feet on the embroidered hearthstool, occupying herself with needlework. Her husband, Arthur, relaxed for once, sat opposite to her reading his newspaper. Upstairs her children were sleeping. The only member of the family who was not safely beneath the roof was Phœbe, who had gone with the Butter children to the orchestral concert in the New Public Halls, or Saint Andrew's Halls as they were coming to be called. Bel had wondered at her bothering to go. The night had been so wet and stormy.

Even now, as she sat here in the warmth, she started a little, as a particularly sharp squall burst against the drawing-room windows, causing them to shudder in their frames, and driving the rain against the glass.

'Listen to the storm, Arthur,' she said, looking up from her work.

'Aye. It's wild,' was the complacent answer.

'I wish Phœbe had stayed at home.'

'She'll be all right.'

'I hope so.' Bel settled back. She supposed there was nothing to be alarmed about really. And Phœbe had been determined to keep her promise to go with her cousins to the concert.

Yes, she reflected, she had had her troubles with the immense Christmas party. That was the worst of being in a family at all kinds of social levels. The Butters were so homely.

The McNairns were so smug. Bel's own mother, old Mrs. Barrowfield, could be so outspoken, with the habit of flaunting her opinions in broad Scotch to make them sound yet more downright. Set against these, there were David and Grace, who were becoming more and more distinguished as time went on; Grace's mother, who met lords and ladies on her various committees, knew what was what, and did not scruple to say so. And Margaret Ruanthorpe-Moorhouse, a daughter of broad acres, who had genuine, blue blood. An appalling hotchpotch of a family really!

Sitting here at peace, Bel wondered how she had ever had the courage to bring them together. And yet, in spite of awkward moments, it had been a friendly gathering, with much goodwill and a display of affectionate indulgence that did everybody credit.

Bel's besetting sins were her preoccupation with the trimmings of life and her obsession with social compatibility. She had worried that William Butter had not been properly dressed; that her mother's speech was abrupt; that the McNairn boys had seemed rude. But she had not taken account of the sense of security and family good-feeling that existed among them, even among the newer members; of the consciousness of each that, should things go wrong, all the others would be there to give support.

There was another shuddering gust against the windows, and, following it, a metallic crash on what sounded like the private carriage-way of the terrace.

'Good gracious, Arthur. What's that?'

'Somebody's chimney-can.'

'What a night!'

Arthur rose, parted the curtains of a window, and looked out. Street lamps were dancing and flickering. Some of them had been extinguished. A torrent of rain was lashing a trafficless Great Western Road. He fancied he heard a branch crack and break off over there in the Botanic Gardens.

'It's as bad as I've seen,' he said, turning back into the room.

Bel looked up at the clock. It was after nine. She felt a genuine stab of apprehension now. 'I wish Phœbe was at home and safe,' she said.

'She'll take a cab.'

'Do you think a cab will dare to bring her?'

'Of course. It's scarcely time yet.'

Bel went on with her sewing, thinking of Phœbe. She had seemed quieter this autumn. Quieter and more contented. She got letters from Henry in Vienna, but said little about them. Bel had begun to think that her interest in Henry was on the wane. But with Phœbe you never knew. When she asked her how Henry was getting on, Phœbe usually said, 'All right,' and left it at that. But she was well accustomed to Phœbe's queerness. She could do nothing but leave her alone.

There was a momentary lull in the storm. They could hear the sound of horses' hoofs, and presently the slamming of a cab door.

Arthur was at the window again. 'It's stopped here,' he said. 'I'll go and let her in.'

II

'Henry! Where have you come from?'

Henry, still in his Inverness cape, stood grinning at Bel.

'From Vienna. From where else do you think? Can I stay here tonight?'

'Of course.' When had Bel's hospitality ever been appealed to in vain? 'But why didn't you tell us? Phœbe is at a concert.'

Momentary disappointment clouded Henry's grin. He began to unwind his thick scarf. 'It's a terrible night,' he went on. 'I thought the cab was going to be blown over when we were crossing Kelvin Bridge. I hope she'll get home all right.'

'Of course she will. Have you ever known Phœbe stuck?'

Another fierce blast struck the house and roared in the chimney. Henry replied with a doubtful 'No', and stretched out his hands to the fire. 'I've never seen such a storm,' he said. 'My porter at St. Enoch's told me that a lot of the glass roof of the station had been blown in. I'm glad I didn't try to cross from Hamburg to Leith. The porter said word had come through that there was trouble on the East Coast. The Tay Bridge. He didn't know yet whether it was true.'

Arthur joined with Bel in pressing Henry to stay at Grosvenor Terrace, which Henry had fully intended to do. But why was he in Scotland, and what was the purpose of this surprise visit? Henry avoided the answer to this question. He had things to see to at home, but he must return to Vienna within the next fortnight.

As he sat with them talking of his work, Bel and her husband could not help noticing that, in so short a time as three months, Henry's character had undergone many not quite definable changes. He was more of a man. The lines of his face were more mature. It was the old Henry who, gesticulating and excited, was telling them of his struggles in the strange, far-off city where his calling had now taken him; of his difficulties with a strange language; of his troubles with the kindly, almost Oriental lethargy of the Viennese workmen – a lethargy that the people of Vienna themselves, prepared to excuse everything, especially their own and everybody else's shortcomings, dignified by the name of *Schlamperei*. It was at once obvious to Bel and Arthur that Henry was developing. He had been given authority, and he was able to take it. He had said do this to this one, and do that to that other. People had taken his orders as an expert, and neither he nor they had questioned his right to give them. This was fixing his character. Was it also colouring his eagerness with tinges of conceit?

'And what kind of place is Vienna? Is it as wonderful as they say it is?'

What was the meaning of the smile that flickered in Henry's face? Was it the smile of a cosmopolitan, who has returned for a moment to the ignorance of his native province? Was it a faint smile of patronage?

And yet, what had he done in the last months? Gone to Vienna and lodged in a workman's suburb with a family who were less educated than he. Schemed and laboured to set up a factory for harvesting machinery. Studied the German language. Gone for walks, written letters home, suffered from sharp fits of loneliness. The real life of the City had scarcely touched him. He had been quite unaware that a part of the cultural history of Europe was being written under his nose.

He had seen the Emperor Franz Joseph make one of his paternal appearances at his study window at the midday changing of the Palace Guard. He had seen him wave to his people. He had, here and there, caught glimpses of military splendour. But that was all. He had viewed such happenings with little curiosity, and no sense of romance.

And yet the Imperial City had worked a change in him. It had given him a consciousness that lay beyond the horizons of his boyhood. Of lands that took notice of neither his cults nor his creeds; yet seemed to do very well in their ignorance of them, and rise, after their own fashion, to a glory of their own choosing.

The door was suddenly thrown open with the words: 'What a night! We couldn't get a cab and decided to walk.' Phœbe was standing framed in the doorway, dripping and dishevelled.

'Phœbe, dearest, see who's here!'

She stood where she was, looking at Henry, who had risen from his chair. For a time neither of them moved.

Fascinated, Bel tried to interpret the emotions of this strange, unpredictable girl. She saw the colour flood up from Phœbe's neck and set fire to her face. For a moment it wore an expression of softness that Bel had never seen before. Her gipsy eyes shone. Her lips seemed to be exclaiming the word 'Henry!' In an instant it was over, and Phœbe was advancing into the room to shake Henry warmly by the hand, and to kiss him in all friendliness, as though she were his sister.

'Hullo, Henry. What on earth are you doing here?'

'I've come to take you back to Vienna with me.'

The colour began to rise in Phœbe's face again. 'What do you mean?'

'To get married, of course. We've only got a fortnight.'

Phœbe said nothing. She crossed to the mirror over the fireplace and fingered the strands of wet hair that straggled on her cheeks. More, even, than the others, she had already felt the new force that Henry had brought back with him. 'I'm soaking! I must go and change at once. I won't be a minute.' She left the room.

'You never told me!' Bel said as they sat down once more.

'I wanted to tell her first.'

'But, Henry, Phœbe is only nineteen! And you would be taking her so far away! I don't quite see how we can allow it!'

But now Bel remembered how Phœbe had looked a moment ago as she stood in the doorway.

III

Everyone was out at church next morning. The fury had gone out of a wind that had dropped to little more than a breeze. As the

91

Moorhouse carriage, containing Bel, Arthur and their elder son, together with Henry and Phœbe, made its shining way towards town and the Ramshorn Church, a watery sun found strength, for some moments, to pierce a fissure in the low-hanging cloud, filling a wet rain-washed city with a sudden flood of diamond light. Streets were littered with slates and chimney-pots. Shattered glass lay here and there on pavements. Trees, hoardings and wooden fences lay torn and broken.

Already there was early morning talk of a great railway disaster. It was, perhaps, to hear of this that so many people had come out this morning. Being Sunday, there were no newspapers to tell them, but telegrams had been coming from the East Coast. The great middle span of the Tay Bridge had collapsed before the fury of the storm, taking a trainload of some two hundred people with it. Glasgow, along with the rest of the Kingdom, was horrified.

People stood on their church steps, talking of it; declaring it could not be true. And what was the world coming to? – With this dreadful happening; the depression in trade; and last year's collapse of so many banks up and down the country, beginning with the collapse of the City Bank of Glasgow. They shook their heads and agreed that the times were indeed terrible, and that things couldn't be much worse. It was only when the bells showed signs of stopping that they remembered where they were, and turned to hurry inside. In many churches, prayers were offered for the bereaved. And when the service was over, worshippers lingered once more to discuss the disaster further, to tell their friends how their own washing-house door had been torn from its hinges, how a chimney-pot had smashed the glass of garden-frames, or how a tree had fallen on the rose-plot in the front lawn.

Like many another returned traveller, Henry felt himself detached. Those of the family who had come to church this morning expressed momentary surprise at seeing him; then seemed to take him for granted; to forget all about him. He put this down to the all-engrossing news. But in this he was wrong. The imaginations of the Moorhouse family, as of most people, could not stretch beyond the circle of their own experiences. The appearance and customs of the Austrian capital in no way aroused their curiosity; except when they fell to considering if it was wise or foolish to allow one of their number to follow him thither as his wife.

Even on the church steps, Sophia, hearing from Bel that Henry proposed marrying Phœbe and taking her back to Vienna almost at once, was quick to express an opinion. 'But, Bel dear, Phœbe's only a child! Now, if it was my own Margy, I would never think – and I read somewhere that Vienna was a fearfully wicked place! Oh, Henry Hayburn's quite a nice boy, dear; I don't mean he... But you remember we always used to think that his brother Stephen – you know, in David's office – was just a little bit – well, dear, light-minded. Of course, I'm sure he's quite settled down, and all right now, what with his mother's death, and having to work, and everything. Still, the family has a wild streak – and we couldn't have Phœbe...'

At this point Arthur had hurried Bel and their elder son into church, where they found old Mrs. Barrowfield comfortably ensconced in the corner of their pew; her elastic-sided boots on the highest and most comfortable hassock; her special, large print Bible and hymn-book conveniently placed in front of her; and her gold spectacles polished, ready to begin. She was smiling delightedly at Henry and Phœbe, who were already in their places, and she was addressing Henry in loud, unnecessary whispers.

Somehow, Sophia's chatter had stirred up Bel's anxiety. Was she to let Phœbe go? How could she hold her against her will?

Was not Phœbe much too young to marry this impetuous, strange young man, and go to live with him in a great, unknown city? For one of the few times in her life, Bel wished she were better educated – better informed.

Standing, sitting, praying, going through the actions of worship, with elegant, automatic reverence, Bel took in nothing of the service. She was worried by love and anxiety. Phœbe would want to go. Her behaviour last night had shown Bel that.

What, then, had stung Bel to apprehension? Sophia's silly talk? The sense of disaster that hung in the air this morning? But now Bel remembered that Phœbe had once promised to come back to her if she were in trouble. Surely there was comfort in that? Bel stood up for the benediction. For the first time during the service, she found herself receiving some comfort; some quieting of her fears.

IV

'Well, Phœbe? Are you coming back to Austria with me?'

'I think so.'

They had been given possession of Bel's parlour on Sunday evening. For the first time, almost, they were left to themselves.

Henry took her into his arms and kissed her, with a force, a lack of apology, that Phœbe had never met in him before. His former love-making, when, indeed, there had been any, had been boyish, tentative, and virginal. These were the embraces of a man.

95

'No, Henry. Go over there and sit down. That's better. Did you miss me when you were away?'

'Yes. Did you miss me?'

'Of course.'

It was impossible for these two to be arch or oblique in their utterance, the one to the other.

'You know, you've changed,' Phœbe went on, looking across at him.

'For the worse?'

Phœbe considered this for an instant. 'Not for the worse. I think you're a bit older. That's all.' And then after a moment: 'No. I'm glad you went. It's been good for you.'

For reply, Henry allowed a flicker of indulgent amusement to show itself upon his snub features. She had never seen this look of masculine patronage before. Yes, Henry was changing.

'Tell me about everything.'

There was much of the old Henry left. Indeed, now that he was in full cry, chasing his ideas, following his plans, the old Henry seemed livelier than ever.

She was accustomed to these outbursts. Henry, she knew, was launched. A semblance of listening, a word or two of assent, and he could go on like this for hours. And meanwhile she would sit, hearing his voice, basking in his enthusiasm, testing the strength of the bond between them, seeking the answers to the questions of her own unquiet heart.

What had brought her together with this strange young man, who sat here gesticulating happily before her? An uprush of emotion, when, that night two autumns ago, she had seen he was at breaking-point?

She sat watching him, summing him up behind the mask of her smiles. The attitudes of his body. The eagerness of his voice. The graceless expressiveness of his gestures. That was Henry; the Henry she knew now through and through; the Henry she had defended hotly; the Henry she had sometimes quarrelled with childishly; the Henry whose fears she had stifled; whose resolution she had steeled. There was little more now of Henry to know, until she came to know the unknown Henry who was her husband.

Was she ready to go thus far with him? Was she ready to join hands with the unknown Henry, and follow him confidently into an unknown world?

But now, as she sat watching him, his body bent excitedly towards her, it came to her clearly that should Henry leave once more for Austria without her, he would be tearing away a part of her with him. For better or for worse, Henry Hayburn was her own.

'But tell me a little about the *town*, Henry. What does it look like? In what kind of house shall we have to live?'

The will to adventure had never been lacking in Phœbe. And now that she had settled essentials, she was prepared to let excitement do what it would. Henry could tell her that Vienna was a great, important city; a city of spectacle, consequence and glitter. When they got back it would be lying under the white, mid-European winter. But while they settled in, it would be moving forward towards the spring. And people had told him that there was nowhere comparable to Vienna then.

She tried to see Vienna in her mind. But she could not. She had never been in London, and like so many people in the West of Scotland, only once or twice in her own lovely capital. But she allowed the prospect of living in this far-off City of enchantment to take hold of her. Life would be new. She could not believe that it would not be beautiful. And now that she felt sure of her heart, her doubt was banished. This passionate girl could look to nothing but adventure and fulfilment. Her lover saw her eyes were dancing; that her face was flushed with happiness.

'Will they let you come, Phœbe?'

'They'll have to.'

'You're not quite twenty yet. They might say...'

'I'll run away with you if they try to stop me.'

98

'I hope it doesn't have to come to that.'

Presently they found themselves in the drawing-room having tea. David, who was spending the weekend with Grace in Mrs. Dermott's lately acquired house in Kelvinside, had come across to pay Henry his respects.

Grace was doing splendidly, he told Henry. But did not much care to be out of the immediate reach of her mother and the best professional attention now.

Talk at once turned to the disaster. Yes, it was fully confirmed. David had special information. The papers would tell everything in the morning.

Now Henry was all questions. What had happened? Where had the weakness been? What was the speed of the train as it crossed the bridge? What was the force of the wind? Questions that David could not answer.

'I think I'll run through to Newport tomorrow and have a look at the damage myself,' Henry said.

Bel looked at Phœbe. She did not seem to mind.

V

Bel had come to call upon her mother for several reasons this morning. The first one was filial. The old lady had a sharp attack of

99

gout, and had, at the last moment, sent apologies and regrets that she felt unable to attend the wedding of Phœbe to Henry Hayburn, which, hastily arranged, had taken place in the drawing-room of Grosvenor Terrace yesterday. Bel had felt that it would be the next thing to cruelty not to drop down to Monteith Row, on this the morning after, to enquire for her mother's health and give her the gossip.

Again, having assured herself that the tradesmen had already done their part in restoring her house to its usual, Bel had felt it more tactful to leave her maid-servants, tired and out of temper, to take their own time to dust, sweep and add the final polish.

But there was yet another reason for coming out this morning; one she had not yet defined to herself. There had been a feeling of emptiness in the house; a feeling that Phœbe was gone. Presently, when she got back for lunch, she would have to face this fact. But here, sitting drinking tea in her mother's familiar room, the truth could be pushed away for a little longer.

Bel sat, willingly telling the old lady what she expected to hear. Yes, Phœbe had made a beautiful bride. Mrs. Barrowfield's own grandchildren had been the best behaved. Mary McNairn was getting ridiculously fat. George McNairn must have something organically wrong with him. If Bel were

Mary, she would have George thoroughly examined again. Sophia had actually brought that dreadful muff. And in other respects had looked quite inexcusably shabby. After all, William was not a pauper. Yes, Mrs. Dermott had come too, having shed mourning for the occasion. She had been majestic, but amiable, and had renewed her Christmas-dinner friendship with Margaret Ruan-thorpe-Moorhouse, which had been all to the good, as they had mopped each other up. David had come with his mother-in-law, Grace being indisposed and disinclined to come. Stephen Hayburn, looking more settled and sensible than formerly, had been his brother's best man.

'And Henry himself would be looking gey glaikit?'

Bel stiffened a little. Really, her mother used some very old-fashioned expressions sometimes. Why couldn't she say 'rather stupid'? Her daughter wished she wouldn't. The children would be picking them up, and their little school friends in Kelvinside simply wouldn't know what they meant. Broad Scotch was so unrefined. But she knew that remonstrance would merely rouse opposition, and contented herself by saying primly: 'No. I don't think Henry *did* look specially awkward. But his work has changed him, you know. He's much more of a man than he used to be.'

The old woman sat ruminating for a moment. She was thinking of Henry's visits on those frustrated, impatient evenings last summer. It was odd how this young man, a comparative stranger to her, had made for himself a place in her affections. Odd, when she considered how set she was in her ways. Yet Henry's sudden need of her, coupled with his almost simple-minded honesty, had won her over. She looked at her daughter.

'Phœbe is very fond of Henry,' she said at length.

Bel looked at the clock. She stood up. 'Yes, I realised that for the first time on the night Henry came home.' She drew on her gloves and took up her furs. 'Still, Phœbe is so young, I dare say people will blame me. But I felt I was taking too much responsibility if I tried to stop it. Arthur felt the same. And Phœbe can be so self-willed. She might even have taken things into her own hands.'

Mrs. Barrowfield smiled. This side of Phœbe appealed to her.

She kissed Bel, patted her on the shoulder, and assured her that, knowing the young people as she did, there was nothing else to be done; that they were good bairns; and that everything would turn out for the best.

VI

Little Isabel and Thomas Moorhouse were standing on the doorstep as their mother arrived back at Grosvenor Terrace. Sarah had, in spite of upheavals, found time to take them for their morning walk in the Botanic Gardens, and they were just come back. The children jumped and waved at the sight of the carriage, and at once begged Bel to allow them to climb up beside McCrimmon into the driving-seat and drive round to the coach-house in the lane. Bel cautioned them that it must be nearly their dinner-time, told them to hurry and passed on into the house.

Everything was put back and in order. All the signs of Phœbe's wedding had been removed. Yet the house was strange. Bel caught herself humming a tune to keep her spirits up, as she went from room to room inspecting. The dining-room, the back parlour. And on the first floor, the drawing-room. Everything had been set aright. On the top floor she hesitated. Out of cowardice, she went into the children's rooms first. The nursery. Where, by the way, was her son Arthur? His school bag was lying in his room. She called his name but there was no reply.

At last she turned the handle of Phœbe's room and went in. It, too, had been put into some kind of order. Cardboard boxes and tissue paper had been stacked on the bed. On a chair there was an old dress, that seemed almost part of Phœbe herself. Bel took it up to shake it out, then, surprised by a quick emotion, laid it hurriedly down again, telling herself not to be a fool.

As she turned to go she was startled by a sound. She cast her eyes about her. There was nothing to be seen. She looked behind the window curtains. Then at last beneath the bed, where she found her eight-year-old son Arthur lying on his stomach.

'Arthur, what are you doing there, frightening the life out of me? Why didn't you answer when I called?'

The boy crawled out reluctantly. His face was swollen, grubby and tear-stained.

'Arthur, what's wrong?'

He did not answer.

'Did you get a whipping at school this morning?'

He shook his head.

'Are you ill with eating too much yesterday?'

Again he shook his head.

'Well, it must be something. What is it?'

Arthur did not reply. He stood looking red and sheepish. His mother examined him, puzzled. Arthur was getting a big boy now. He didn't often cry.

'Is it because your Aunt Phœbe's gone away?'

A fresh welling of tears gave Bel her answer. Really, this was ridiculous! She felt herself going, too, now! She held her son to her, and indulged herself for one long, luxurious minute. Suddenly she had an inward picture of Phœbe looking at them, glum and scornful, as only Phœbe could look. In the middle of her weeping, she began to laugh.

'Arthur,' she said, 'do you know what your Aunt Phœbe would say if she were here?'

'What, Mamma?'

'She would tell us both to stop being silly and go and wash our faces!'

Chapter Seven

They had arrived last night, and had come to this inexpensive little hotel in the Domgasse. It was after nine on their first morning in Vienna. Now, as they stood in their bedroom, they could hear the outside wings of the double doors open, and then a knock. Henry Hayburn, engineer, of Glasgow, Scotland, not quite loath to show off his accomplishments before this, his newly acquired wife, shouted in German: 'Come in!'

A homely young porter in a striped waistcoat and a green baize apron, with thick blond hair tumbling over his sweating, over-worked brow, begged pardon a thousand times, but might he inform the gracious gentleman that there was yet another gracious gentleman awaiting his pleasure in the hall downstairs.

All this fine speech, rendered less formal by the slovenly, endearing dialect of Vienna, conveyed nothing to Mrs. Henry Hayburn, but her husband took care to show her that it conveyed something to himself. He took the card the boy held out and read the name: 'Maximilian Hirsch'. The gentleman downstairs had said it would give him great pleasure to be presented likewise to the gracious lady, the porter added, quite un-bashfully casting approving, friendly eyes over Phœbe.

'That's the boss. You had better come down and see him,' Henry said, turning to his wife. 'Immediately,' he added, addressing the porter, who thereupon bowed himself out.

As Henry and Phœbe made their way downstairs, Maximilian Hirsch came forward, to greet them. He had not seen Phœbe on the day of his visit to Duntrafford. The sight of this beautiful child Henry had brought back filled him with interest.

'Mrs. Hayburn!' He bent over Phœbe's hand and raised it to his lips.

Phœbe blushed scarlet. This behaviour

106

was so very foreign. Her look sought help from Henry. Henry shut one eye.

Like many of her race, Phœbe was suspicious of extreme politeness. But this dark-skinned man of fifty, with his shock of black hair, his coat with its astrakhan collar, and his carefully pronounced, foreign English, seemed friendly enough. Besides, Henry's employer must be shown respect. Awakening to her responsibilities as a married woman, Phœbe did her best.

Yes, they had arrived late last night at the Nordwest Bahnhof, she told him. It had been a somewhat cold journey, but interesting. They had sailed from Leith. They had spent a night in Hamburg and a night in Berlin. Yes, it was all very new to her indeed. No, Phœbe had never been out of Scotland before.

She seemed a very direct sort of young woman, this, Herr Hirsch decided. Her first embarrassment had passed at once. It had, obviously, been superficial. There was no need to set her at her ease. She was at her ease already. Her figure was girlish and appealing in the close-shaped dress of dark green stuff with its prim little cuffs and collars. Her beauty was unusual. She seemed neither forward nor reserved. And she had charm. Not the warm, sophisticated charm of Vienna, but rather the cool, inconsequent charm of a half-wild thing.

'I am sorry, Mrs. Hayburn, I must take your husband away with me now. But it will give me great pleasure if you and he will have supper with me some evening soon.'

Phœbe smiled assent.

Mrs. Hayburn was not overtired after her long journey?

Mrs. Hayburn laughed. Of course not. Everything was far too interesting for her to be tired.

Well, very soon, then. Herr Hirsch bent down and raised her hand once more to his lips.

Henry kissed her. 'You're sure you'll be all right, dear?' he said possessively.

Again Phœbe laughed. 'Of course! What would you do if I said I wouldn't be all right? Take me back home?'

Maximilian Hirsch had already swung himself through the outer glass door into the street. Henry hurried after him. As they went, Phœbe, much to the surprise of the head porter, turned, and, forgetting she was a married lady with a dignity to maintain, caught her skirts and bounded upstairs with the agility of a cat.

Back in her room in a matter of seconds, she stood in the centre of it humming to herself. Then she turned to the double windows, flung them open, and stepped out on the crisp, dry snow which lay on the little balcony outside. She was in time to see

Henry striding round the corner, out of the Domgasse.

Standing there in the glittering snow and sunshine, Phœbe was suddenly, astonishingly, caught up in a flame of tenderness – tenderness for the young man she had just seen disappearing. She had never felt so light, so uplifted. With surprise it came to her that, for this instant in time, she was completely happy. That a joy, new, yearning and radiant, had taken possession of her.

She loved Henry, then. She had never before been quite sure. She had been sorry for Henry; had faith in Henry; fought for Henry. But now all these feelings were as nothing to this shining, consecrated joy, that was to stamp itself upon her memory and remain with her for ever.

For a time she stood in the blinding, winter sunshine, taking in nothing of what she saw about her, wrapped in this unexpected ecstasy. But at last the sting of the cold air brought her back to the world. She returned to her room, flung her long travelling coat round her, and came out again to see what was to be seen.

She leant on the balustrade looking up and down the street. It seemed strangely quiet here, to be in the heart of a great city. One or two children hurried along chattering; as little understandable as monkeys. Strange little children, in unfamiliar clothes. She could see a fat woman in the house opposite, with her hair in curl-papers, plumping just such another feather-balloon as they had on their own bed here. From a passage-way at the top of the street a man appeared. He must certainly be an officer. He came down towards her. What a magnificent creature he looked in his long black cloak, swinging open to reveal his green uniform, his slim-drawn waist, and his trousers cut so tight that they revealed his leg muscles! He might have been a figure in an operetta. But he had too much of an air; too much insolent distinction. As he passed beneath her he cast up black, questing eyes.

Bells that seemed to come from the sky joined themselves to the jangle from other churches, then struck ten. Phœbe twisted herself about, and just managed to see a tall spire almost above her. Filled with curiosity, she withdrew from the balcony to find out her whereabouts in a guide-book Henry had left with her. That must be the spire of the Church of Saint Stephen. Now the cobweb-patterned map of this new city had become a challenge in her hands. She must go out! Out into Vienna!

II

She must go out into this snow-clad, glittering city, into the sunshine to meet the new life that was to give her so much happiness!

But first she must set their luggage to rights. They had come late last night, and gone to bed very tired. She must tidy up this queer room, with its red plush sofa, its worn carpet, its shabby gilt chairs, its stove instead of a fireplace, which was to be their home until they could make better arrangements. An odd room, but not unfriendly; and the centre now of her universe.

She picked up the clothes that Henry had thrown off after his journey. They were new – hastily bought while he was at home. But already they were redolent of Henry's soap, Henry's tobacco, Henry's person. Already they had taken on creases from Henry's body. It pleased her to touch them, to fold them away. Life must go on like this. Things must never change. But with the thought of change, a breath of doubt blew through her mind. No, that was ridiculous. Of course things must change. Yet they need not change for the worse. Besides, no one expected to live on pinnacles for ever.

But she must hurry into her outdoor clothes, and have a first glance at this city she had come to live in. As she descended, the porter came round from behind his desk in the entrance, and asked in halting English if he might call a *Komfortable* for Madame. A *Komfortable*, he condescended to inform

111

Madame's ignorance, was a one-horse cab. Madame thanked him – no. She was just going out for a walk. He bowed, held the door open for her, then returned to his desk.

She was charming, this girl, with her good but not quite fashionable clothes, and her fearless eyes, he said to himself, conducting one of his many little one-sided conversations, as was his habit to alleviate boredom. Now, if she were Viennese, what couldn't she look like? But, then, British women seemed to take a delight in throwing away their assets.

In a few moments Phœbe had found herself in the square surrounding the Cathedral of Saint Stephen. People were hurrying across it. Some two or three were going into the great church itself. Was a service beginning, or did the churches here, quite unlike the churches at home, remain open all the time? She must ask, because she wanted to have a look inside. What beautiful flowers in that window, still half-clouded with morning frost! Hothouse flowers they must be. Presently she was examining with rapture the shops, some of them world famous for their elegance, first in the Graben and then in the Kärntnerstrasse. She went from one window to the other, her face glowing with cold, her heart singing within her. She was young, she was feminine, she was having her first sight of Vienna. And in an hour or two she was going back to have lunch with her husband.

Now what was this great building on her right? She crossed and walked round to the front of it. She looked at her plan. It was the Opera House. Sometime she and Henry must go to a performance, just to see the inside of the building. She looked at a playbill and was able to deduce the words 'Lohengrin' and 'Wagner' from the angular Gothic scrip. 'The new music,' she said to herself, feeling gaily erudite.

And this must be the Ringstrasse, if she were following her book aright. What a great, beautiful street! How wide and imposing, with its fine buildings and its young trees sparkling in the snow!

What a strange little tram-trolley, with the bells of the horses jingling all the time! It was stopping near her. Should she get in and let it take her where it chose? No. Her husband had warned her not to lose herself. She must, she told herself demurely, do what her husband told her. And there was more than enough to see if she merely walked about.

Tingling with adventure, Phœbe went along the Opernring. The air was cold but exhilarating. The snow flew up in a dry powder at the touch of her foot. Presently she came to the Hofgarten. The wintry branches of its trees stood up like white coral.

The new palace was still only on paper, and thus Phœbe, looking across the immense open space made by Palace Gardens, parks and squares, to the distant heights of Kahlenberg, wondered if she had suddenly come to the edge of the city. But glimpses of other, distant buildings through the snowy trees prompted her to continue along the Burgring through that quarter of the city which, more than any other, had but lately come to be the final expression of Habsburg magnificence.

Even now, as she passed along, Phœbe could see that some of the public buildings were not yet completed. There was scaffolding, but little work appeared to be going on. Winter must have brought it to a standstill. But what grandeur! There was so much to see! To explore!

It was strange Henry had said so little of all this. But then, of course, Henry had been preoccupied. And who, better than herself, knew just how preoccupied Henry could be? That was a part of his make-up. And on this shining morning she would not have changed a hair of her husband's head.

At the corner of the Volksgarten she halted for a moment to look about her. Inside the garden itself old women were sweeping the paths clear of their latest powdering of snow. In the stillness she could hear the voices of children playing. She would go in, cut across it, and get back to her hotel through the Inner City.

The air was so still that the slenderest twigs stood motionless, each one bearing upon it its feathery burden of snow. Their pale tracery glittered against the blue of the sky. Brought to life by the burst of sunshine, starlings chattered in the evergreens, and among the fir-trees whose dark branches sagged beneath their white burden. Now and then a bird would fly into the open, making a little cloud of silver dust, as the powdered, displaced snow hung for an instant in the sunlight.

Here in this magic garden it was almost hot. Would she be crazy if she brushed away the snow from one of these seats and sat down for a moment? Three pale, over-disciplined little boys, in dark green coats with sable collars, passed her walking hand-in-hand beside a fashionable governess. A young man, who might be a student, arm-in-arm with a young girl, both of them smiling as they went. A soldier of some cavalry regiment, in long coat and spurred boots. He turned to look at the young woman, sitting here unattended in the winter sunshine, and permitted himself the homage of a smile. The strange, blue eyes remained cool and impersonal as he passed on. Then two women, very elegantly dressed, deep in gossip.

It was beautiful in this hushed, foreign garden, with its strange, snow-covered temple. Beautiful. Far away. Unreal and strange. What was she, Phœbe Moorhouse, doing here? No, not Phœbe Moorhouse, Phœbe Hayburn. At this time exactly a week ago she was dressing for her wedding. All the familiar faces had been about her then. Now, in this place of white stillness, Phœbe asked herself if she would choose that the past week – the week during which she had been Henry's wife – should be taken back and forgotten. She smiled to herself. Her strange moment of ecstasy on the balcony this morning came back to her. No. Something would snap now, if Henry were taken from her. Her husband. The impetuous, yet oddly sensitive male creature, who took her into his arms in the darkness; who was grateful to her for being a woman. A new Henry. But one she would not change. He had shown forbearance and a great tenderness, and out of these things her love for him had put forth a hot, Maytime bud, and burst – it would seem suddenly – into full bloom.

A puff of wind brushed the garden, blowing a light cloud of dry snow before it. She must not risk taking cold through sitting here any longer. She passed by the Ballhaus Platz and the Michaeler Platz into the Kohlmarkt. Here there were still more fine shops to be examined. Italian silk. Bohemian glass. Hungarian leather. Everything that was rich, elegant, unusual. And now here she was in the Graben once more! Phœbe laughed to herself. She had actually recognised it. She was getting to know Vienna! The pealing of bells warned her that it was midday. Henry had said he hoped to get back early. Another look at those shops she had already seen. That fine china. That strange embroidery. Those flowers.

But Henry might have come back, and would be wondering where she had gone to. As she turned into the quiet of the Domgasse, she saw her husband at the front door of their little hotel, waiting for her, bareheaded in the sunshine.

Chapter Eight

It was a quarter to seven in the evening two days later. Maximilian Hirsch pushed his way through the glass doors of a restaurant in the Kärntnerring. He stood for a moment, blinking in the light, while a waiting doorman hastened to relieve him of his heavy fur coat. He thanked the man with what would have been stiff formality, had his thanks not been spoken in the Viennese dialect which proclaimed him one with the fellow-citizen he was addressing. Was the restaurant full?

he asked. There was still room for the gracious gentleman in this dining-room, the man said, indicating a door.

Maximilian thanked him. And there was just one other thing. A foreign young lady and gentleman would ask for him about seven. Would the man be so good as to let him know when they arrived? Meantime he would see about a table.

Maximilian came here only when he had people to entertain. At other times he ate at a restaurant of long standing in the Griechengasse, where he was a *Stammgast* or regular diner. There he found comfort, pleasant familiarity, his own table, and cooking to turn the brain. But this townman's restaurant was no place for strangers. Indeed, a young lady like Frau Hayburn, who, along with her husband, was to be his guest tonight, would have been more than out of place among the sybarites of the Griechengasse.

Besides, this here, was one of the famous restaurants of Vienna. It was a place for Frau Hayburn to see. He called for an aperitif – a pleasant, un-Viennese custom he had learnt in Paris – and sat holding it in his plump white hand, sipping it now and then and looking about him. Yes, all these mirrors, this gilt, brocaded furniture, these glittering gaseliers, that soft music, was far more for a young woman than the subtleties of cooking.

As he sat waiting, his black eyes met the eyes of one or two acquaintances, and each inclined towards the other with conventional bows. This place was the restaurant of finance and wealthy business. It was of the first class, but the aristocracy did not haunt it, as they haunted Hopfners in the Kärntnerstrasse or Sacher's near the Opera. Here Maximilian was on his own social level, and, as a typical man of Vienna – that city of so many sharply defined grades of society – it had never occurred to him to risk the unpleasantness of a snub. His wealthy, middle-class bachelorhood suited him excellently. He much preferred savouring life to wrestling with it.

The strong waters he was tasting gave him a comfortable glow. The hidden orchestra was playing a homely, old-fashioned waltz. It might have been written by Lanner, or his partner the elder Strauss, Maximilian reflected. At any rate, it wasn't a waltz such as, in these days, the younger Strauss was writing – heady, compelling stuff, that was sweeping the town. No; it had the heavy, simple rhythm of a peasants' round dance. Maximilian beat a finger thoughtfully on the damask table-cover. He encouraged the music to rouse the pleasant ache of memory.

Thirty years ago. He had been twenty, and he had gone with fellow-students to Grinzing to drink the fresh-pressed grape, mix with the workpeople, and dance with the girls. Perhaps they had played this tune then. It seemed elusively familiar, and brought things back. It had been early autumn, and he and his girl of the evening had stayed all night in the woods. He remembered the dawn as it came up out of Russia. He remembered the early morning birds, and the sunshine beginning to strike through the beech leaves. He even remembered the face of his blonde companion. Why did that music bring back these things so clearly?

And yet he had had a very good fifty years of it. During the first forty of these he had stayed with his mother in a villa in Penzing near the Palace of Schönbrunn. At her death, and now being a man of substance, he had removed his easy existence to an expensive flat in the Inner City. His windows had a view of the Minoriten Church and the open space that surrounded it. In addition to being within walking distance of the bank, he was now within walking distance of the Opera and most of the theatres. Like most educated Viennese, his interest in these places was fanatical.

Thus he had fashioned the pattern of his life – a pattern easy for an intelligent, wealthy citizen to weave in this graceful, culture-loving, pleasure-mongering city. Some imperial pride; a real and perceptive interest in the art of the opera singer and the actor; much excellent eating; some selective drinking. Kindness and good manners; some cynicism; much self-indulgence. No attempt to pierce the iron defences of circles, intellectual or aristocratic, to which he did not belong. Pleasant affairs – a sin hidden is quite forgiven – and just as much work as would keep him going.

The band had finished its nostalgic music. Maximilian Hirsch pulled out his fine gold watch, flicked it open, and looked at the time. It was after seven now. What had happened to the Hayburns? Oh, there they were! He jumped to his feet. As they were led towards him, he saw that they had seen him and were grinning, a little gauchely, as they came.

A broad smile of welcome overspread his smooth, dark face as he advanced to greet these two denizens of another world.

II

Maximilian liked to think of himself as a taster of life. He liked to see himself, a highly civilised citizen of a highly civilised city, sampling, appraising, measuring – places, peoples and manners – with his own urbane, tolerant yardstick; savouring the bouquet of them as he would savour the bouquet of a wine he did not know.

Tonight he was enjoying himself. They were something fresh for him, these two. The quality of the young man he already knew. He was quick and decisive in his work. He had enterprise, and that strange, British seriousness that had no play-acting about it. So far as young Herr Hayburn's work was concerned, Maximilian was receiving what he paid for. He had been no dilettante when he had engaged this young man. But Maximilian had long satisfied himself about this. It was not Henry's constructive talents that filled his mind now.

He sat in his corner smiling genially upon his guests, rotating the stem of his wine-glass with his finger and thumb, and looking on the luxurious stir in the room beyond. At a nearby table, a party which had dined early in order to reach their box in the Opera before the first act was over was rising to go. Laughter. Perfume. The rustle of silks. The aroma from long Viennese cigars. Discreet music. Waiters hurrying to and fro. Stacked plates. Service wagons. Pails of ice. Flowers. Well-dressed men, prosperous and polite. Their women; charming, young, and dependent; or old, influential and bedizened. If, like Maximilian, you understood some of the relationships behind these good manners, it was all the more entertaining. No; his business relationship with the Hayburns did not concern him tonight. He saw them as a new and amusing type, lit with a flame that gave forth, somehow, a different light from the brilliance around them. They did not conform to the Anglo-Saxon pattern he was accustomed to. Particularly the girl, with her dark blue, strangely set eyes, that were avidly taking in everything around her. He must find out what she was thinking.

And they seemed so simple, so artless. At their naïve request that he should choose for them, he had ordered a meal of *Backhendl* followed by *Salzburger Nockerl*. They were eating these things with appetite, but no special show of interest. Their glasses of *Voeslauer* were scarcely touched.

The orchestra was playing snatches from a Mozart opera. Unconsciously, Mrs. Hayburn was beating time as her hand lay on the table.

'Do you like Mozart, Mrs. Hayburn?'

'I beg your pardon? Do I like—?'

'Do you like the music of Mozart?'

'Yes, I like all music.'

He saw that she did not recognise the composer of this fragment. 'Perhaps you did not hear much music in Glasgow? But now that you have come to Vienna—'

'Oh yes, we had splendid concerts in Glasgow. We used to go sometimes.'

'But here, in Vienna, you can hear everything! The best! Opera, concerts—!' Maximilian shrugged and cast eyes of wonder and appreciation heavenwards.

'Yes, I hope we'll have time.'

Time! Would a young woman with a single drop of Vienna running in her veins have talked about having time? 'My dear young lady! It is your duty!'

For reply Phœbe smiled with respectful indulgence. After all, she could not be expected to argue with Henry's employer. Besides, foreign though Mr. Hirsch might be, he could not possibly be quite serious.

Maximilian drained his glass, asked them if their food and wine were to their taste, received quite formal assurances, and decided it was no easy matter putting himself into accord with these strange young people.

And yet she was lovely, this child. Put her in the hands of a good dressmaker, teach her to moderate, to mix with graciousness the suddenness of her manners, let her pick up the small change of conversation, and she would become enchanting.

He was following this train of thought when he made his next remark. 'I must present you to my aunts, Mrs. Hayburn. They are much older than you, of course, but they can teach you about our wonderful Vienna.'

Phœbe murmured that she would be very pleased.

No. A strange, gauche creature, who had everything to learn. 'And where are you going to stay, Mr. Hayburn? You are still in your little hotel, yes?'

Phœbe answered for him. 'Henry had quite a nice room before he was married. He thinks we might go back there.'

'What! To the Quellengasse in the Favoriten? Impossible!'

She was looking at him directly now – regarding him gaily with those strange eyes of hers. 'Why?'

'But it is a workmen's quarter! You have your lives to live! The shops! The theatres! You will make friends! You cannot receive in the Favoriten!'

'But, Mr. Hirsch, Henry and I are here to work, not to play!' She was so earnest, so charmingly young, that he leant over and patted her hand.

'But you must play, too, my dear child. It would be much waste for you only to be serious, here in Vienna.'

A cloud he did not understand passed across her face. 'Henry has his way to make,' was all she said in reply.

But her host was quick to note that, a moment afterwards, her eyes were full of eager amusement as a bejewelled woman entered the room flaunting a scarlet ostrich fan.

'Henry! Would you look at the size of that fan!'

At last she was understandably charming. Her eyes were sparkling now like those of any other young woman. He wondered what she would say if she knew this woman's history, and the aristocratic names of those who had given her her finery. Yes. He must do something about the education of this lovely barbarian.

III

It was a very few days after this that Phœbe had an envelope handed her by the porter of her hotel. She had just come back from one of her many solitary walks of exploration. It was time for lunch, she was very cold and hungry and, remembering that Henry had said he would be too busy to have his mid-day meal with her, rather more lonely than she cared to admit.

The envelope was addressed to her in a strange, spidery hand. She tore it open. For a moment it was difficult for her to make out the writing. But reading it through more than once, the full sense became plain. It was a message in stiffly phrased, imperfect English, inviting her to come to the Paulaner-gasse in the Wieden on the following day. The writer signed herself Stephanie Hirsch, described herself as the aunt of Maximilian Hirsch, and hoped that Mrs. Hayburn would do her sister and herself the honour of taking the midday meal with them. Further, the writer asked Mrs. Hayburn's pardon for inviting her thus informally, and might she assure her that no disrespect was meant? But, as her sister was no longer young, and as she, the writer, was inclined in winter to a chest complaint, they neither of them went out any more than was quite unavoidable. Being 'English', perhaps Mrs. Hayburn would find it easier to overlook this unconventionality, and dispense with the ladies' failing to pay a first ceremonial call upon her. If Mrs. Hayburn accepted, the carriage would be sent for her tomorrow.

Mrs. Hayburn had no difficulty whatever in overlooking the daring unconventionality of the aunts of Maximilian Hirsch. From the letter, she suspected that the ladies might be somewhat alarming, but already she was becoming tired of being left so much to herself. She sat down, then, to write them a note of grateful acceptance, which her friend the porter undertook to have delivered.

At half-past eleven next morning a carriage, drawn by handsome Russian horses, came to a standstill before the door of the hotel in the Domgasse, and Phœbe was conveyed to the apartments in the Wieden.

An avuncular house-porter, middle-aged and benign, and treating her with that combination of respect and approval which is one of the charms of simpler Vienna, led Phœbe up the old-fashioned stone stairs to the flat on the first floor.

Presently Phœbe found herself in an ante-room, the window of which overlooked the street. Being alone, she gazed about her. It was a very strange sort of place indeed. More a museum than anything else, she decided, and certainly the last sort of room she had expected two elderly ladies to possess.

It was essentially a male room. Apart from the curtains at the window of double glass – the inner ones elaborately looped-up lace, the main ones of plain red baize – there was little that would not have been appropriate in a mountain hunting-box. The chairs were stretched with worn leather, and studded with many brass nails. A skin took the place of a rug on the floor of polished hardwood. But most amazing of all to Phœbe were the heads of foxes, the heads of chamois, the antlers of stags, and even the head of a wild boar, which hung from the walls. There were several daguerreotypes in plush or gilt frames, depicting an old, but apparently vigorous gentleman in Tyrolese costume. Occupying the place of honour in the midst of these was an oleograph of the young Emperor Franz Joseph himself, wearing a Styrian hunter's hat, with its shining black-cock plumes, and a long grey hunter's cape, from beneath the fold of which the muzzle of a sporting gun protruded.

Phœbe was examining these things with

curiosity, when she became aware of the rustle of silk behind her. She turned in confusion. A tall, thin lady of sixty-five was standing very erect, holding out her hand and smiling.

'Mrs. Hayburn, no? It is a pleasure that you come!'

She was surely the most civilised human being Phœbe had ever seen. Her stiff black dress was bustled, although this was not the fashion of the year; it was severe and un-adorned – unless the little crucifix on a fine gold chain might be called an adornment. Her poised head, with the well-tended grey hair cut to a fringe that came low on her brow. Her smile that seemed just to have won the battle for kindly tolerance against instinctive disdain. Her white hands. Phœbe felt uncouth and provincial.

'You look at the picture of our dear father, yes? He is dead already twenty years. He hunted very much. He arranged this room, and we do not change it. This is the Kaiser, Franz Joseph, no? My dear father had allow-ance to hunt several times in his private lands.'

The tall lady seemed inordinately proud of this fact, as she led the way through the door, whence, presumably, she had come. As she followed her, Phœbe did her best to respond by making appropriate, awestruck noises.

Now they were in a larger room, carpeted and more feminine. At a round cherry-wood table, a little bent lady, who seemed much older, was sewing.

'My sister, Helene, Mrs. Hayburn.'

The elder lady did not get up. She merely gave Phœbe her hand, and bestowed upon her a smile of benignity resembling her sister's. 'Do you speak German, please?' she asked in a voice of great gentleness using the German tongue.

Phœbe shook her head.

'Tell her I can't speak English, Stephanie,' Fräulein Hirsch said to her sister, once again taking up her embroidery. 'You must be our interpreter.'

'You look at this room, too, Mrs. Hayburn?' Fräulein Stephanie asked, seeing Phœbe look about her.

'It's beautiful!' Phœbe's eyes went every-where. The cherry-wood furniture, elegant and frail; the faded striped coverings; the china and bric-à-brac; the coloured glass in its special cabinet; the silhouette portraits and miniatures hung in thin gilt frames against striped walls; the faded carpet of lime green with garlands of roses; the white porcelain stove. It was a room of pale tones, but, with many fresh spring flowers, it was friendly and charming.

'I am glad that you like it.' The Viennese woman was pleased. 'It is old. Our mother was young in the Biedermeier times. Except for photographs and piano, we keep this room old, too. Most young people who come–' She shrugged and smiled with sad indulgence. '*Na?* You will come now, please?'

Lunch had been announced.

IV

Phœbe found herself in the dining-room of the flat. It, too, was old-fashioned, but elegant, and there was no doubt about its dignity. A very old man, who had been their father's personal servant, waited upon the ladies. She noted with interest his blue tailcoat, his brass buttons and the white cotton gloves he wore as he handed dishes.

All this was old, established and strange. But Phœbe found herself responding; enjoying this new adventure; taking pleasure in the company of these stiff, but not uncharming women. The yellow muscatel wine, that the man-servant had poured out for her unasked, expanded her senses.

'I'm very new to Vienna,' she found herself saying. 'If I make mistakes, you must tell me.'

'No. A young lady so charming is not able to make mistakes, Mrs. Hayburn.'

She was beautiful, this girl, Stephanie Hirsch decided. Beautiful, and likeable. And

131

although her manners seemed casual, they were not rude, neither were they quite English. Did the Scots, then, differ from the English in these things? Phœbe's youth moved her as she had not been moved for long. It would give her pleasure to take her guest under her wing, help her, if she would allow it. Max, their nephew, had been quite right to ask them to receive her.

'No, please! You do things so differently. It would be very kind of you to tell me.' (What would Bel have said to this? Phœbe begging to be taught manners!) 'You see, there are so many things I don't know. You could help me so much.'

It is flattering to be asked for guidance. And none the less so if one is old and conventional, with the best of life beyond recall. And especially when she who asks for guidance is young, quick and full of red blood. Fräulein Stephanie knew that most Viennese young women of Phœbe's looks and age would have taken little pleasure in coming here to her backwater in the Paulanergasse. But she guessed that this foreign girl might be somewhat lonely, somewhat bewildered, somewhat directionless, despite – or perhaps, indeed, because of – her very recent marriage, and the great changes it had brought her.

And thus an unlikely friendship between Phœbe and Stephanie Hirsch sprang up.

After their meal the elder sister went to rest, while Phœbe, pressed to remain, sat with the younger, listening and learning.

The relatives at home would not have known this Phœbe. And yet it was the same Phœbe, impelled by a sudden new enthusiasm, enjoying a new experience – a feeling of play-acting, perhaps, a feeling that now she was doing something that those at home would never do.

She had drunk her afternoon coffee, said her farewell, and promised to come soon again and bring her husband with her. Now she found herself once more sitting in the well-preserved, old-fashioned carriage.

As it clattered over the snowy cobbles, Phœbe smiled to herself. She was delighted – childishly gleeful, indeed – over her visit. Her husband did not know everything about Vienna! She was opening up ground on her own account now, learning customs she had known nothing of. Her long talk with Stephanie Hirsch had been warm and instructive.

In the last days she had been secretly doubtful of what the future would hold for her. It was very well to be brave and spirited. But these things did not make up for lack of experience, nor, for that matter, for quite blank ignorance. Today she had found another woman she could turn to. A strange, rather stiff foreign woman, perhaps, but one with whom she found herself in sympathy. And she was grateful. The thought, indeed, gave more comfort than Phœbe's courage liked to admit to Phœbe's nineteen years.

Chapter Nine

Their first quarrel since their marriage. Before it, Henry and Phœbe had spent much of their time together in adolescent bickerings, as two much attached school friends might bicker.

But now their new awareness of each other made disagreement different. These hot young people were now so much of one flesh that the inevitable divergences which, sooner or later, must arise from the clash of their strong wills could not but cause them surprise and pain.

The quarrel took place after Phœbe's return from the Hirsch ladies. Henry had come back to the hotel in the Domgasse with news. His tutor and interpreter, Willi Pommer, had appeared this morning, and he had gone out to lunch with him. Herr Pommer had brought word from the Quellengasse. The good Herr and Frau Klem were well; and Pepi, despite some show of what Willi was solemnly pleased to call high spirits, had, at last, consented to become formally betrothed to himself.

Even Henry, who was no reader of other people's hearts, wondered a little at the point of view Willi was taking; at the Austrian's strange, and what seemed almost insensitive satisfaction over his now nearly certain hopes of becoming the possessor of a modest dowry, and the pretty little wife that went along with it. But Henry had long since learnt to accept divergences of outlook in this unaccountable city, and if they did not directly concern himself, he saw no reason to harass his mind with them.

And Herr Pommer had brought a message from the Klems to Herr Hayburn. They hoped that he would do them the great honour of coming to see them, and of bringing the gracious lady with him. The Klems had become very attached to Henry Hayburn, Willi assured him – rather to Henry's surprise – and naturally they would be much interested to meet the wife he had so recently brought back. In addition, there were books, papers and clothes belonging to Herr Hayburn at the Quellengasse. Frau Klem was a little surprised he had not been to see after these, and would be glad to know what he intended to do about them.

Henry now took the opportunity of asking Herr Pommer's advice. Would it not, didn't he think, be a good idea if he and Phœbe went back to the Quellengasse to live for a time? Since he had returned to Vienna, Henry had been so much occupied with his work at the factory, with showing his wife Vienna, and in settling down to marriage generally, that he had had little time to think of more permanent lodgings. Now he had come to a point where everything must be sacrificed to his work. His wife understood this perfectly; and did not Herr Pommer think that she would do better to be under Frau Klem's wing, than struggling alone, or more doubtfully befriended, in unknown rooms elsewhere?

Herr Pommer certainly thought so. The gracious lady had the language to study. He would find her a suitable teacher, and Pepi, of course, would help while she was still there, which would not be – his face flushed with complacent self-consciousness – for very long, he hoped. And when she was gone, perhaps they could have Pepi's room as well. He was sure that his future mother-in-law was anything but grasping. She would be glad to let them have it for very little more.

If Willi seemed, at this point, rather to have taken upon himself the role of calculating son-in-law, Henry was too well aware of the advantages he was setting forth to let this disturb him. Yes, Frau Klem's was certainly the place for Phœbe and himself. He was in no doubt about this whatever. Though the room he had occupied would be somewhat cramped, Phœbe was as anxious to save money as he was. Indeed, she, herself, had already spoken of going to the Klems. If the good Frau Klem would but have them, Henry was certain his wife would be as delighted with the idea as he was.

But in that certainty he was wrong. And this was not the reason for their quarrel.

He had no sooner suggested that they should, this very evening, settle their permanent headquarters, than he was made aware of the fact that Phœbe had been having ideas put into her head by the aunts of Maximilian Hirsch.

'But, Henry, the younger Miss Hirsch says that only working people live out in the Favoriten.'

'Well, we're working people, aren't we? We're here to work, anyway.'

'Oh, you're trying not to understand me! You know perfectly well what I mean.' Phœbe, flushed and angry, turned from the long glass in front of which she was brushing her hair before going down to supper.

Henry was on the edge of their bed, still in the thick, fur-lined coat the Viennese winter had forced him to buy. He got up and began to struggle out of it moodily. 'We haven't come out here to live like swells, anyway,' he grumbled. His wife's unexpected opposition in this, his new world of tenderness, shocked his senses more than he cared to admit. But that was no reason for giving way.

'Of course not, Henry. But after all, as Miss Hirsch says, we're young and have our lives to live.'

'Lives to live? What does she mean?'

'Well, enjoy ourselves a little, and cultivate our minds, Henry!'

'I never heard such rubbish! The way to live your life is to do the work you have to do – properly and well!'

Phœbe turned back to the mirror, brushing her hair savagely. At another time she might have smiled at her own glum reflection. But now she was too angry. She knew that when Henry spoke of his work, he was speaking of something that was his obsession. So long as he was left to that, he did not care where he – or she – lived. It was his enjoyment. But what about herself? What did she get out of it? No. This was downright hypocrisy. As his wife, she must not allow it. He had no right to treat her like this; pushing her into the house in the Quellengasse so that he could conveniently forget about her!

Phœbe was not yet twenty. Rights and wrongs were still black and white. She had not yet learnt that the colour of compromise is grey. And she had come back so uplifted, so enchanted, as only a young girl can be,

138

with the new friend she had found today – a friend who must know so much more about life in Vienna than Henry possibly could. She turned to Henry once again: 'But, Henry, surely we can afford–'

'How do you know what we can afford?'

'You told me yourself before we were married that we were earning enough to live comfortably.'

'But not enough to squander!'

'Oh, of course not! But Miss Hirsch says–'

'Damn Miss Hirsch!'

'Henry! Don't you dare!' Phœbe stamped her foot. Arthur and David would never use language like that! She stood close in front of him, her hair down, her colour high, her eyes blazing.

Suddenly this new facet of her strange beauty, joined to his own trembling feelings, overcame him. He caught his wife's lonely unwillingness into his arms – unwillingness which did not last.

And when they came to descend for their evening meal, Phœbe, a hand through Henry's arm, had promised she would go with him to visit the Klems that evening. They would decide everything after they had been there.

II

Like many who glory in the adventures of the mind, who are inventive and bold in their vocation, Henry felt a timidity, a dislike of change in the background of everyday things. His homing instinct was strong. It had been a wrench, an uprooting, for him to come to Vienna in the autumn. Only the strongest pressure of circumstances could have forced him to the step. But, having got himself there, and having found a room in the Quellengasse, his homing instinct had reasserted itself. It was there he had managed to settle down.

Frau Klem had been kind. She had looked to his comfort almost fanatically. Recognising him to be eccentric, she had cooked his meals at whatever times of the day or night he had chosen to appear, regardless of the fact that he might have spared her by eating at the suburban restaurant nearby. She had looked to his mending and his linen. And, when the cold came, seen that the fire in his stove burned brightly. It is doubtful if Henry noticed any of these attentions. But it had made him aware that the Klems' was a very good sort of place to have a room in.

Besides, there had been Pepi. Gay, light-headed and ridiculously pretty, she had run about, serving him as her mother did; helping him with his German when he asked her;

teasing him when she thought his mood was dark. Deep in his preoccupations, Henry had taken almost as little notice of her as he had of her blond, leonine father. They were, one and all of them, part of a convenient background – nothing more. If Pepi had conceived an interest in the gesticulating, innocent young stranger, the last person who had been aware of this was the stranger himself.

What, then, could be better than the Quellengasse, if Frau Klem would have them? Thus, in the evening, after their meal, Henry set out with Phœbe.

The night was cold and brilliant. There had been a powdering of snow earlier. As they crossed the Stephansplatz, they could see smooth drifts, new, white and unsullied, blown into corners of the great cathedral's walls. Looking down the Graben, they saw that a full moon was flooding the white roofs of the central booths and the straw-covering of the rococo fountain, with a light that seemed almost blue, against the yellow warmth of flaring, gas-lit windows. Overhead there were stars.

Despite the cold, the evening promenade in the Kärntnerstrasse was in full swing. Shops and restaurants were blazing with light. Even on this winter night, the street was teeming. Men and women wrapped in heavy furs. Officers of line regiments. Demimondaines

141

in the height of winter fashion. Personal servants brought from the further parts of the Empire, bearing themselves proudly in the full consciousness of their magnificent regional clothes. A Slavonian woman, her many petticoats ballooning out beneath her heavy sheepskin coat, and wearing hessian boots and a turban. A Polish woman, seen through the plate-glass windows of a famous coffee-house, wearing a white skirt braided with gold, red-leather boots, a white fur-lined attila and a lancer's square-topped cap. Hungarians. Bohemians. Transylvanians. All of them aware of the spectacle they made in this incredible, glittering street. All of them adding to the brittle brilliance of their Empire.

Phœbe hung on Henry's arm. Her heart was singing. It was a far cry from here to Grosvenor Terrace. Tonight Henry and she were very near to each other. The storm had blown up between them, changed to a tempest of the feelings, found its appeasement, and now there was a tender, shining calm. She stopped at one of the several toy-shops in the Kärntnerstrasse. There were dolls dressed in the absurd peasant costumes of these men and women here in the street. She must buy one and send it home to little Isabel.

It was typical of them that they did not think to hire a *Fiaker* or a *Komfortable* to take them out to the Quellengasse. A cab was an expense, a luxury in Glasgow. Unless you were old, or ill, had much luggage or were very self-indulgent indeed. Phœbe and Henry were none of these things, so why hire one, even in Vienna? A tram ran from the top of the Kärntnerstrasse at the Opera house up into the Favoritenstrasse, and they could walk the rest of the way.

All entertainment was early in Vienna, and the opera made no exception to this rule. Thus an hour of the performance must already have passed as they reached the stopping-place near the Opera House and stood waiting. Yet even now fashionable people were arriving, alighting from hired *Fiakers* or private carriages, and passing on into the lighted building.

It would have pleased Maximilian Hirsch to see Phœbe now, as she stood, her shining eyes taking in the extravagance of this lovely, flaunting city. She hugged her husband's arm. It was all so strange, so unreal, so enchanting! Everything was new, everything adventure. If there was another side to Vienna's glamour, Phœbe had not yet even thought about it.

Now the little horse-tram was coming, the many bells on the horses' collars emitting a continuous metallic sound, a cascade of brassy rustlings, as the steaming horses came along the moonlit Ring. Now she was sitting close to Henry in the dim, oil-lit car.

Now they had turned and were heading uphill towards the Favoriten suburb.

III

The Klem family made a picture of domesticity this evening. Joseph Klem lay, stretching his comfortable and corpulent length, on the plush sofa, that stood to one side of the stove. Now and then he withdrew a plump hand from behind his head to stroke his side-whiskers, smooth back his thick, blond mane, or remove from between his teeth for a moment the carved meerschaum pipe he was ruminatively engaged in smoking. He wore a patched jacket and embroidered slippers, that had once been worked for him by his schoolgirl daughter, Pepi. The colours of these had been of a child's bright choosing, but a homely dinginess had long since claimed them, and now they were merely comfortable. A shaded lamp stood on the round, baize-covered table, where Pepi and her mother sat sewing. Their busy hands, and the rough, coloured table-linen they were hemming, were caught in the circle of bright lamplight. Their faces, as they bent over their work, were thrown into the warm glow made by the coloured shade.

Though her hands continued steadily

occupied, now and then Pepi's mother raised her eyes to look at her daughter. Pepi's behaviour was somewhat unaccountable these days. The child was so demure, so well-behaved. Was her daughter, Frau Klem wondered, feeling the weight of the responsibility betrothal had brought with it? Joseph and Martha Klem were well aware that they had rather forced this betrothal to Willi Pommer. But they did not take blame to themselves for that. Pepi's future had to be provided for. And Willi, if he was not the Apollo Belvedere, was at least diligent, honest and, they judged, sufficiently in love, or at all events, good-natured enough to put up with Pepi's tantrums.

But now, almost alarmingly, there were no tantrums. Almost alarmingly, for it was so unlike Pepi. What had happened to the child? What did all this docility mean? Pepi – their temperamental, sparkling, naughty little Pepi – had, since Christmas, turned herself into an obedient mouse. Frau Klem's plump face wrinkled with anxiety, and she scratched her greying head with a thimbled finger. No. She knew Pepi too well. She could be a deep little creature when she liked. Now the waters of the girl's behaviour were running so smooth that her mother could not but think they must be running deep.

Yet what could Pepi be hiding? What was

she up to? But she must stop indulging these maternal fears. The child was growing up, that was all – accepting the unexciting life they had chosen for her; persuading herself, at last, that thus she would find happiness.

'I see, from a bill, that Lisa Fischer has been given a part at the Karl Theatre,' Joseph said, taking his pipe out of his mouth and staring placidly at the ceiling. And, as no one replied to this, he added: 'I didn't know she had a voice for anything but the chorus. She must be getting on with her singing.'

'She must be getting on with somebody who has paid down the money for the part,' his wife said tartly.

'Oh, I don't know.' Joseph stretched himself comfortably.

'Well I *do* know!' Frau Klem was not at all averse to talking scandal, especially such scandal as diligently and shamelessly generated by this black sheep of her husband's family. Only yesterday she had caught a glimpse of Lisa skating on a flooded lawn of the Stadtpark, her hands crossed with those of an elegant, slim young man who wore fair, cascading side-whiskers, a light beige bowler hat and a modish, short overcoat of much the same colour. Lisa herself had been flaunting a wax-red cashmere skirt, the pleats of which flared becomingly as she skated. And how her sable bonnet and the sable muff she carried

146

on her arm had been come by, the good, but gossipy Frau Klem did not dare to think! She would have been more than glad to discuss with her husband all that this implied; been glad, indeed, to invent further implications if necessary; but she was not prepared to do this in in front of their daughter. The seeming success of her cousin Lisa Fischer had in times past had its unsettling effect upon Pepi. The less Pepi knew about toilettes that must certainly have come from Maison Spitzer, Drecoll or Marsch, the better.

'Oh, but Lisa is singing much better. She's gone to a new teacher.' For a sudden, eager instant Pepi looked up to say this, then she quickly dropped her eyes again, and went on with her sewing.

Her mother put her work down on the table, and turned to her daughter. Had Pepi been in secret contact with this, quite literally, scarlet woman? Anxiety made Frau Klem's voice severe. 'Will you please tell me who told you about Lisa Fischer's voice?'

For the fraction of a second Pepi's expression might have seemed to betray confusion. But it was only a fraction. And her face was so much in the shade that it was hard to tell if her colour had risen. 'Really, Mama! Why are you looking at me like that? *I'm* not Lisa Fischer! It was the little Schani Fischer who told me. I met him in the Stubenring the other day. I see no reason to walk past him just because he's her brother! The boy can't help that, can he?'

If this was intended as a red herring, Pepi's mother followed it obediently. 'The Fischers would do much better not to talk about Lisa to their younger children,' she said, taking up her sewing and masking her relieved anxiety in righteous indignation. 'The children will learn all the whys and the wherefores soon enough.'

Pepi did not reply to this. When, in a moment, her mother ventured to glance at her from the corner of an eye, she appeared to be sewing, as quietly diligent as ever.

On his sofa Joseph Klem had fallen asleep.

IV

Presently they were roused by a knocking at the door. Frau Klem went. There was the noise of welcome.

Pepi dropped her work and rushed to rouse her sleeping father. 'Quick! Quick, Papa! Visitors.' She shook his shoulder in her agitation. 'It's Herr Hayburn's voice!'

Joseph had only time to rise to his feet before Phœbe and Henry came into the cheerful little room. Martha Klem was genuinely pleased to see them. She had come to feel almost maternal towards Henry while he was with her in the autumn. And, even

148

making allowance for his preoccupations, she had been a little hurt that he had not come back to see her. But now the warm-hearted Viennese woman had forgotten everything but the excitement of his arrival with his wife. She fluttered about, taking their coats, scolding her husband for looking untidy, bidding him change his jacket and brush his hair, smiling encouragingly at the young lady, asking her in dumb show where she would like to sit, calling to Pepi to clear up the table, and telling her to go at once and make coffee.

Pepi did as she was told. She was glad to be in the kitchen by herself. As she put the beans into the coffee-mill and turned the handle, she could feel the sullen beating of her heart. She had dreaded this. And it had come. So that was the other girl he had gone to fetch. Her eyes had told her that Frau Hayburn was beautiful. And they had told her that Herr Hayburn was conscious of his wife's beauty. This was a marriage of love; it was no marriage of convenience.

As she bent over the cooking-stove a tear fell, and was turned by the heat into a puff of sizzling steam. There was little of reason in Pepi's make-up. She was a thing of instinct and emotion. She could not have defined what Henry had brought her in the last few months. A strange, gauche friendliness. A vivid interest in his troubles at the works. An absurd masculine helplessness that was, somehow, engaging. And, above all, his foreignness; the novelty of him. He came from a golden, outside world, far beyond the confines of the Favoriten. He was young. He was clever. One day he would be rich. He had made no love to her. But that, perhaps, only added to his interest, in this city where love was almost a matter of politeness; where pretty girls like Pepi could find amorous young men two for a *Kreutzer*, and reject or accept their advances as the mood took them.

And so, with a young girl's light-headedness, Pepi had woven her fantasies and dreamt her dreams. She had always known that Henry was betrothed, but that might be a mere loveless arrangement. Such betrothals were the rule in Vienna. Here, in this gay city, it was the custom for love rather to overflow its banks than to remain within them. It was dull and stupid to go without adventure, if adventure was yours for the taking.

Why she had accepted her own betrothal to Willi Pommer, Pepi could not have said. It had been pressed upon her, and for the sake of peace, perhaps, she had allowed it. Perhaps she had been waiting to find out if Henry loved his wife; to see if there was still hope of intrigue. By the illogical, frivolous standards of this, the most seductive of cities, it did not strike this light-hearted little moth, dazzled by the brightness of her native candles, that the feelings she allowed herself were wrong. But, right or wrong, the sight of Henry together with his wife had given her her answer. And it was an answer she did not like.

Pepi wiped her eyes, examined her face in the kitchen mirror, and picked up the coffee-tray. Life was a thing to be lived. If you could not live it in one way, then you must live it in another. She had nearly given herself away tonight about Lisa Fischer. What a fool she had been!

She kicked the sitting-room door open with one foot and went in with the coffee-tray. Frau Hayburn, first to see that she was heavily laden, jumped up to help her.

Phœbe, still in her mood of honeymoon pliability, felt herself forced to admit that this was a pleasant place. Mr. and Mrs. Klem seemed so pleased to see her husband and herself. Their kind faces were overflowing with interest and pleasure. Henry was interpreter, and, with his three-months-old German, things went slowly. But they had turned this slowness into a good-natured game, and there was friendly laughter, and much dumb show. As, this afternoon, she had been uplifted by the distinction of the Misses Hirsch, now she was uplifted by the warm simplicity of the Klems.

She began to wonder why she had been so silly as to quarrel with Henry about their coming to live here. Henry, of course, had been much wiser than she. She must, she told herself, remember this in future when she felt like opposing him. Her friend Stephanie Hirsch would understand when she explained to her more thoroughly just what their circumstances were. (Phœbe had a very hazy idea of them herself, but this did not now occur to her.) And their stay here would not last for ever. She would have time to learn to speak a little, and Mrs. Klem would teach her to keep house in the Austrian way. And perhaps in some months Henry and she would have an apartment of their own.

Thus, before they left, their stay was arranged. In a week's time they were to come out here from the Domgasse. The spring would be coming, Frau Klem said, smiling, and out here the gracious lady would find herself almost in the country, which would be very healthy for her. The room that Herr Hayburn had occupied this autumn was a little small for two, she was afraid, but the gracious lady did not, perhaps, mind. Besides, they could have Pepi's room before so very long, she added, giving her daughter's arm a brisk little pat. In the springtime? Was that not so, Pepi?

But when Phœbe and Henry, together with their belongings, arrived in the Quellengasse at the end of eight days, Pepi's room was already empty.

Chapter Ten

A relentless day in mid-March. The east wind, crossing Scotland from Edinburgh to Glasgow, blew steadily as though it blew from a fan. Smoke trailed from the chimneys horizontally. In the streets, dust and torn paper played games. Warmth and comfort were difficult to find.

But Bel had found them. The fire in the back-parlour of Grosvenor Terrace was stacked high. She sat with her feet on the fender, busying herself over family mending, and watching her six-year-old daughter Isabel, who was occupied in cutting out scraps. Every now and then Bel took her eyes from her work to look down upon the little girl's industry.

Isabel was crouched on a stool set on the hearthrug, her fair ringlets dangling in front of her, her protruding tongue following the twisting scissors this way and that, cutting and snipping in an ecstasy of concentration. In addition to her little serge dress, she was wound in an old nursery shawl, the ends of which had been secured behind her small shoulders by one of Sarah's, the nurse-housemaid's, hairpins.

For a moment the child stopped, straightened her back, sighed, pushed away those troublesome ringlets that Sarah was forever re-shaping with a hairbrush round her large, red fingers, then she bent down again and went on with her snipping. But she had given her mother a glimpse of a flushed face.

'Don't you think you should stop and have a rest now, dear?' Bel said, a little anxiously.

Isabel had been allowed to get up only this afternoon. For a week she had been in bed with fever and cold. Perhaps it was not good for her to occupy herself so intensely.

'But I want to finish this,' came non-committally from the tangle of fair hair.

This highly-coloured sheet of the members of the Royal Family had been a stealthy gift from Cook, who had her own ways of worming herself into the children's affection behind Sarah's somewhat jealous back. She had waited until Sarah had wrapped up little Thomas and marched him off for a bleak afternoon walk in the chill, unblossoming Botanic Gardens, then she had appeared above-stairs, plump, affectionate and triumphant, and handed over this present she had secured to celebrate Isabel's convalescence.

Isabel had received it with a child's solemn radiance, thanked Bessie demurely, promised rather pompously to kiss her later on, when there was no chance of giving her infection, then gone off to cut out the scraps before the parlour fire. Cook had returned to her kitchen, glowing with the sense of her own generosity, her importance, and her ability to demonstrate her attachment to the children, Sarah or no Sarah.

'Well, after you've finished that one, I think you should go on the couch for a little and play with the Austrian doll your Aunt Phœbe sent you. I'll get it for you,' Bel continued, in answer to her daughter's last remark.

Isabel did not see any point in replying to this. She wished, indeed, that her mother would stop trying to carry on a conversation. It hindered concentration. As a result of this last interruption her somewhat inexpert scissors had cut off the late Prince Consort's nose. That meant cutting out the nose and pasting it separately, which would be a great nuisance, and very difficult to do properly so that it did not show.

Isabel was not pursuing art quite for art's sake. She was hoping to have something really remarkable to show her brother Arthur when he got back from school this afternoon. Her six years were ever anxious to measure themselves against Arthur's nine, her femininity against his masculinity. Isabel adored Arthur. Now this misfortune with the nose. It was most provoking. If only her mother–

The front door banged. Could that be

Arthur home from school already? Should she hide her unfortunate slip away, or should she ask him to help her to patch the poor Prince Consort?

II

But before she had time to decide, her Aunt Sophia came into the room.

'Bel, dear! And wee Isabel! How are you, lovey? Your Auntie Sophia has just come in to see how you are. Wil told me just this morning at breakfast that Isabel had been ill, Bel. And he said he had known for days! Aren't boys awful? Someone had told him. I forget who it was. Now, had he met Arthur? Or did he tell me he had run into Sarah buying a newspaper? No. No, I'm sure it was Arthur. But, then, why should I think of Sarah? Or am I thinking of her in connection with something else? Well, anyway, I'm glad to see you up again, dearie. And what are you busy with?'

Isabel, having bestowed just as hurried a greeting upon her aunt as her mother's ideas of a little girl's politeness would permit, continued with her scissors contemptuously. If her Aunt Sophia had any sort of eyes in her head, it must be perfectly obvious to her that she, Isabel, was cutting out scraps. There were times when grown-up people asked the most nonsensical questions.

Bel was not displeased at seeing Sophia. The searing winds had kept her in this afternoon. Sophia was, at least, an excuse for early tea. Sarah's second-in-command could bring it, or Cook, indeed, if it came to that. There was no need to split ceremonious hairs over Sophia. She pulled the bell-cord, invited her to lay aside her bonnet, the singed muff, and her outer wrappings and bade her pull the arm-chair opposite close to the fire.

'And what's the news, Bel dear?' Sophia, now in full certainty of the cup of tea, which had been one of the stronger strands among the tangle of motives for her coming, bent forward and warmed her hands at the fire.

'Nothing very much,' Bel answered, intent once again upon her mending. Then, as though she had found a crumb to throw to her guest, she added: 'We had David here last night. He begged a bed. He had to attend some meeting that kept him too late to get home to Aucheneame.'

Bel was little surprised that Sophia received this information with no great show of interest. The smallest piece of family news usually set her tongue wagging. But now, she was merely leaning forward, holding out her hands and gazing expressionlessly into the fire. 'How are Grace and the baby?' she asked presently.

'Oh, very well. Grace is up and about again.' Bel's surprise increased. The mention of a new baby, especially a new Moorhouse baby, was the topic of all topics to open the floodgates of Sophia's chatter. But Sophia still sat silent, her face, middle-aged and moody, glowing red in the firelight. 'He seems very proud of his son,' Bel added, throwing the bait yet again.

'That's good.' Sophia sat back in her chair, her eyebrows raised defensively.

Bel was mystified. Had Sophia something to tell her? She gave her another chance. 'Have *you* seen anything of David lately?' she said, looking up from her sewing.

A motion from Sophia gave Bel to understand that she had no wish to say what was to be said while sharp little ears concealed by tangled ringlets sat between them.

But at this moment the door was thrown open, and Cook, who, having admitted Sophia to the house, had gone to make tea unbidden, brought in the tray and set it down on the parlour table with a self-satisfied smile – a smile that demanded of the ladies where they could find a better anticipator of their wishes than herself? And, following on this, Sarah arrived back with little Tom. And on their heels came Arthur home from school. There were handshakes and boyish, March-cold kisses on Aunt Sophia's hot, fire-baked face, then Sarah, having added Isabel and her scraps to the cavalcade, swept all the children upstairs to their nursery tea.

In the wake of the storm Bel rose to pour out for Sophia. She was still wondering about David and the Butter family. 'Two lumps, isn't it? Did you say you *had* seen David, Sophia?'

Sophia stirred her tea reflectively. 'No. But William went to see him. Oh, I shouldn't be telling you this, Bel dear; it's really nothing, but I know you won't repeat it. You see, dear, William and I are just a little disappointed with David. Now, I wouldn't dare to say anything about this if David wasn't my own brother. But you know you can say things about your own people, without anything – anything very – well, serious, dear, being meant. You see what I mean, don't you?'

There was really nothing yet for Bel to see. But, as curiosity was now thoroughly aroused, she hastened to encourage Sophia by assuring her that, of course, she saw everything.

'Well, it was this, dear. You see, Wil is more than sixteen-and-a-half, and we've been thinking about his business training. He's been getting splendid reports from the Glasgow Academy. Oh, I know it's not as – well – fashionable, dear, as the new Kelvinside Academy, where you're sending Arthur, dear – but some quite important people send their sons there.'

As there was a momentary pause here, Bel, all ears now, further encouraged her by saying: 'Of course, Sophia, very important people.'

'Well, you see, dear, William wrote to David and told him all this, and asked him if he couldn't possibly make a place for Wil in Dermott Ships. He explained our own business wasn't suitable for a boy to have a training in, and a shipping office like David's would be so wonderful and everything. And that it wasn't a case of a large salary, or a permanent appointment. And that times were so bad, it was difficult to get a young man into anything nice. It was a beautiful letter. William showed it to me before he posted it. And you know, dear, William is the least well-off of all the brothers-in-law. Not that I am complaining about that, of course.' Sophia stopped. Her face was flushed with vexation.

'But what happened, Sophia? What was David's reply?'

'He sent no reply. And then William went to see him.'

'But David's not like that, Sophia. There must have been– What did he say to William?'

'He made an excuse about his mind being taken up with Grace. It was at the time of the baby's birth. But he must have come to the office every day. He must have written other letters.'

'But what did he say to William about giving Wil his training?'

'He put on a far-away look and said that times were so difficult that he couldn't make any promises just now. That perhaps later on–' Sophia put down her cup, pulled a handkerchief from her belt, blew her nose and added: 'There won't be any later on, Bel. If it had been the son of one of David's grand friends–' To recover her poise she took up her cup once more.

'Do you think Grace knows about this, Sophia?' Bel asked after a pause of bewilderment.

'Oh no. I don't suppose so. Besides, Grace is not like that.'

'No, Grace is not like that.'

There was a silence for a moment, then Sophia burst out:

'Do you know what about my brother David, Bel? He is getting mean and pompous! I would never have believed it! All Grace's money has been bad for him!'

'I've always been very fond of David.'

'I know you have.'

'He was quite like his old self last night, Sophia,' Bel said rather lamely, pouring out fresh tea for both of them.

She sat herself down by the table, reflecting. It was difficult to judge the rights and wrongs of this. It did seem a little thing for David to take his sister's boy into a great office where there were already so many. Was it true, what Sophia said of David? Was a large fortune taking away the gift of understanding? Blunting him to the hopes and fears of others? Robbing him of the common touch? It was a pity if the rudimental weakness of his character should betray him in this way; should destroy the quick sympathy she, Bel, had always loved in him. Could he really be afraid that his coltish nephew should not seem presentable enough to do him credit? Was snobbery sapping David's courage?

She felt a self-accusing pang. In this respect she, too, was not without stain. She had to admit it. But now her own snobbery – a snobbery that was constantly breaking down before her womanliness – allowed her to understand David and be sorry for him. No. It would be a great pity if, with his large way of life, he should begin to grow small.

'Perhaps if Arthur spoke to David, Sophia–' she began, coming once more to the surface.

'No, Bel dear. If David can't do that for his own flesh and blood–'

'But perhaps there was some mistake.'

'I don't see how there could be. No, dear, please leave it.'

'Or Grace, Sophia?'

'Not for the world, Bel! We are not proud. You know that very well, dear. But there are limits.'

'I'm sorry, Sophia. I do hope it will come right.'

For reply, Sophia held out her cup. 'But it *is* all right. We've forgotten already. Don't bother any more about it. I shouldn't have told you, Bel dear. And we're not going to make a family quarrel out of it.' She took her cup back from Bel, thanked her, then asked: 'And when did you have a letter from Vienna last?'

III

Bel was glad that Sophia had changed the subject. There was nothing more she herself could say without appearing to take sides. And she had no wish to do this. She was grateful to her that she had not tried to engage her sympathies more deeply. Later, when she had Arthur to himself, she would ask him what he thought.

'We had a letter from Phœbe this morning,' she said, following Sophia's example and having a third cup of tea. 'We were glad to get it. She doesn't write very regularly. We were beginning to wonder.'

'And how is poor Phœbe getting on?' The

adjective 'poor' as applied by Sophia to the Phœbe of these days denoted a regret that her sister should have married so rashly and so young, should have attached herself to such an odd, erratic husband, and that she should be forced to live anywhere that was not Glasgow.

'Oh, she's getting on very well – in a way.' Bel looked about her. 'I should have the letter somewhere.'

'Why "in a way", Bel dear? She's in rooms, isn't she? I was very pleased to hear it. How could poor Phœbe keep house for herself? And with all these foreigners about! I was glad to hear she was being looked after.'

The thought crossed Bel's mind that Phœbe's wit might, with little trouble, quickly bring her skill in housekeeping well above Sophia's. But she merely went on: 'I say "in a way", Sophia, because I'm not too sure about the people she and Henry are staying with.'

'I thought he was a respectable bank clerk.'

'Yes. But there's a daughter. Phœbe mentions her in this letter. She ran away from home just before Phœbe and Henry went to stay. Her parents had no idea where she had gone. It was a week or two before she was found singing in a theatre in some small Austrian town. I don't like houses that daughters run away from, Sophia.'

'No, indeed, Bel dear. They must be light-minded sort of people. Have they brought the girl home?'

'No. She wouldn't come.'

'Better not.'

'Much better not, Sophia.'

'There could have been no question of Phœbe staying on if she had come, Bel.'

'No.'

'Especially running away to a theatre,' Sophia added.

Bel *had* heard that there were worse places than theatres for daughters to run off to. But, according to Moorhouse ways of thinking, not much. 'Well, anyway,' she said, 'they're talking of finding a place for themselves before long, and that would be best. Oh, here is the letter.' She had found it in her work-basket.

Sophia took it and settled down to read. She read slowly, punctuating her reading with mild exclamations of sympathy, surprise and bewilderment. Once she laid it down on her knee, looked across at Bel and exclaimed: 'You would wonder from all this what kind of place Vienna is, at all,' then picked it up and went on reading.

The part about seeking a place of their own came at the end of the letter. Sophia re-read it aloud:

'It's all right here. But Henry's books and papers take up a great deal of room. And we may want more accommodation for all

165

kinds of reasons later this year.'

Sophia folded the letter, and, looking at Bel, repeated the words: 'All kinds of reasons.' She was surprised. For once, her own pedestrian wit had moved more quickly than Bel's. 'So there's to be a Hayburn baby, is there?'

'What do you say, Sophia?'

'Well, it looks like it, doesn't it? That's what Phœbe's trying to tell you.'

'I didn't think of that.'

'Well, I must say you surprise me, Bel dear. Remember, Phœbe's very young, and it will be the first. I remember I didn't know how to tell anybody when Wil was coming. And if I had had to write it! Poor Phœbe! So far away! Dear me! It's that o'clock already? How the time flies!' Sophia got up and began putting on her things without breaking the flow. 'Well, it's been lovely, just what I needed to cheer me up. And you won't say a word to anybody about our little difficulty with David, will you, Bel dear? You see, William was just saying he couldn't bear–' Bel accompanied her to the door. If Sophia had remained sensible she would have discussed Phœbe's letter further with her. But the sluices looked like opening. And there was nothing now to do but bid Sophia and her flood of chatter good afternoon.

166

IV

She shuddered as she closed the door behind her. The wind cut like a knife. Bel bent down and stirred the hall fire. Its reflection jumped and glittered on polished brass and varnish. But even here it was chilly.

She hurried back to the warmth of the parlour, her mind full of Phœbe's letter. She took it up and read the end of it once again.

Yes, almost certainly Sophia was right. Odd, that she had missed the sense of it when she had read it this morning. Now she must write to the child at once to make sure.

Bel crossed to the parlour window and looked out thoughtfully upon her own back garden. The door in the wall by the side of the coach-house leading to the lane had been left off its catch and was blowing back and forth. The grass was powdered with March dust. Bleak, shrivelled leaves eddied against a corner of the garden wall. There were shouts of children playing. They must be McCrimmon the coachman's children playing with their kind in the lane. Presently a half-grown kitten ran into the garden, and was immediately followed by the eldest McCrimmon child, who caught it up in her little purple hands, clutched it to her, and carried it out of the back garden, shutting the door behind her. Bel wondered that the child could bear to play so gaily in this cold wind. But, except for her hands, she was warmly, if somewhat miscellaneously clad, and health rounded her cheeks. A different child from the pale little creature Phœbe and Henry had brought from the slums that Saturday afternoon over a year ago.

Phœbe. Bel realised now that she had really been thinking about Phœbe all the time she had been standing here; that she had been apprehending what she saw at the merest surface level.

Phœbe to have a baby without herself being with her? It was unthinkable. Had this been her fear from the beginning? Yet what could she have done with this headstrong couple? And it might be that Sophia was wrong. She must write to Phœbe at once, demanding an immediate answer.

But, if Phœbe said yes? How could she go to her? With this house, a husband and three children? Gazing before her, Bel twisted the blind-cord in her fingers, her eyes gazing out on the walls, roofs, and swaying naked trees, all of them a monotonous grey in the bleak evening light.

But her heart held the glowing picture of the stormy girl who, now that she had gone from her, Bel was coming to miss more and more.

Her mother had told her just the other day that she, Bel, was too possessive; that she tried to manage everybody; that she was too sure of her own judgments. That might be, Bel muttered, tangling the blind-cord and arguing with herself defensively, but Phœbe wasn't everybody. She was almost her daughter. She was someone very dear. And she was young and foolish. And Bel didn't even know if she was with respectable people.

The walls and windows began to tremble in Bel's vision. She dropped the tangled blind-cord, and, coming back to the fireplace, leant her brow on the mantelpiece, gazing into the fire.

No. She must write to Phœbe tonight, and if things were as she suspected, Phœbe must come home. She was having no nonsense. Henry would have to bring her. Or, if that was impossible, she could join with some other woman who might be travelling. Phœbe had written that she and Henry had taken to going of a Sunday to a Presbyterian service conducted by a missionary of the Free Church of Scotland. Bel had regretted that it was the Free Church and not the Established Church of Scotland. Moorhouses were all Established Church people. Still, on the whole she had been glad. Surely Phœbe could find a respectable companion among the congregation.

Bel was a planner, and this burst of planning soothed her. Now she felt she was getting things into some kind of order in her mind. Her sense of tidiness reasserted itself. She rang for tea to be removed, went to the window, disentangled the cord, pulled down the blind, then drew the heavy curtains. The afternoon was almost gone. Arthur would presently be home, and, anyhow, she had had enough of the cold, comfortless light of the long March day.

Now the darkened room glowed in the firelight. That was better. She took a taper from the mantelpiece, held it to the fire, lit a wall-bracket beside her chair and sat down once again to her mending.

Tonight, when things were quiet, she would write to Phœbe.

Chapter Eleven

Mrs. Robert Dermott was so enchanted to find herself a grandmother that her friends were beginning to think her a menace. Even at the committee table, where it was her habit to assume a manner that was forthright, purposeful and stern, she had, more than once, softened, changed colour and, catching at the straws of her importance, referred to the fact that it had been somewhat difficult for her to see to everything just recently on account of family ties. After that she would look around her with an expression which proclaimed that of course she couldn't go into that sort of thing here, thrust her spectacles back on her nose, and sharply demand of the secretary what was the next item on the agenda.

Outside of her committee work, Mrs. Dermott's obsession was completed. If she were not at Aucheneame instructing the monthly nurse in her duties, and explaining to her just how she herself had felt when Grace was born; then she was visiting friends, and even mere acquaintances, in order to keep them posted in the progress of the new Robert David Dermott-Moorhouse. With a flash of his old humour, David had taken to teasing his mother-in-law about the baby. He was forever pretending to receive letters from his brother Mungo reporting the progress of the Ruanthorpe-Moorhouse baby, and how surprisingly his mind and body were developing. But Mrs. Dermott would have none of it. She affected to meet David's teasing with the coldest of disinterest, and returned his rally by telling him that, if his nephews were going to matter more to him than a son of his own, then it was a pity Providence had bothered to send him one.

All these pleasantries pleased Grace. Everything about the advent of this child was a matter for gratification. And not least that her mother had taken a new lease of life, and was beginning to find some compensation for the loss of her father.

But if there was endless patience for the new Robert Moorhouse at Aucheneame and at the smart little house in Hamilton Drive, where his grandmother now had her home, patience was not quite so endless in other quarters.

Bel had had rather a lot of Mrs. Dermott. Being in the process of successfully rearing three children of her own, she was not without the necessary small talk on the subject of babies. But she had long since learnt to take her family, its ailments and its nourishment, in her stride, and the infatuated grandmother, however important Bel might consider her to be, was in danger of becoming a bore.

When, therefore, on the day following Sophia's visit, Mrs. Robert Dermott's card was brought to Bel, together with the information that Mrs. Dermott's carriage was standing at her front door, and would Mrs. Arthur Moorhouse drive into town with her, Bel, catching still the overtones of command in Mrs. Dermott's invitation, could not but feel a sense of persecution.

But she had planned to visit her mother this afternoon to discuss the problem of Phœbe. And as her own carriage was at the coach-builders having Arthur's monogram painted discreetly in yellow on its shining doors – there had been a battle with Arthur's modesty about this – Bel decided to take the line of least resistance and accept Mrs. Dermott's offer.

It was as cold as it had been on the previous afternoon. Mrs. Dermott's hackneys stamped the ground impatiently as Bel mounted the carriage-stone and entered the carriage.

'Oh, there you are, Bel, my dear. I am so glad you were able to come with me. Bitter weather for late March, isn't it? Now, take this spare rug all to yourself, Mrs. Moorhouse. You mustn't get chilled.' Since Grace's marriage, her mother had announced that she was going to call all Grace's brothers and sisters-in-law by their Christian names – a gesture which, on the whole, pleased everybody. But Mrs. Dermott's memory was like a defective fly-paper. Sometimes things stuck; and sometimes they didn't.

By this time Bel was well used to being pulled forward into a first-name intimacy, only to be thrust back later to the level of plain Mrs. Moorhouse. She thanked Mrs. Dermott, and wound the rug about her as the horses swung round into Great Western Road.

'I'm just going down to Albany Place to visit Mary,' Mrs. Dermott said, triumphantly remembering Mrs. George McNairn's name. 'She sent me a very nice letter the other day, with a little subscription I had asked her for, and also hoping the baby was thriving. I acknowledged it at once, of course; but I suddenly felt I ought to drop down and pay her a little visit, and tell her just how the baby was. I really must say, Bel, everybody has been most kind and interested about Grace and David's child.'

Bel dug her hands into her muff, smiled a misty, elegant smile, and said: 'Such a dear little baby!'

'Yes, indeed, my dear. Now, Mrs. Moorhouse, when your children were as young as that, did you–?'

Bel was engulfed until the horses were standing before Mary's house in Albany Terrace.

'You know, I'm a terrible old woman! I've never even asked you where you were going!' Mrs. Dermott said, preparing to descend herself. 'But of course you'll come in to see Mrs. McNairn, too, before I take you anywhere else?'

But Bel stood firm. She had no wish to see Mary's embarrassment at Mrs. Dermott's sudden descent. And, in addition, she felt she had paid for her drive handsomely in pandering to Mrs. Dermott's pride and interest in her grandson. The least Grace's mother could now do was to send her to her destination. She hastened to tell her, therefore, that her mother expected her at Monteith Row at the earliest possible moment this afternoon – a lie which was not, perhaps, white enough to leave Bel's conscience quite in peace – and that she could easily get out here and pick up a hansom.

Mrs. Dermott gave her coachman instructions to take Mrs. Moorhouse to Monteith Row and call back here for herself at a stated time later.

II

There are many reasons for gossiping. And not all of them are bad. Sophia was sitting comfortably with her sister Mary this afternoon gossiping over David's unhelpfulness with young Wil, all unconscious that David's formidable mother-in-law was about to descend upon them. Sophia was not ill-natured. She was gossiping to distract her sister Mary's anxiety, quite as much as to relieve her own feelings.

For this afternoon Mary's spirits were low. Her husband was ill with an illness that was becoming more and more evident. It was beginning to show itself in the diminishing plumpness of his naturally heavy body, in his sallow skin, in the lack of spring in his gait. In his forty-fifth year, George McNairn was quickly turning into an old man. And the worst of it was, as Mary had just told her sister, George would admit none of it; would not even discuss it with her. But his placidity had given place to a very uneven temper, and he had taken to working at his business like a fanatic, spending his diminishing energies in a way that distressed his wife acutely.

Having heard Mary's recital of her troubles, therefore, Sophia's good-nature, rather than her reason, had prompted her to apply David and his iniquities as a counter-irritant. She was thus in full flood when David's mother-in-law broke in upon her.

If it had been anyone other than Mrs. Dermott, she must have wondered why Sophia's face was bright scarlet, why it wore an unmistakable expression of guilt. But Grace's mother, large in body and mind, had little proficiency in subtle deduction – prided herself, indeed, in the lack of it.

She advanced into Mary's stuffy drawing-room beaming with pleasure. 'My dear Mrs. McNairn, how cosy it is in here! And Sophia! How nice to see you! I've just taken the liberty of coming in for a moment to thank you for your very kind letter about the baby, Mary, and to tell you how he was getting on. And how is your family, Mrs. Butter? I seem to hear of nobody but ourselves these days.'

The two sisters did not see so much of Mrs. Dermott as Bel did, but even they were becoming accustomed to her confusing modes of address. They stood up, received Mrs. Dermott with the best grace their embarrassment would allow them, and Mary, leading her to the fire, insisted that she should take tea and making the excuse of giving orders, hurried from the room, leaving her over-powering visitor with Sophia.

To be left alone with Mrs. Dermott was like being left alone with a friendly battleship. She sat leaning forward warming a large, red, diamond-ringed hand at the fire, and launching benevolent broadsides at Sophia.

'I'm so pleased to find you here, too, my dear. How is your nice husband?'

'William's very well, thank you, Mrs. Dermott. I wish I could say the same for Mary's husband. She's just been telling me that poor George–'

'I brought your sister-in-law, Bel Moorhouse, down into town with me in the carriage. Such a dear woman! So kind and straightforward!'

'We all like Bel, Mrs. Dermott.' Then, feeling she must, however guilty her feelings, Sophia added: 'And how are Grace and her wonderful baby?'

Mrs. Dermott went solemn at this, a little. 'Oh, I don't know that he should be called a *wonderful* baby, Sophia,' she said, almost stiffly. 'Indeed, only the other day I was giving Grace and David a lecture: telling them they must keep some kind of proportion; that the baby might be everything to them, but they must really remember not to bore other people about him.' And, still further to Sophia's amazement, she added: 'But why did you say *poor* George? Is Mary's husband ill?' The reference to George McNairn had, after all, become stuck to the fly-paper of Mrs. Dermott's mind.

Sophia had just time to tell her of Mary's apprehensions before her sister's step was heard outside the door. For a moment Mrs. Dermott's eyes filled, and her large face took on a soft uncertainty that gave her, of a sudden, a strong likeness to her daughter Grace. 'Poor Mrs. McNairn,' she said. 'I know what that is. It's just over a year–' and then, as she saw Mary, she added with a heartiness that could deceive nobody: 'There you are, Mary! Taking all sorts of trouble about me.'

And thereafter her behaviour was odd. Her sympathy seemed to keep wheeling round Mary in strange, wide circles. As was to be expected, she spoke much of her grandchild as she drank tea. But every now and then her mind swooped down to ask Mary questions. How did her boys do? How were the little twin girls? Were they at home, and might she see them? When they came, she kissed them majestically, bestowed half-crowns, gave each a pat of dismissal and a far-off smile as they scampered off giggling, then she turned as though they had never existed to go on with what she had been saying. Of George McNairn, it seemed, she could say nothing whatever to his wife.

III

Suddenly the door was thrown open and Mary's schoolboy sons came in, bringing with them their cousin, Wil Butter. And as suddenly the noise of their entrance was muted at the sight of their Aunt Grace's formidable mother. At the unexpected appearance of Wil a feeling of guilt returned to Sophia. She well understood her own son's heightened colour. She stood up to say she must go, and demanded of Wil if he were coming with her.

Wil's cousins claimed him. They had brought him to show him a model steam-engine they were attempting to build, and they begged their aunt to allow him to stay and share their schoolroom tea.

'I'll take you home, Sophia. I want to talk to you. See if my carriage is there, will you?' Mrs. Dermott said, turning to Sophia's son and smiling to herself at his Moorhouse good looks that so much reminded her of David – looks that even grubby adolescence could not quite extinguish.

'I'm distressed to hear about Baillie Mc-

179

Nairn's illness,' she said to Sophia, as they settled back in the carriage some minutes later. 'I felt I couldn't say much to his wife, but if there's anything I can do, you'll tell me, won't you, Mrs. Butter?'

Sophia, a little overcome at finding herself alone with Mrs. Dermott, and touched, perhaps, at what she had just said, told her, with rather less periphrasis than usual, that she would certainly let her know, and that she was being very kind indeed.

With a 'Don't talk nonsense, Mrs. Butter,' said with what sounded so like rudeness that Sophia blushed once more, wondering what now she had said to offend, Mrs. Dermott turned her head away, and seemed for a moment to have found some object in the street at which to gaze intently.

Sophia waited. For a time there was nothing but the movement of the carriage and the trotting of the horses.

Suddenly Mrs. Dermott turned. 'That's a handsome boy of yours, Sophia. What are you going to do with him?'

Sophia found herself forced to collect her wits before she answered. Obviously David's mother-in-law knew nothing of David's refusal. 'Well, Mrs. Dermott, you see, William has been trying to place him in a nice office. Oh, just for training. After that, of course, he'll– '

'Then why on earth doesn't he go into

180

Dermott Ships? Surely that's good enough for him?' The tone of her voice sounded in Sophia's ears almost like insolence.

'Well, we thought of that, but–'

'I'll speak to David.'

'Oh no! Please!'

Mrs. Dermott turned her bulk round and looked at Sophia's confusion. 'My dear Sophia! Why ever not?'

'Please, Mrs. Dermott! I don't think William would like it.'

'But why? My husband's office is the best in Glasgow!'

'Oh yes, we know that. But–'

'Well, then, Mrs. Butter! Isn't your own brother, now that he–? My dear girl! What's upsetting you?'

Sophia, beaten, had extracted her handkerchief from her shabby muff and was wiping her eyes. Her companion sat looking down at her, as much at a loss as she was. Again there was a pause. The carriage swayed and rattled.

'I wish you would tell me, Sophia,' Mrs. Dermott said at last. Now her voice was not so peremptory.

'William did ask David. But there wasn't any room.'

'Room? Room for his own nephew!'

Sophia did not answer. How could she accuse David to his wife's mother? How could she explain her own humble, good-natured estimate of herself and hers, to this commanding, wealthy woman?

'David must have misunderstood.'

Sophia merely shook her head and blew her nose.

The horses had come to a standstill before Sophia's house in Rosebery Terrace. The footman had jumped down to open the door for her. His mistress motioned him to re-close it.

She sat contemplating David's sister. She was used to managing people, and here was a situation to be managed high-handedly. It was very well for David to be carrying on a quarrel with Sophia, or Sophia with David, or however it was. But all that must be nothing to her. She was forever dealing with contention on her committees. She had better deal with this family one, or young Wil Butter would lose the chance of the best business training in Glasgow. In the eyes of Robert Dermott's widow, there could be nowhere like Robert Dermott's office.

She laid a hand on Sophia's arm. 'I'll speak to David, and get it all arranged for you at once.'

'Oh no! David doesn't want him!'

'Doesn't want him, Mrs. Butter? I don't think it's very nice of you to say anything so unkind about your own brother. Of course David must want a splendid boy like that! Who wouldn't? I'm proud to have him as a relative. Why shouldn't David be? I never heard such nonsense!'

Sophia's wits were confused with this alternative slapping and patting. But her modest pride held. 'We couldn't have David think for a minute that we had come to you.'

'And why not? I belong to your family, don't I?'

'But William and I are not asking favours!'

'Asking fiddlesticks! It seems to me the favour is to David. And even if it were a favour, surely I, at least, may ask a favour in the business I watched my own husband build up?' She paused for a moment, then she added: 'I don't think David will want to refuse me.'

Sophia brightened enough to smile. 'It's very kind, Mrs. Dermott,' she said. 'But I don't like the idea of my boy going into Dermott Ships, then feeling uncomfortable because he's forced his way there.'

'Really, Mrs. Butter, you talk as if your brother David was a monster! You know very well that if *I* ask him he won't have the – well, anyway, my dear, the horses are getting cold. I'll have this all seen to, and let you know.'

In another moment Sophia found herself standing on the windy pavement waving her muff at the retreating carriage and wondering if the word Mrs. Dermott had omitted to say was 'courage'.

IV

For a terrible moment old Mrs. Barrowfield, looking down by chance from a window in Monteith Row, thought that Mrs. Robert Dermott had come to call. She knew her carriage, for she had seen it more than once at Bel's. But, strong-minded herself, she had no wish for closer acquaintance with Mrs. Dermott's forcefulness. Bel's mother thought she was doing quite enough if, when she met her by chance in Bel's drawing-room, she managed to be civil. Once, indeed, calling spades spades, she had bluntly said to her daughter: 'Now, Bel, see that ye don't bring that upsettin' old body here!'

Bel had promised; smiling to herself a little, that her mother had called Mrs. Dermott old, despite the fact that she, herself, was eight years older.

Behind the lace curtains of her sitting-room window, however, Mrs. Barrowfield's perturbation faded as she saw that her daughter's fashionable bonnet was the only one to emerge from the carriage. Indignation, alarm and thoughts of a hasty change into her best shawl subsided pleasantly, and now she was standing, a poker in her hand, stirring flames of welcome from the fire.

Seated opposite her mother now, Bel answered questions. She gave the reasons for coming as she had; how little Isabel's cold was keeping, and how everybody else at Grosvenor Terrace fared. These preliminaries having been got through, Mrs. Barrowfield rang for the tea-tray and astonished her daughter by saying:

'So Phœbe's expecting?'

'Now, Mother, how on earth did you know that?' Bel jumped up, and leant against the mantelpiece.

Mrs. Barrowfield was delighted with the effect she had made. It gave her a feeling of still being in things; of not being laid aside. She smiled triumphantly. 'How do you think? I had a letter.'

'From Phœbe?' There was a ring of jealousy in Bel's voice.

'No. Henry.'

'From Henry!'

'You forget that Henry's a friend o' mine.'

'Has he been writing to you regularly, Mother?'

'Well, I wouldna say regularly.'

'And you never told me.'

For reply, Mrs. Barrowfield gave a chuckle that her daughter considered both offensive and sly. 'Am I not to get keepin' anything to myself?'

Bel's colour rose a little. 'No, really, Mother! A thing like that!'

'But I just got it yesterday,' the old lady

said, by way of laying a resentment she had naughtily striven to arouse.

'I had one from Phœbe. I've got it here,' Bel said, feeling there was much too much of importance to talk about to indulge in childish annoyance with her mother. They compared letters. Henry's was the more explicit.

Phœbe's child was expected in October. Presently they laid down the letters they had exchanged and looked at each other.

'She's young,' was Mrs. Barrowfield's comment.

'She's far too far away!'

Old Maggie, who had come in with the tea-tray, wondered who was far too far away, and why Miss Bel had spoken the words in tones of vexed exasperation, standing, flushed, before the fireplace, her bonnet thrown carelessly down, a strand of her smooth, fair hair straggling out of place.

'Listen, Mother. Phœbe must come home.'

Mrs. Barrowfield said nothing. She rose heavily to her feet and began pouring out tea, forgetting in her abstraction that her daughter might very well have done this for her. She liked Phœbe Moorhouse; always had liked her – ever since, indeed, she had seen her, a little girl of ten, help to push her own luggage up the hill to Ure Pace. But Phœbe could look after herself.

In a drawer in her bedroom she had a little

pile of letters written in Henry Hayburn's strangely adolescent hand. Letters written before his marriage. Letters of homesickness, of self-distrust, of crushing loneliness; or again, of self-praise, of over-confidence, of boyish boasting – according to his mood. She had held her tongue about them. Why should she expose these raw confessions of his heart? Better than anyone, she felt she had understood his arrogance at Christmas. It was an armour his half-developed poise had forced upon him before the family.

Little did Bel and Arthur know that it was she who had urged him to come home and marry Phœbe. She had guessed from his letters that his loneliness in Vienna was stretching him to breaking-point. And she had felt responsible. She had told him to go. His marriage was, as she saw it, the remedy. And the happy and few letters he had written since had told her she was right.

She sat gazing into the fire, her tea untasted. Why had she, an old woman, become so attached to this young man? It was strange and unusual, but it was so. Was it because he needed her?

And now here was Bel, her own daughter, but yet in very essence a Moorhouse, proposing to take his wife once more from him. She raised her eyes to meet Bel's.

'Well, Mother?'

'Phœbe had better stay with her man.'

'What? And have her baby in Vienna?'

'Well? What for not?'

'Oh, how can she, Mother? The girl's not quite twenty!'

'And what about Henry?'

'Henry will want his wife to have the best of attention.'

Mrs. Barrowfield looked again at her daughter glumly. This was Bel back at her high falutin. Carried away by her own fine phrases. Taking upon herself the right to arrange for everybody. Never for once doubting the soundness of her own judgment.

'And what do the other women in Vienna do?' she asked. 'I havena heard that they all come to Glasgow.'

'Oh, Mother! What am I to say to you? I thought you would be reasonable about this! I came down for your advice.'

'Well, you're gettin' it! Leave man and wife alone. Don't interfere. They're young, but it's their business. Not yours. Don't try to be a Providence for everybody, Bel!'

'But don't you understand that Phœbe will be quite alone?'

'Dear me, Bel, she'll have her man!'

'A lot of use he'll be, Mother.'

'Well, it was *your* father I wanted when you were coming.'

'But you were at home, Mother! And father was a doctor!' Bel was almost shouting now. And there were tears. 'And don't you understand, her life may be in danger?'

'I was forty-one when you were born. So was *my* life in danger. And yer father was ower old-fashioned to let them use chloroform!'

Oh, it was no use talking to a woman of seventy-five about these things. Bel smoothed her hair, wiped her eyes and sat down to drink her tea. For the remainder of her visit her demeanour towards her mother was sweet, tactful and controlled, as though she were talking to a child of twelve.

And presently, when she rose to say goodbye, the old lady found great difficulty in withstanding the temptation to box her daughter's ears.

Chapter Twelve

A fine, unusually warm morning in Holy Week. Henry Hayburn sat in one of the great coffee-houses on the Ring. On account of the unexpectedly warm weather, the large plate-glass window near which he found himself was thrown open. From where he was, Henry could have put out his hand and touched the shoulders of those who passed him down there on the pavement.

It was not yet April. Easter was early. But

today there was bright sunshine. Already there were one or two straw hats and parasols in the street.

Mrs. Barrowfield had been right. Henry's marriage had given him the background his work demanded. Now that he had a wife to accompany his scanty leisure, to listen to him, to fulfil his manhood, Henry's mind was free.

His work fascinated and engrossed him. The adventure of setting up a factory in a strange land, employing foreign workers and meeting new technical difficulties, filled him with a keen sense of romance. An odd kind of romance, perhaps, and one little known in this, the romantic city. But romance nevertheless.

A light wind blowing down from the Vienna Woods ruffled the fringe of the striped awning that hung out over the sunny pavement. To Henry it was just a breeze. But to the natives – to those tarock players at the table behind him, to that old man with the Barbary organ over there on the far side of the Ring, to that stiff dowager sitting in her carriage beneath her tussore parasol – it was a promise and a harbinger. All of them breathed a little more deeply, caught, or imagined they caught, the scent of damp earth and rising sap from the sprouting woodlands up there in the blue distance, and told themselves that spring was about to invade their city.

Somewhere a clock struck eleven. Henry looked about him. Maximilian Hirsch had given him this place of meeting, and eleven was the time. Henry, from his point of vantage, leant forward and cast an eye up and down the pavement. Maximilian was not yet to be seen. The morning was growing warmer, the scene more animated. Shop-girls in bright colours. Plump City men, hats in hand, mopping warm brows and looking about them for a table where they might sit and cool themselves. A flower-seller passed by, her basket laden with Parma violets and mimosa arrived from Italy overnight. Out in the expanse of the Ring itself, carriages, hired and private, were becoming more numerous. Many of them were moving in the direction of the Aspern Bridge on their way to the Prater. Some of the trams had open trolleys now, and, as the stocky little horses trotted back and forth along the Ring in the sunshine, their bells added a joyful noise to the other sounds of the City. It was difficult to believe that the passengers were everyday people merely going about their business. They wore an air of gaiety as though they were holiday-makers, out to see the sights.

Henry ordered his coffee, and when it came sat sipping it moodily. What had happened to his employer? Why was he keeping him waiting? He had more than enough to see to when he got back to the factory. It was maddening that he should have to waste the morning like this, merely to see some papers that he could just as easily have seen in Herr Hirsch's private office at the bank. Herr Hirsch knew very well that he, Henry, hated wasting time. Why then had he asked him to waste this morning dawdling in a coffee-house?

II

As he sat stirring his coffee, stroking his beard and mechanically following the come and go of the traffic, Henry became aware that his eye had fixed itself on the figure of a young woman sitting in an open tramcar. As she came nearer, he saw that there were parcels on her knee, together with a bunch of flowers that might be mimosa or yellow tulips.

Suddenly he came to his senses. The girl was Phœbe. His own wife. As she passed him by, he could see her sitting, sunk in her own thoughts, far away from the animation about her, pensive and tired, perhaps, with her morning shopping.

A quick uprush of tenderness, of passionate excitement, took hold of him. He waved to her but she did not see him. Now he felt that he must run out into the street, race after the trotting horses, and climb into the car beside her. But already the tram had gone on. He would never catch up. He would only look ridiculous. He sat back regretfully, and took another sip of his coffee.

Why this excitement, when he had seen her at breakfast, only a few short hours ago? She had sat out there, unconscious that his eyes were upon her. Why should this sudden glimpse of her thus, unattainable, pensive and alone, stir him so deeply? Was his conscience chiding him with neglect of this wife of his, who was now to bear his child? Should he have given her more of his companionship? Of his support? Had he been taking all and giving little?

He was glad that Hirsch was not yet with him. He wanted to sit here alone, examine himself and think.

After their first quarrel, there had been strangely little friction between them. Knowing Phœbe and his moods as he did, her patience had been remarkable. She had told him not to worry, that she did very well meantime, that he must give everything to his work. But had he any right to take her at her word? Did not his wife come before all else? Phœbe could be so remote, so independent, that it was easy to forget she must need him, as any other woman must need her husband. Especially in this foreign place.

For a newly married couple, his wife and he had spent far too little time together. On many days he was so busy that he saw nothing of her until late in the evening. But Phœbe had not complained. And her time seemed full. She seemed to be occupying herself picking up Austrian marketing and housekeeping; in learning the language; in amusing herself with the shops and the sights of this endlessly amusing city. That she should be exerting patience until such time as he should find himself established, had not before entered his mind.

Now Henry was stricken with a sense of guilt. His feelings rose, quick and hot, to blame him bitterly. He had failed Phœbe! It was no use trying to find excuses in his in-experience! He was nothing but a thought-less monster!

An old man in a moleskin cap, with a tray of primroses hanging from his neck by a string, stopped and held up a bunch. Henry, in his agitation, was quite unaware that the man was there. The old creature shuffled off, muttering to himself that the strange young man in the coffee-house was, as the Austrians say, 'heavily' in love.

He was not wrong. Henry was 'heavily' in love with his lawful wife. And he was full of youthful doubt and a sudden sharp self-criticism of his conduct towards her.

He drained his cup and drank some of the fresh water that, after the Viennese custom, stood in a glass beside it. Yes, he would talk to Phœbe tonight.

But where the devil was Maximilian Hirsch? The precious morning was almost gone. He leant out once more and looked about him. Why were people standing gaping by the edge of the pavement?

The ring of distant hoofs on granite slabs told him. A squadron of Hussars were coming back from morning exercise in the Prater. Now they were in front of him, coming down the Ring. The horses were dark and gleaming with sweat. Each rider, in his blue tunic with its yellow frogging and his fur cap, held himself proudly, in the knowledge that Imperial Vienna was watching him go by. Brass buttons sparkled in the sunshine as attilas, hanging from square shoulders, swayed to the rhythm of the walking horses, as they passed, row by row.

And, good heavens! There was Maximilian Hirsch standing among the mob watching the horsemen – a sight he must have seen hundreds of times. Watching them with the innocent interest of a child! Truly, the Austrians were an unaccountable, time-wasting people!

III

Now the last row of mounted Hussars had passed. The watchers by the kerb were breaking up and moving off. The pavement in front of Henry regained its spring-time animation. Gaily dressed ladies. Fashionable men. Milliners' girls. Flower-women. Clerks in shabby, light-brown overcoats. Peasants' wives in vivid regional colours. Officers in bright uniforms. Countrymen in chamois shorts and short jackets. Bareheaded porters in striped waistcoats and baize aprons. The cheerful, surging, colourful mob that might be seen in Vienna on any sunny morning.

Maximilian Hirsch had turned, too. In a moment he had spied Henry, given him a signal of greeting, and presently he stood beside him, offering him his hand.

'Good morning, Herr von Hayburn. Wonderful morning, isn't it?' He said in the Viennese dialect, at the same time sitting down and looking about him, hot and smiling. He took off his hat, wiped his brow, and looked at Henry quizzically. This young man was altogether too solemn. Maximilian knew that Henry hated to be called von Hayburn. It was ridiculous to be so young and yet so serious. Henry needed teasing.

'You will have a quarter with me?' he asked, raising his finger to attract a waiter. 'I can't drink coffee now: it's too near lunchtime.'

Henry drank little wine, and it was part of his creed that he must drink nothing at a time of day when there was still work to be done. But he did not dare to offend Maximilian.

While the wine and mineral water were being brought, Maximilian gave him the papers to look through. As the young man was doing so, the other took out a long Viennese 'Virginia', drew the straw from it, lit it and sat puffing contentedly, following the passing show outside the window. After a moment his eyes wandered back to Henry.

'Understand?' he asked, indicating by his question that Henry might still have some difficulty with German.

'Yes, thanks.'

A clever boy this. There was little that he did not grasp. Henry was bent forward, reading the sheets with concentration. Maximilian examined him afresh. His straight black hair straggled over his sallow brow. His young beard needed trimming. His hands were rough and stained with oil like a workman's. The nails were closely cut, and none too clean. How did his young wife like this? What sort of life was he giving her?

Henry laid down the papers.

'All right?' Maximilian asked him.

'Yes, I think so.'

'You'll manage to deliver on time?'

'I'll see that we do.'

'Good.' Maximilian gathered up the papers out of the way of the waiter who was waiting to put down the little tray of wine and mineral water, and thrust them back into his pocket.

He picked up the carafe, poured out for both of them, touched glasses with Henry and sat back once more. 'How's your wife?' he asked, after a sip or two.

'Quite well, thank you.'

But Maximilian wanted to know more than that. 'How is she liking Vienna?'

'Very well.'

Maximilian regarded Henry for an instant, the beginnings of a smile just showing; then, with no unfriendliness in his tone, he asked his next question. 'How do you know? Do you ever ask her?'

Henry's colour deepened. 'Well – she seems all right. She knows I'm too busy to go out much. She understands. The land-lady we're staying with takes her about.'

Still Maximilian's eyes were upon him. Still the teasing smile. 'Von Hayburn, you're a hypocrite. I don't believe you're looking after her! It would serve you right if she took a lover!'

This was the kind of Austrian joke that Henry's Puritanism did not think funny. But Hirsch had touched on a sore spot. Had he not, as he sat here ten minutes ago, blamed himself bitterly for neglecting Phœbe? He sat now confused and silent.

'Where are you going to live during the heat of the summer?'

'We don't know yet. Where we are, probably. For a time, at least.' Then, answering a question in Maximilian's eyes, he added: 'You see, it's all uncertain. She's going to have a child in the autumn.'

The elder man leant across the table, took his hand and shook it warmly; thus merely adding to Henry's confusion. 'But, my dear boy, she must be looked after! Why hasn't she seen more of my aunts? They were horrified when they heard she had gone to a district like the Favoriten. Oh, I dare say the old ladies in the Paulanergasse are not very interesting. But a young woman in that condition must have women friends!'

Maximilian swallowed down the dregs of his wine and again looked at Henry. This was ridiculous! Preposterous! Indeed, it made him angry! He set down his glass on the marble table and launched forth. Henry was behaving like a thoughtless boy. Why had he brought this girl from Scotland if he were going to treat her thus? She must see his aunts at once, and have their help and friendship!

And why should not the Hayburns spend their summer in a little house on the edge of the Vienna Woods where it would be cool and pleasant for Phœbe, yet not too far for

Henry to come to work?

This he said, and much more. And, as he spoke, he was glad – if a little surprised – to see that Henry looked ashamed of himself. But well he might! It was not before time! He did not deserve that beautiful child for a wife!

Maximilian finished his tirade and stood up. 'Now, you'll look after your wife, von Hayburn, won't you?'

Henry's reply was the ashamed grin of a schoolboy who has been scolded and forgiven.

Herr Hirsch handed the waiter a coin and drew out his watch. It was a quarter past twelve. He had invited a crony to lunch with him in his pet restaurant, the 'Reichenberger Beisel', in the Griechengasse, at twelve o'clock. But a quarter of an hour in Vienna was neither here nor there.

He gave Henry his hand, saying he must go, and took his leisurely way across the Inner City.

IV

A few minutes later, Henry also found himself in the Inner City. Like Maximilian, he, too, could call himself the *Stammgast* of a Viennese restaurant, although it had never occurred to him to do so. But Maximilian's restaurant in the Griechengasse and Henry's restaurant in a passage-way off the Herrengasse were very different places. Henry had come upon his one day quite by chance, as he was taking a short cut through one of the rights-of-way or *Durchhäuser* which abounded in the Inner City; relics of earlier days when Vienna was a closely crowded labyrinth inside protecting walls; when much time and inconvenience were saved to those who went on foot, that they were given rights to pass through other people's courtyards.

In one such passage-way off the Herrengasse, Henry had found a little eating-house. He had come here in the first place merely because he was hungry, because it looked cheap and because he happened to be passing by. It consisted of one large stuffy room, constantly lit by gas-flares, since, from its position, there was never enough daylight. If the regulars – clerks, students and *Fiaker* drivers – had at first resented a foreigner's presence, Henry had certainly not noticed this, any more than he had noticed the grease-spots on the checked cloths or the all-pervading smell of *Gulasch*. But in a short time custom had set aside a table for him, and 'der Mister', as he came to be called, was to be seen sitting solitary in his accustomed corner, papers or a book propped against a carafe of untouched wine, deep in his reading, and munching abstractedly anything that happened to be put before him.

But today Henry had no reading propped up in front of him. He felt unhappy, and his conscience was not clear. The sight of his wife passing him by in the tramcar. The scolding he had just had from Herr Hirsch. The thought of the child that was to be.

Henry was a simple creature. Now that he had thought of it, he was filled with self-reproach at his treatment of Phœbe. She had been too much alone, too little with him. He had been very busy, of course, but, in the full flood of his penitence, he could look back and think of many times he might easily have spent in her company.

The elderly restaurant-keeper, having served everybody for the moment, leant against his little service counter watching his customers eat, and conversing with the plump lady who combined the occupations of wife, cook and cashier. Now he gave it out as his firm opinion that something was on 'der Mister's' mind. She nodded sympathetically. Yes, he looked troubled as he sat there, forgetting his soup, looking about him, and crumbling rye bread with his long, stained fingers, his bony wrists protruding from his sleeves.

Should he apologise to Phœbe? Henry wondered. No. Somehow that would merely be awkward and unnatural. But tonight he would talk to her and put things right.

And now, having reassured himself a little, Henry remembered the vegetable soup that stood before him, took up his spoon and allowed his eyes to range about the room while he ate.

In a far corner, dim in the gas-light, there was a table of young people, most of them regular customers, who came and went, making this their common meeting-place – students from the music or medical schools, judging from an occasional fiddle-case, or from the fact that at more hilarious moments stethoscopes were brandished, and even, on more than one occasion, amid the screaming of the girls, a human skull. Today the din was at its height. There was gaiety and laughter, and, as was the unself-conscious custom of Viennese youths, bursts of song.

Henry, well used to this behaviour, sat watching them, incuriously. But now a single voice piped up. In some way it sounded familiar. He looked across, and saw that it came from a young woman who sat conducting herself with a fork as she sang. He had heard this voice many times singing about the house in the Quellengasse. It belonged to Pepi Klem.

She finished, bowed exaggerated acknowledgement of her companions' applause, then her eyes caught Henry's. She smiled and waved her fork. Henry, surprised and embarrassed, smiled in return.

So Pepi was back in Vienna? He fell to wondering about her. Her mother, he knew, had been much troubled at her disappearance. Willi Pommer had for a time been inconsolable. But Henry had, just then, had more than enough to think of on his own account. Having heard that she had been found working in some provincial theatre, and that her parents had accepted the inevitable, Fräulein Klem and her problems had passed from his mind.

Now the party in the corner was standing up to go. They were teasing their host as they paid – or begged him to mark up – their modest reckonings. There was laughter, banter between young men and women, and noise. Presently Pepi said goodbye to her friends, came across to Henry, and sat down facing him, her elbows on the table.

V

'Well, Herr Hayburn? Aren't you pleased to see me?' She was laughing at his surprise, his flushed face, his obvious embarrassment as he stammered out:

'Oh, how are you?'

His innocence amused her now, as it had always amused her. But now there was

recklessness in her amusement – recklessness born of the jealousy that had driven her
from home, of the careless informality of
her life in the theatre, of her new, defiant
independence.

She offered her hand in a formal handshake across the table, rather with the
affected air of a prima donna.

'I suppose you are still in the Quellengasse?'

'Yes, we are.'

'And how is the gracious lady?'

'My wife is very well.'

'She must be quite Viennese now.'

'Oh, no. I wouldn't say that.'

'No? Well, she had better learn. If she
doesn't want to be hurt in Vienna.'

'I don't understand.'

Pepi shrugged. She had picked the bundle
of wooden toothpicks out of the glass that
contained them, and was making squares
and triangles on the table-cloth.

Henry watched her, puzzled. Here was a
Pepi he had not expected. She was gaily
dressed, confident and full of high spirits.
There had been tears, tragic predictions and
endless talk in the Quellengasse at the time
of her going. Phœbe and he, when they had
mentioned her to each other, had spoken of
her as a brand gone to the burning. Now
here she was, delighted with herself. His
artlessness could not believe that she was in

any way changed. She seemed the same friendly little Pepi she had always been. He was glad. Last autumn she had been a very good friend to him.

'I've been in Lemberg, in Galicia,' she said at length, looking up from her game with the toothpicks. 'The Mama has probably told you. It wasn't much of a place, but I got an offer of work in the theatre there. I had to start somewhere.'

And, as Henry had no comment to make, she added, with a glint of mischief: 'Besides, it might have been worse. It's the Head-quarters of an Army Corps. The officers helped to amuse us.' Her eyes dropped to the table once more, and she continued with her squares and triangles.

'And what exactly were you doing?' he asked for the sake of saving something.

'Singing in the chorus. Doing anything. Studying.'

What would he have expected, had he been told he was going to meet her? A weeping magdalen? A broken creature who could not raise her eyes to those of an honest man? But now her eyes as she raised them regarded him humorously and calmly – the eyes of a young woman who is no longer afraid; who has taken the measure of emotion and knows where it leads.

But she wasn't establishing the old friend-ship with him. She must try again.

'Were the poor Papa and Mama very anxious when I went away, Herr Hayburn?' she asked, with exaggerated sympathy.

'Yes, they were. They thought you were murdered or something.'

She laughed. 'Well, it didn't last long. I wrote whenever I could. I had always wanted to make a career on the stage. But they would never hear of it. Now they realise that I'm in earnest.'

'Then you'll come to see them?'

'Of course! I only got back to Vienna yesterday. I'm staying with my cousin for a few days. I've got a summer job in the Prater. It's only the chorus again, but I want to be in Vienna to have singing lessons. You see, I want to study and turn into a real artist.' She looked at Henry, sighed and added: 'The poor Mama! If I don't manage to see her today, please give her all my love and say I'll come tomorrow.' She stood up, tied the green ribbons of her bonnet, pulled on her gloves and held out her hand. 'Well, then, dear Herr Hayburn. Until very soon.'

Henry had risen, too. He stood now at the door of the little eating-house, watching her as she took her way across the paving-stones of the shadowy passage towards the arch of white sunshine at the open street. Now he could see her standing framed in the light for an instant, as though she were halted by the sudden brightness. Now she had flicked open her frivolous green parasol, gathered her skirts in one hand and tripped off up the Herrengasse out of sight.

Henry turned back, paid his bill and looked at his watch. Already he was a little later than he liked to be. It was bad for discipline to give the impression that he had allowed himself a leisurely lunch.

He made his way towards the Neubau, walking fast and taking as many short cuts as possible.

So that was Pepi? He had not disliked seeing her again. She had always been a friendly little thing, and had helped him through those first lonely months when he had not had Phœbe. He would be glad to tell her mother she was in Vienna once more, if she herself had not already appeared and done so. And he could assure Frau Klem, too, that she looked very well and seemed rather the better than the worse for her adventure.

Chapter Thirteen

To Phœbe it seemed as though in the last day or two a curtain had been lifted – as though the strange, dull veil of commonplace that had, somehow, so quickly fallen between herself and Henry – between herself and the first, shining happiness of her marriage – had suddenly been torn asunder and they were back once more in the radiance of their first days in Vienna.

How had it come about? From the sudden burst of warmth and sunshine that had taken possession of the city as though the weather knew what was expected of it in Easter Week? From the extravagance of joy that now was reigning in the Quellengasse? From the fact that the simple father and mother Klem, having had a visit from Pepi, and having received her assurances that she was really studying and would one day be a great prima donna, had – rather inconsequently, the Hayburns thought – turned right about and, instead of making a tragedy of Pepi, had decided to make an idol of their prodigal daughter?

Or was it merely that Phœbe felt, during these bright days, that there was now no need to be jealous of her husband's work? For a change had taken place in Henry. He had become boyishly tender towards her; gauchely apologetic. The mask of self-importance that Vienna had given him fell from him now when he was with her. Once again they had come very near.

Phœbe found herself wondering how this had come about. Even when, some days ago, she had told him she hoped to be the mother of his child, Henry had not perhaps responded with the tenderness she had expected. Now in his own way he sought to serve her lightest wish, as though he were seeking to right some wrong he had done her. To Phœbe it was incomprehensible. But it was pleasant, and she was uplifted and happy.

And this Eastertide in Vienna enchanted her. It was as though this ancient capital of the Holy Roman Empire had set aside her frivolity, and let herself be washed clean for the festival of Death and Resurrection. Her church spires stood up, hard and pure against the pale Easter sky. Behind them the outline of the mountains. And in the streets everywhere, the Viennese in their holiday clothes. Some mere promenaders; others going to church. Fashionable men and women. Comfortable burghers with their wives. Harassed mothers with worn prayer-books. Children with gleaming, holiday faces. Officers and soldiers wearing their white linen tunics for the first time this year. A cheerful crowd of high and humble. Shop-windows full of coloured Easter eggs, Easter presents, Easter food.

Sometimes by herself, sometimes in the company of Henry, Phœbe visited the churches. She had, in these months abroad, lost her Puritan and provincial hesitation – almost fear – of entering a popish building. And, though it never crossed her mind to question the rightness of her own faith, she found herself taking pleasure in these foreign churches; even in their ritual. She had come to love the smell of incense, the guttering candles, the sacristans with their keys, the dim, praying women, the solemn bursts of music. Even the beggars at the church doors holding back the leather curtains and begging alms. To her it did not mean religion; it meant romance.

And now for Easter, that the simpler people might better remember the story of the Agony, each church had set aside a chapel, and there had arranged, in effigy, the Holy Tomb. In the great churches, in the Votive Church, the *Hofkapelle*, the Church of Saint Stephen, the arrangement was elaborate and rich. In lesser churches it was simple. But each, according to its resources, had its Tomb, its plaster Roman soldiers and angels watching over the effigy of the weary, bloodstained Redeemer who now, His agony over, lay at rest.

It seemed strange to these young Presbyterians that sometimes people could be seen turning away from these stiff images, the tears shining in their eyes. These Holy Tombs appeared to the Hayburns unreal, foreign and strange.

Henry had told Phœbe of his plans for finding a little house somewhere on the edge of the Vienna Woods. He had mentioned it as though the idea were quite his own. He did not tell her of the scolding he had received from Maximilian Hirsch, and his consequent feelings of penitence. And with this planning for her, Henry was pleased with his own new-found sense of responsibility, his protective masculinity. The Klems might be sorry to lose them, he argued; but, after all, Pepi had reappeared in Vienna, had made her peace.

Further, he suggested that Phœbe should call once more upon the ladies Hirsch, tell them of her condition, and beg their very kind advice. At this Phœbe was really astonished. She had taken Henry to call on the ladies some weeks ago, and when, after a very formal cup of coffee, they had found themselves once again in the street, he had told her bluntly that she must not expect him to visit these 'old tabbies' any more.

Phœbe was almost as little a reader of hearts as was her husband. But now even she began to suspect that someone had intervened to change his mind.

II

It was into this pool of re-established happiness that Bel's letter, bidding Phœbe come home to Scotland, dropped like a stone. But they did not allow it to do more than ruffle the surface. There was nothing now quite real to the young couple except each other.

She held out the letter to him one evening as he arrived home.

'Here's a letter from Bel.'

'Any news?'

'Nothing much. Except that she wants me to go home if there's to be a baby.'

'Why?'

She was surprised at the rush of colour to Henry's face; at the quick, angry question. It was as though she had touched the trigger of a gun.

'It's all right, dear! I'm not going! Do you want to read the letter?'

'No.'

She folded it up, and that, for the time, was the end of the matter. She would write later and tell Bel how they both felt about it. It was natural enough, perhaps, that Henry should not see things through Bel's eyes; that he should want to keep his wife by him. She would say no more about it.

And now, in and around Vienna, the tide of spring was rising – fresh, sprouting days that had little to do with the springtime of her comic operettas. The thrushes were singing in the Volksgarten and Votivpark. In all green places, flowering shrubs were budding. Presently there would be laburnum – golden rain, as the citizens call it – and lilac in profusion. When the fitful sunshine appeared for long enough to make its presence felt, there was the scent of lime and elder. In the Haupt Allee – the great main drive of the Prater – with its double row of giant chestnut-trees stretching, as it seemed to Phœbe, to infinity, the pale green leaves had begun to fan themselves out above the now-emerging fashionable world, whose ritual it was to drive in their elegance beneath them. In the People's Prater the booths and merry-go-rounds had received their yearly coat of paint. The voices of showmen – good-natured, crude and coarse – could be heard insisting that all and sundry should walk up and try their luck or find amusement.

Times had been bad this winter here in Vienna, as in most other towns in Europe. But what was that to a young Viennese, who could find *Kreutzers* enough to take a girl to have fun in the Volks Prater?

On more than one fine April Sunday, the young couple, having done their duty by attending the Scotch service in the morning, had gaily agreed that in Rome one must live as the Romans, and had spent the remainder of their day in the Prater. If their behaviour towards each other was a little ashamed, a little conscience-stricken, a little indulgent towards the reckless, laughing inhabitants of this carefree city that had not seen the Presbyterian light, it did, perhaps, no harm to anyone, and may even have given spice to their own enjoyment.

On one of these occasions they encountered Pepi Klem. She was in the company of a spirited young man, whom she was pleased to introduce to the Hayburns as her cousin. He seemed a gay, affectionate sort of cousin, and, on Henry's suggestion that they should drink a cup of coffee together, readily assented. Before the Hayburns had done with them, they had made the round of the People's Prater. They saw the traditional Viennese Punch-and-Judy show, made up of two clowns and a rabbit. They had visited fat women and strong men. They saw 'the lady without a body' – a young and cheerful head and shoulders on a stand; like an animated barber's dummy. They saw the ladies of an Eastern harem. Henry had swung Pepi so high in a red, plush-lined swing-boat that she had screamed to Phœbe and her 'cousin' to stop him. On a merry-go-round they had rotated to the Miserere music from 'Trovatore', Pepi riding side-saddle on a spirited wooden horse painted and harnessed to look like one of the Emperor's Lippizaner horses from the Spanish Riding-School; Henry was seated on a pig; the 'cousin' occupied a large and comfortably upholstered giant model of a teacup; while Phœbe rotated demurely in a comfortable seat set between the wings of a giant swan.

It pleased Phœbe to see Henry in this mad

mood. This crazy, dare-devil Henry. It was a Henry she had never seen before, a Henry she had not even suspected. Pepi Klem and he behaved like children. The switchback railway. The spiral slide. The house of mystery. Where she judged it was prudent for herself, she took part; where not, she stood by and laughed. It was as though her husband had opened a safety-valve of high spirits. Phœbe welcomed it. The weight of the winter seemed to be lifted from him. She was grateful to this madcap girl for breaking down his seriousness; for releasing the boy that was still in him. If they were all a little above themselves; even a little hysterical; then that, indeed, didn't matter.

That night they lay in the darkness side by side, still too excited to sleep. After a time Phœbe spoke:

'Henry.'

'What, dear?'

'Today was Sunday. Isn't it awful to think!'

'Think what, dear?'

'How we've both been behaving.'

'Awful, wasn't it!'

But she could feel the bed shaking as he laughed silently to himself.

III

The Hirsch ladies' reception of her was a

little stiff, Phœbe felt, when next she went to call in the Wieden. The younger Hirsch sister had been so ready to open her formal heart to this foreign girl her nephew had begged her to befriend, that Phœbe's casual treatment of her, Phœbe's disregard of her advice over such matters as lodging and a language teacher, had looked like a rebuff.

And young Frau Hayburn's husband had made none too favourable an impression either. His awkwardness of person, his pronouncements on matters Viennese about which he could not possibly know, his British off-handedness – all these things together did not recommend him. And his table manners were deplorable. He did not seem to have the faintest idea how to manage his coffee-cup, the little cakes or the thimble-glass of cognac, which were provided for his entertainment. Max said he was clever, and this Max's aunts were quite ready to believe. Herr Hayburn's knowledge of German, if it were gained in the short months he had been in Vienna, was quite astounding, mixed though it might be, here and there, with the language of his workmen. Even his grasp of Austrian politics, if unconventional, was remarkable. But he was an odd, angular sort of young man to have paying a visit, and the ladies had been glad when his wife had taken him away again.

But now Phœbe's condition and her need

of their help held an appeal that was irresistible. Of course dear Frau Hayburn must come to them whenever she felt like it! Yes, a little house on the edge of the Vienna Woods was just the place for her to spend the summer waiting for her baby! That was to say, if her dear husband really insisted that he was unable to leave Vienna for a proper holiday, because of all this new and very important work he was organising.

Besides, they themselves would only be out of town for four weeks. They had quiet rooms in Gastein where they went each year, so that Helene might take the cure. For the rest of the summer they lived very well and much more quietly staying at home, taking the air in the Prater, or even, if they felt adventurous, driving out into the surrounding country. If fashionable Vienna was pleased to disport itself in the Salzkammergut, on Tyrolese mountains, or by the Adriatic, that was fashionable Vienna's affair. And so, for the greater part of the summer, these well-intentioned and rather sentimental ladies would be at dear Frau Hayburn's disposal.

Left alone with Fräulein Stephanie, Phœbe spoke of doctors. She told her of Bel's letter insisting she had much better go home.

Her friend called the proposal ridiculous. Why, she demanded, should dear Frau Hayburn leave the city where the most famous specialists in Europe were to be found. Did not the whole world of medicine come here to learn? Where could Frau Hayburn better be looked after? Had she never heard of the great medical school and hospital founded long ago in the time of Maria-Theresa by the great Queen herself? And was there not at this moment an excellent maternity hospital in the Alsergrund?

Phœbe did not know that she had done the one thing that no Viennese would allow. She had implied a criticism of Vienna. She had an idea that doctors in Glasgow were not quite ignorant, that the city in the Clyde had contributed more than its share to the store of medical knowledge; but never having had much interest in these things, she was unable to find names and facts to set against those of Stephanie.

And yet she was glad her friend was so insistent; glad that everything she said supported Henry. For Bel's influence with Phœbe was strong. Stronger, indeed, than Phœbe knew.

Though a week or more had passed, she had not yet brought herself to answer Bel's letter. It was nothing to run counter to Bel's advice in unimportant things. But in this, a great happening in her life, all Phœbe's instinct turned towards Bel's judgment.

She was happy in Vienna. The tenderness that had somehow been re-born between herself and Henry was everything to her. She loved her husband, and had no wish to leave him. Yet, she had kept Bel's letter, wondering.

Now her decision was taken. Tonight she would write to say she was staying where she was. That she had good friends. That everything was available for her well-being. That Henry could not possibly do without her.

Presently she realised that her friend was sitting watching her, her white hands slowly smoothing out the folds of her stiff black silk.

'*Na?* Frau Hayburn? You have come back?' Stephanie Hirsch was smiling with quizzical affection.

'Back?'

'You were not here. You were lost? No?'

For reply Phœbe stood up, smiling herself in turn, embarrassment adding colour to her face. She held out her hand.

With a quick gesture Stephanie put a hand on each of her shoulders, turned her to the light and regarded her for a time with ad-miration.

'You are a dear and beautiful child!' she said, speaking in her own language, and, taking Phœbe into her arms, kissed her first on one cheek and then the other.

Phœbe blushed scarlet and took her leave. Austrians were perhaps sentimental, she told herself, as she made her way down the worn stone staircase. But she would go back soon. For Stephanie Hirsch was kind.

Chapter Fourteen

The Hayburns were present at Pepi Klem's reunion with her parents. Behind a set smile of politeness the Scotch couple considered the episode over-acted.

Pepi threw herself first into her mother's, then into her father's arms. She begged their forgiveness, implored them not to scorn her, and told them her love had brought her back. But she had not, it seemed, retracted one whit from the stand she was taking over becoming a singer and leading an independent life of her own.

Her simple, kindly parents, loving, in the Austrian fashion, this dramatic situation, were delighted. Her father offered, now he was convinced, as he put it, that music really called her, to pay out a portion of what had been intended as her dowry, for the proper training of her voice. The mention of the word dowry caused Pepi to demand in stricken tones: How was poor, poor Willi Pommer? Willi Pommer, it seemed, felt rather a dull dog these days, on account, no doubt, of herself; but apart from that he was very much as usual. This last was the only part of this scene of reunion that did not quite come up to the emotional level of the rest, the Hayburns felt, forgetting that Pepi had merely broken an agreement, and not Willi Pommer's heart.

But it was not for these two young people from an Island where the show of feeling is counted a weakness, to judge this reunion in a land where quick emotion is part of the currency of daily expression. That the Klems exaggerated their joy did not mean that their feelings were hollow.

Pepi, then, was to continue with her cousin Lisa Fischer until such time as the young Herr and Frau Hayburn should be gone. Pepi, greatly daring, had told her parents where she was living at present, guessing rightly that even Fräulein Fischer would be caught up in the present wave of emotion – other aspects of her existence forgotten – and clothed with a halo as a handmaid of song. Thereafter she, Pepi, would return to her father's roof, hire a piano, and add arpeggios and distinction to her home in the Quellengasse.

It was on account of the arpeggios that Frau Klem looked to the Hayburns' going with so little concern. For would not Pepi presently be a famous prima donna and fully compensate them?

If Phœbe and Henry could not, perhaps, read the future with the Klems' eyes, they were, none the less, pleased that the matter should be so pleasantly settled.

II

The month of April was, indeed, to be among the most pleasant Phœbe had known. When it was some days old she wrote to Bel telling her that she intended to stay with her husband in Vienna; that here there was more than the necessary skill – in this she quoted Stephanie Hirsch pompously – and that they were now looking for a little house near the woods in which to spend the summer. When she had posted the letter she felt misgivings. It was not easy for her seriously to flaunt Bel.

But now, with her husband and the Hirsch ladies supporting her own strong inclinations, Phœbe decided that her decision must be right.

She was seeing much of Stephanie Hirsch now. Henry had taken Maximilian's lecture to heart; and, busy though he was, he made time to visit the 'old tabbies' in the Paulanergasse, present them with a bouquet of Italian roses with a formality that sat so ill upon him that they were touched, and thank them for all the kind interest they were

223

taking in his wife.

And so, with the best of goodwill fully restored, Stephanie Hirsch put herself and her carriage at Phœbe's disposal and spent many radiant April days with her, exploring Vienna's lovely surroundings. These were days unique in Phœbe's life. In her memory they were to take on the quality of a dream, long since dreamt. Even as she lived them, she was assailed at times with a sense of their unreality.

The soft air of an unusually mild spring. The shining Russian horses. The much-polished, old-fashioned carriage. The grey-haired, elderly woman in the carriage beside her, whose mid-European elegance owed little to the fashion of her time; whose dignity did not rob her friendliness of warmth. The triumphant consciousness of her own young body, and the magic that her love for Henry was working within it.

More than once their carriage took them up into the woods out of sight of any dwelling, following, perhaps, an alley road by some rushing stream. They drove through regions of pine-trees where squirrels scurried out of sight, disappearing into the gloom of the brown, needle-covered forest floor; through bright regions of sprouting beech, oak or birch, where there were April violets, pale fresh grass and patches of white sunshine. Then suddenly they might come upon an opening and find all Vienna lying over yonder in the crystal distance; its gardens, its palaces, its church spires all to be distinguished in the clear spring light. Days of rapture, of expectation, of young fulfilment, of sharp awareness of the romance and beauty that fed her avid senses.

By mid-April they had found a little house. It had not been altogether easy for Phœbe to persuade Stephanie that she and her husband were seeking anything so simple. Like most other Continentals of her day, the younger Fräulein Hirsch took for granted that the Hayburns, like all the other 'English', were made of money.

It was a house, its upper storey of timber, situated in the forest near Ober Dobling, a miniature Tyrolean chalet, gay with fresh paint, with an upper balcony from which you could touch the pine-trees, a little rose-garden, a motherly landlady, who was, at once, intimately interested in Phœbe, and a benign St. Bernard dog, that bore with sleepy dignity the malicious slander painted on a board nailed to the garden gate, that here there was a fierce creature on the watch ready to tear all tramps and vagrants to pieces.

On the following Sunday Henry went alone to see this house. He grumbled, as a formal show of his authority, at the price demanded for the season, decided, however, that it was healthy and at a distance that could easily be covered twice a day on his 'Kangaroo', and so it was taken.

Phœbe seemed to herself to be moving through this Viennese April on a strange rising wave of happiness. Her heart kept bursting into an ever-brighter blooming, like the lilac and the laburnum in the parks around her. She ran to the Paulanergasse to tell Stephanie that Henry had taken the house, and that they were moving out on the first of May.

Stephanie Hirsch bent to kiss Phœbe, and as she did so, there were tears in her eyes. At no time in her own life had it been given to her to know ecstasy. The sight of it in Phœbe aroused in her a strange, unnamed compassion.

'But, my dearest,' she said, 'the first of May you cannot go. You are coming in the carriage with me.' And as Phœbe looked blank, she added: 'On the first of May is the May Corso in the Prater. It is very important that you see these things, if you will live in Vienna.' And she went on to explain to Phœbe the nature of this May Day ceremony. Nothing would make her sister Helene and herself happier, than that Phœbe and Herr Hayburn should drive in the Prater with them.

They accepted the invitation, and Phœbe's month of April moved on joyfully to this fitting end.

III

The first of May dawned serene and misty, promising a full continuation of the fine weather. Henry, accustomed to early rising, awoke at his usual time. It was almost with a sense of annoyance that, as full consciousness returned, he came to remember what day it was. He was an industrious young man, with work to do, and a day of holiday seemed to him at this cool hour of the morning, nothing but a needless and frivolous interruption.

He turned to look at his wife. She lay beside him, still breathing deeply and steadily. Her face was rosy with sleep. The black plaits of her hair were straggling on the pillow beside her. That he might not wake her, he slid gently from his side of the bed, crossed to the open window and stood in his nightshirt looking about him.

The Quellengasse beneath was almost empty. No workmen, it seemed, would be working on the unfinished buildings today; but further down he could see a woman on her knees scrubbing an entrance. Nearer by, a peasant woman was delivering milk from a cart drawn by a great, yellow ox. A small baker's boy, in a white coat, passed beneath, bearing so large a tray on his head that, for a time, it seemed to Henry, as he looked down, as though this tray of *Kaisersemmel*, salt sticks and *Gipfel* moved along the pavement of its own accord. In a kitchen near at hand someone was roasting coffee. Its sharp aroma mixed itself with the smell of last night's *Gulasch* and the May-time scents of lime and plane-trees.

He gave a sudden start as he became aware that his wife was standing in her nightdress beside him.

'Oh, hullo. I thought you were asleep.'

'So I was. But you've been standing here for hours, Henry. What are you looking at?'

'Nothing much. The weather.'

'It's going to be glorious today!' She looked about her eagerly.

'Happy?'

She turned to him and nodded, her eyes dancing like a child's. Suddenly her face flushed, and as though to cover some other feeling, she laid a hand on her husband's arm.

'You silly boy,' she said quickly, 'you've let yourself get as cold as a puddock. Go back to bed and warm yourself.'

As they sat up in bed, Phœbe talked with animation of the day that lay before them. He had never seen her so uplifted. He watched her, wondering. She lay propped against her pillow looking at a beam of morning sunshine as it crept across Frau Klem's coarse window-curtains.

'If our baby's a boy,' she said presently, 'he's going to be called Robert Hayburn after your father. Just that. Robert Hayburn. None of your Ruanthorpe-Moorhouses or Dermott-Moorhouses or any of that nonsense.'

Henry laughed. It was impossible to follow the train of her thinking.

'I don't see what there is to laugh at,' Phœbe said, turning to look at him. 'And, by the way, this morning I must go out and find some flowers for the Hirschs. I meant to order them yesterday.' And, as he had protested at her extravagance, she added: 'We really must, Henry; they've been so kind.'

While Phœbe was buying flowers, Frau Klem brought Henry a letter. It was in the handwriting of Bel Moorhouse. To his surprise, it was addressed to himself. He tore it open with curiosity. As he read it his face darkened. So Bel was writing to *him* now? To tell him it was his duty to send Phœbe home! But his wife wasn't going! What business had Bel to interfere? He folded the letter angrily and thrust it into his pocket. He would not mention this to Phœbe today.

IV

Stephanie Hirsch felt inclined to laugh at

Henry as, along with his wife, he presented himself in the Paulanergasse at three o'clock. He wore his best clothes as though they belonged to someone else, and his dutiful, self-conscious bearing suggested anything but lightness of heart. But his wife, with her arms full of roses, her glowing cheeks, and her summer dress, seemed to bring with her everything that was young into the old-fashioned room of the Paulanergasse.

The Hayburns were given sweet wine and the inevitable chocolate cakes with cinnamon, while the Hirsch ladies put the finishing touches to their stiff finery. At last, with an amount of fuss that was a severe trial to the young man of the party, they were seated behind cockaded flunkeys in the family landau.

Stephanie had looked forward to this year's Corso with keen anticipation. It is always pleasant to show off what one has known and loved to the young and the eager. And to this Viennese woman there was nothing so precious as Vienna and its pageantry. She sat beside Herr Hayburn facing Phœbe, who was in the place of honour on her sister Helene's right hand.

The carriage made its way out of the Wieden and down that part of the Ring that leads to the Aspern Bridge. Already it was noticeable that all the smarter traffic was making in the same direction. As they passed the Stadtpark, with its shrubs hanging heavy with blossom, they noticed it was unusually empty. The fineness of the weather was drawing everybody to the Prater to see the world go by.

Presently they had crossed the Danube Canal and found themselves in the Praterstrasse, the wide and handsome street that leads to the entrance of the Prater itself. Here carriages were coming in from all sides, and the traffic was heavy as it moved down towards the famous pleasure-grounds.

Workpeople on holiday crowded the sidewalks; some of them standing, hoping to see a celebrity pass; more of them walking towards the Prater, where they would see the parade in full swing. There were many families, the plump fathers and mothers carrying baskets of food to be eaten later. Even if times were bad, and there was no money for the roundabout or even a cheap restaurant in the People's Prater, you could always take the children's bread and sausage to the Prater meadows, and have all the fun of watching and criticising the rich and the aristocratic, as they displayed their finery to each other in the Haupt Allee – or main drive. The weather of the first of May was kind this year. Little children trotted, chattering and excited, after their parents.

Now the Hirschs' landau was at the Prater

Stern, where seven streets meet and the great park begins. Here the press of carriages was so thick that they could move round the circle only slowly, almost completing it before they reached the entrance to the Haupt Allee. Now they had passed under the railway bridge and were in the great carriage-drive itself, with its double rows of giant chestnut-trees, planted three and a half centuries before, in the days when the Prater was an island of the Danube, and the private hunting-grounds of Austria's rulers.

As they found their place in the glittering stream of carriages, Phœbe looked at her companions. The elder Fräulein Hirsch had taken on a quite special dignity, now that she found herself in this parade of Vienna's society. She sat like royalty, alert and stiff, ready to return the formal salutations of acquaintances as they passed her coming back down the Haupt Allee in the opposite direction. Henry was sitting, glum and unhappy-seeming, as many Scots do when they are excited. Stephanie made weak attempts to appear dignified like her sister, but she was flushed and happy, and intent on pointing out everything.

Phœbe had seen the parade of carriages in the Prater many times already, but never thus, at its height. And it would have taken someone who was much less avid of life, much less eager, to remain cold before this astonishing spectacle.

Now, leaving the entrance, they were passing the Kaisergarten, where the Court, ever conscious of the spectacle it must provide for the people, had come to be seen and to take a ceremonial luncheon. Now their coachman had cracked his whip, the horses had dropped into a trot, and the landau was holding its place in this river of vehicles that flowed between towering, leafy banks of fresh green chestnut-trees with the candles on them bursting into bloom – banks that seemed to stretch into infinity in front of them.

Thousands of *Fiakers*. Poor and prosperous. Cabriolets. Phætons. A four-in-hand driven by some sensation-mongering grandee. A closed carriage with a regal old man looking through its windows. A shabby *Komfortable* with its single tired horse, lumbering along, bearing a numerous and vulgarly joyful City family. An open landau with a French governess and three young children in white, holding coloured balloons. One or two featherweights, with officers driving high-stepping English hackneys tearing back towards town from the May Day races in the Freudenau at a showy speed that was very dangerous in this traffic. A famous actor with his wife in a discreet, blue coupé. Aristocrats, financiers, men-about-town, demi-mondaines, gourmets, foreign ambassadors, artists, actresses – a swaying, garish flood of elegant humanity.

There were high spirits and laughing salutes. There were women dressed in the best of taste, and women whose every garment was an exaggeration. There were feathers and parasols; elegant, light-coloured top-hats and carefully trimmed whiskers. There were faces thick with paint, and faces lined with sorrow. There were carefree, reckless faces, and faces stiff with ambition.

It was astonishing how Stephanie seemed to know everyone, although she came out so little. Her eyes went everywhere, seeing everyone, seeming to miss no one. There, on the riding-track beneath the trees, was the Count Egon Taxis. And with him was the Archduke Franz Salvator. There, in her carriage with a friend, was the prima donna Pauline Lucca. And there, coming down in the other direction, was the Princess Metternich, sitting in a coupé with an elderly woman, who looked like a professional companion. And look! Over there, being greeted by Sonnenthal, the actor, was Fräulein Charlotte Wolter of the Imperial Theatre. And the fair young lady who was with her was Fräulein Kathi Schratt! And there again, on horseback in the riding-track, were the Barons Albert and Nathaniel Rothschild.

Stephanie mentioned the names of many

famous figures as they passed them by. Counts and princes. Fashionable singers and artists. Nobles and aristocrats from the Crown lands and the Empire. But she did not mention the great hinterland of struggling peoples inside the ring of Habsburg influence, whose labours went to build up this unique three miles of glittering pageantry. Peasants from the Hungarian Puszta. Sub-Carpathian gypsies. Jewish artificers from Galicia. Swabian tobacco-planters from the Bacska. Horse-dealers from Moravia. Bohemian weavers. Mohammedan trinket merchants from Servia. Podolian shepherds. And many more. All contributing to the display in this, their Emperor's capital city. A city that was, in the main, only hazily conscious of their remote existence.

But it was not the names of celebrities, of which she knew nothing, this brilliant froth, floating on a sea of some fifty million souls, that made the shining afternoon for Phœbe. It was the perfume of the trees, the low-hanging blossoms, the glimpses of green meadows and sunlit ponds, the carriages with their freights of elegance and colour, the flunkeys in traditional family uniforms, even the moving forest of whips, the smell of harness and of foaming, high-mettled horses.

And, when at last they had come to the end of the seemingly endless Haupt Allee, and their horses, rounding the Lusthaus, dropped to the traditional walk for the beginning of the return journey, the glimpses of the distant town through the green, the circle of blue mountains behind it, with the Habsburg-warte standing plumb above the centre of the Haupt Allee like the sight on a rifle, and the spire of Saint Stephen's dreaming in the sunshine a little on the left.

As again she lay in the darkness that night, sleep did not come at once. Still she was milling in the colourful traffic. Still she saw fashionable gloved hands raised in salutation. Still the endless line of giant trees bearing their candles. Still the perfume. Still a brassy phrase of distant music from the People's Prater.

Henry, from his breathing, did not seem to be asleep either.

'Henry.'

'What is it, dear?'

'Wouldn't Bel have enjoyed seeing everything today?'

But Bel's letter was still in the pocket of the jacket he had not so long since taken off. Tonight he did not feel particularly well disposed towards Bel.

'Yes, I dare say she would,' was his only comment. Then he added: 'I must get to sleep. I want to be at the works early tomorrow.'

Chapter Fifteen

The beginning of June found Bel unsettled.
Things were not going as she would have
them go.

In the first place there was the question of
holidays. Both the Arthurs, father and son,
clamoured to go back to Arran. Her mother,
who seemed, these days, to be determined to
go against her, took their side. This year Bel
had wanted somewhere more conventional.
The freedom of Arran was demoralising.
Each September, when she got the children
home to Grosvenor Terrace after two
months of running wild, it took her some
weeks, and a strictness she had no pleasure
in exerting, to bring them back to the ways
of gentility.

Then there was George McNairn. Now,
when he did go to business, it was only to
drive down in a cab for a couple of hours,
and come back utterly exhausted. Bel had
never liked Mary and George much; but
Mary was her husband's sister, and very
much a part of her life. Mary must be helped.
George could not leave Glasgow this summer, and Mary would not, of course, leave
George. That meant seeing to the children,

237

providing for their holiday and taking them off Mary's full and sorrowful hands. Sophia was too muddle-headed to help. Good-natured though she might be, she was no rock for Mary to cling to.

No. Mary's children must be removed, kept well and happy and forgotten about during this unhappy summer of their father's illness.

Arran, then, was the place. So the farmhouse was retaken; and Mrs. Barrowfield stoutly undertook to keep house throughout the two months of occupancy, bringing with her her own old and none too willing maids. Sarah would go down to look to Bel's children and also the little McNairn twin girls. Grosvenor Terrace and Albany Place must remain open. If the Arran contingent were packed together like sardines; if young cousins and maids from different households fought with each other like wild cats, then that was quite in the Arran tradition. Her mother, Bel assured herself a little callously, was more placid than she was, and would survive.

Sophia, having heard of this arrangement, announced, irresponsibly, that she thought she would like to go to Arran too. 'You see, Bel dear, I'll be able to help with the children when you have to be in town. The only thing is, of course, that if I take my little maid with me, I don't know what I'll do with

William. I don't suppose Arthur would like his company when he's by himself in Grosvenor Terrace?'

Bel had looked to having Grosvenor Terrace as a sanctuary to which she might run from the pandemonium of Brodick. Now even the sanctuary was to be invaded. But if the summer was to be ruined, let it be ruined thoroughly. Yes, William and everybody else might come to Grosvenor Terrace!

When she told Arthur, he was furious; which did not improve her own temper. She pointed out to her husband, not without some heat, that she had made all these arrangements to help his relatives – not hers; that the thought of this summer made her sick; and that the least he could do was to hold his tongue and go through with it.

But something quite other than these things lay at the source of Bel's discontent. It was her anxiety over Phœbe. Not content with Phœbe's reply, that she intended to stay in Austria with her husband, Bel had written to Henry, lecturing him on his responsibility towards so young a wife. She had waited for more than two weeks, then had received this reply:

'DEAR BEL,

'I would have written to you sooner, but both of us have been very busy getting into this small house. We have taken it for the summer. Our friends say that it is the right place for Phœbe to be, and that the heat is never too much up here in the woods. But Phœbe will have told you that already. About her coming home. There is no question of it. There is every kind of help in Vienna when the time comes. It is said they are further advanced in these things than we are. So please do not write to us about this again. Our minds are made up. We both join in sending our love to everybody.'

'Yours affectionately,
'HENRY HAYBURN.'

This letter made Bel very angry. She, the centre and pivot of the Moorhouses, did not like to find herself thrust back into her place, and told to stay there, by this, the newest and certainly the least-loved member of the family. No, Henry was adding impertinence to Phœbe's stubbornness.

Bel rang for the carriage. She would show this letter to her mother. Wounded self-importance and baffled anxiety heaped themselves high upon her already blazing annoyance. She thrust the letter under Mrs. Barrowfield's nose.

'There, Mother. What do you think of that?'

'Dear me, Bel. What is it?' Mrs. Barrowfield took up her spectacles and rubbed them with deliberation. What was Bel in such a to-do about now?

Bel watched her as she stood reading the letter. When the old woman looked up, there was actually a grin of mischief in her face. Her daughter could hardly believe her eyes.

'That's one in the eye for you, my lady,' she said, handing Bel back the letter. 'Did I not tell ye to let them alone? – No! Here! Stop!'

But Bel had flounced out of the house again. Now her mother, looking down, could see her getting back into the carriage! Silly girl! She might have stayed for a cup of tea. But Mrs. Barrowfield was not unduly troubled. In her teens Bel had done this kind of thing quite often. And she had always come back repentant. She wasn't a really bad-tempered lassie. The old lady called to Maggie to bring only one cup.

II

On the same evening Arthur came, bringing his brother Mungo with him. Mungo, following upon a visit of compassion to Mary McNairn, had appeared at the office this afternoon. Arthur, who wanted to talk over the McNairn situation, had persuaded him to send a telegram saying he would remain at Grosvenor Terrace for the night.

Bel, dark as her mood was, was not displeased to see him. He brought with him an air of the country. He was solemn, responsible and friendly. Mungo, at least, was neither troubling her spirit nor needing her help. His good-natured simplicity, combined with his dignity and his solid bank balance, recommended him to her. His coming tonight and his preparedness to do what he could to help poor Mary in her difficulty was a great comfort. Bel felt that everything was not being left to Arthur and herself. Mungo, in this family of plaguey relatives, was one relative who did not plague.

He had scarcely arrived before he brought out a letter from Margaret addressed to herself. On edge, Bel opened it a little apprehensively. The other letter she had opened today had brought her no pleasure. This one ran:

'MY DEAR BEL,
'I give this to Mungo to hand over to Arthur if he does not see yourself. I do hope he remembers. I am writing to say what a great pleasure it would be if you could come down here to the Dower House for some days; indeed, for as long as you can. You have shown me so much kindness, which I have never yet had any opportunity to repay. I know you are a busy person, but *do* try to find time to come. If Arthur can manage a weekend, that will make it perfect. At least

we can offer you a rest. I shall see to it that our noisy son is not allowed to disturb you. The gardens are beginning to look lovely. I should so much like you to see them. We are most distressed to hear about George McNairn. He is the reason for Mungo's coming to Glasgow. I hope your family is well.

'Your affectionate sister,

'MARGARET
RUANTHORPE-MOORHOUSE.'

Normally, going by herself to the Dower House to spend some days would not have appealed to Bel. She had never reached intimacy with Margaret. But just at present Bel was sick of intimacies. Margaret's cool good-nature, her unpossessiveness, even the fact that she could write of her year-old-son, Charles Mungo, without doting, appealed to Bel. The idea of well-bred simplicity and rest at the Duntrafford Dower House suddenly enchanted her.

Mungo added his invitation to Margaret's. She had told him to bring Bel back with him if, by chance, it could be managed. To Arthur's surprise, Bel accepted.

Bel, immaculate as always, was astonished a little at Margaret's appearance next evening. She had driven the pony-trap to the station herself. She wore a helmet-shaped fishing-cap of faded tweed that had originally belonged to Sir Charles. It was skewered

243

to her somewhat untidy head by several formidable hatpins. Fishing-flies clung to it.
Her Inverness cape was patched and faded,
too, and her strong gauntlet gloves looked as
though she had used them for weeding. Her
handsome red face became even redder, and
her fine teeth flashed resplendent, as she
bent to give Bel one hand, while she held the
reins in the other.

Clearly, here in the country Margaret was
in her own element. Her manners were
much more warm and not nearly so stiff.
Could she be shy, and at some loss, when
she came among her husband's relatives in
the City?

'My dear Bel, how are you? This is very
nice of you indeed! I'm so glad Mungo has
persuaded you!' And as Mungo got Bel into
the trap and followed after her himself, Margaret went on: 'I'm afraid you're going to
have a very dull time with us! Still, I've got
one or two surprises for you. And tonight I
am taking you over to the House to have dinner. Mother would be furious if she thought
I was keeping you to myself. I promise you,
it's only the family! I won't say any more!'
She looked slyly at Mungo now. Bel wondered why. 'Oh, is this your luggage the porter is bringing? Thank you, Macmillan. Yes,
pile it all in here. That's splendid! What a lot
of people we know at the station tonight,
Mungo! Of course, it's Friday. Oh, hullo!

How are you? On Sunday afternoon? Well, I think we'd like to very much. Oh, this is my sister-in-law, Mrs. Arthur Moorhouse. Oh, hullo! And how are you? When? On Monday to dinner? No, we've nothing.'

And so it went on. Margaret seemed to be holding court in the pony-trap – presenting Bel, announcing triumphantly that she could not possibly let her go for a week at least, as she would miss this invitation and that. Bel wondered if this was the country's idea of a rest. But it was impossible for her to refuse, with the givers of the invitations standing there hanging upon her reply.

At last Margaret turned the pony's head and they were off. As she did so she laughed. 'The thing is,' she said gaily, 'I don't often drive to the station like this. And when I do, I seem to run into everybody. And they all seem ready to pounce. You see, Mungo and I are frightful recluses really. And it makes it worse when we do appear. Still, we have to go sometime, and I'm so pleased we have you here to go with us. I was afraid Duntrafford might be dreadfully dull for you after Glasgow.'

As the pony trotted downhill in the warm June evening, Bel sat silent, fatigued and apprehensive. Must she go the round of all these grand people she did not know, whose loud voices and high falutin manners seemed to her genteel, City Scotchness, as

though they were all acting – rather self-con-
sciously, but much delighted with themselves – in some charade? She had been
lured down here with the promise of peace,
rest and a garden. Now it would seem she
was in the middle of a whirl such as she did
not know at home. She was glad she had
packed her best evening dress, just on
chance. It would be put, it seemed, to much
use.

III

There was a chatter of voices as Bel, following Margaret, and attended by Mungo,
ascended the staircase to the drawing-room
of Duntrafford House some hours later.

'Now, my dear,' Margaret announced as
they stood aside to have the door thrown
open, 'this is surprise number one.'

And a surprise it indeed was. For, as Bel
advanced to take Lady Ruanthorpe's hand,
she saw that the room held David, Grace
and Mrs. Dermott.

'Look who's with me!' Margaret called
triumphantly.

Bel, as ever, rose to the occasion. Her sudden shyness gave her cheeks colour, and to
her confident, somewhat provincial manners,
a charming – almost a young girl's hesitancy.
For a moment as he watched her, David

246

caught a glimpse of the young Bel Barrow-field his brother Arthur had presented to him more than ten years ago. Her close-fitting dress of lace and lilac satin. Her fair, carefully arranged hair. Her fine eyes and elegant mouth. Her clear skin. The effect she made was excellent.

Bel, sensing the surprise and pleasure at her unexpected appearance, paid back this friendly homage with a full measure of charm.

Lady Ruanthorpe kissed her for the first time in her life. 'This is wonderful, my dear! But why didn't you tell us, Margaret? Charles, ring for Campbell. He must lay another place.'

But old Sir Charles paid no attention. He left arrangements to his daughter. He was advancing to meet the lovely Mrs. Arthur Moorhouse. A smart girl, this sister-in-law of Margaret's. He wished his own women could get the same kind of spit and polish on themselves. He gave her both hands, and likewise, quite unexpectedly, bestowed upon Bel an avuncular kiss. Thereafter he called to Margaret to order up champagne.

Mrs. Dermott, too, hailed her with plea-sure. 'You didn't expect to find me here, did you, Bel? But Lady Ruanthorpe very kindly asked me with David and Grace. You see, Mrs. Moorhouse, we've been writing to each other about the Indigent Mothers for years, and we both felt it would be such a good thing if we could really meet and thrash them out. I promised not to quarrel with Sir Charles about our grandsons.' Mrs. Dermott manoeuvred herself round in her chair to look slyly – if anything so large as Mrs. Dermott could look slyly – at her host.

But Sir Charles did not hear. He was delightedly filling a glass of sherry to give to his beautiful guest.

Had Bel known these relatives would be at Duntrafford, she certainly would not have come. But now their presence – as the familiar so often does in an unfamiliar setting – reassured and pleased her. To meet Grace and David, smiling and affectionate, seemed to her like suddenly meeting her own children.

And as she sat at Sir Charles's right hand at dinner, basking in his approval, even Mrs. Dermott did not seem so dogmatic and tiresome.

It was hard work responding to the flatteries of her host. But it was a pleasant labour. For so long now, no one else had required a like effort of her. Her beloved Arthur merely grunted at her and accepted her as part of the furniture. She was grateful to the old man for bothering to remind her that, conscientious mother and busy house-wife though she might be, she still had a reasonable measure of good looks and charm. Yes, tonight she would indulge herself. She would allow herself to be as wilful and petted as she pleased.

During a pause in the conversation Mrs. Dermott bent forward to ask her: 'Did you know, Bel, that David has just taken Sophia's boy into Dermott Ships?'

Bel was amazed. She could only repeat: 'Dermott Ships?'

'Yes. Sophia spoke to me about it, and I mentioned it to David. He was delighted to have his own nephew, of course. And he says young William has made a very good start.'

Had Bel been less anxious to keep up the façade of charm before Sir Charles, she would have asked questions. But her tired and flattered head was swimming a little from the unaccustomed glass of sherry, and now at the table a sip or two of champagne.

She had spoken to Arthur about David's behaviour, and Arthur had said it was neither for himself nor Bel to interfere. Now it seemed Mrs. Dermott had taken things in hand and the matter was settled! In spite of herself, Bel wondered how. For a moment she felt a stab of jealousy; a shaft of resentment piercing the glowing cloud of well-being that enveloped her. She must ask Sophia about this later. But almost at once her thoughts, rather inconsequently, floated off yet again into her rosy surroundings.

'I'm certain he's a clever boy,' Mrs.

Dermott said after a moment, puzzled, a little, at Bel's smiling unresponsiveness.

'Oh! – Wil? Yes, I'm sure he is.'

But Sir Charles felt the ladies had said enough about their own affairs. He frowned a little, swallowed some champagne, and turned to Mrs. Dermott, demanding:

'What school have you put your grandson down for? We've put Charlie down for Eton.'

IV

In the drawing-room before the men came, Bel found herself alone with Mrs. Dermott and Lady Ruanthorpe. Grace had carried Margaret off to see the rival baby, Robert David, now asleep upstairs.

If, thanks to black coffee, her thoughts were rather less misted than they had been at the dinner-table, Bel was still a little above herself; a little drunk with unaccustomed flattery; a little too confident that Bel Moorhouse could do no wrong.

For a moment, as they talked, the nagging pain which was Phœbe pulled at her heartstrings. She sat silent, watching Mrs. Dermott and Lady Ruanthorpe: the forceful, shipping prince's widow, and the sharp old lady of the county with her natural habit of command. They were strong personalities, both of them; more informed, more travelled, better bred than herself. Bel's snobbery was prepared to think them wiser than they were.

Should she not ask their help about Phœbe? Beg them to advise her what she must do? Had not Mrs. Dermott straightened out the difficulty between David and young Wil Butter, in a way that could only leave her astonished?

As though in answer to her thinking, Mrs. Dermott turned. 'And how are the young people in Vienna, Mrs. Moorhouse? I hear Mrs. Hayburn is expecting a baby.'

Bel blushed as though she had been detected in some misdeed. 'So far as I know, they're very well.'

'Are you talking about anybody I know?' Lady Ruanthorpe demanded, her hands clasped over her ebony stick.

'Yes, Lady Ruanthorpe. We are talking about Mungo's sister, Phœbe.' Bel raised her voice a little.

'Oh, Phœbe? I know Phœbe. Nice child. She's a friend of mine. How does she like Vienna?'

'She's going to have a baby.' Mrs. Dermott repeated this information with unnecessary loudness.

Her hostess was not deaf. Like many of the old, she was given merely to indulging herself in fits of inattention. She stabbed an

251

immense lump of coal in the fireplace. It fell to pieces, flaming brightly. She looked at the end of her stick. 'Charles is always scolding me for doing that. He says it will ruin the end of this. But I don't care.' She settled back, looked at the others and said, 'Now what were we talking about. Oh yes, Phœbe. So she's having a baby? Dear me! What a lot of babies! My daughter, your daughter, and now Phœbe.' And, as no one had anything to say to this, she added: 'She's coming home to have it, of course?'

'No, I don't think she is,' Bel said, delighted that the subject had thus opened itself.

'I don't see how she can have it there. Her husband ought to send her,' Lady Ruanthorpe said, with indignation.

'They have been writing to say that everything is better arranged in Vienna.'

'Everything fiddlesticks! What do *you* think, Mrs. Dermott?'

'If it had been my daughter, I would never have considered such nonsense for a moment!' Mrs. Dermott breathed all the indignation of a Victorian matron.

'Phœbe isn't my daughter, unfortunately,' Bel said. 'I've been terribly worried about it. You see, I brought her up.'

The old women looked at Bel. She had spoken with emotion. There were tears in her eyes. Lady Ruanthorpe blinked like an old parrot. Mrs. Dermott's face went red, a little, and she said:

'I know, my dear. Of course you have.'

They were all three quiet for a time. The large ormolu clock on the white marble mantelpiece ticked quietly under its glass dome.

'Mungo is her eldest brother. He had better write to her husband,' Lady Ruanthorpe said with decision. She believed in the direct attack.

'Henry Hayburn is very stubborn,' Bel said elegantly, wiping her eyes, and pleasantly aware that the sight of her tears had had its effect on the others.

In reply, Lady Ruanthorpe merely grunted.

Bel looked at Mrs. Dermott, the planner of campaigns, the skilful shepherdess of committees.

'I've been thinking,' Grace's mother said presently. 'And it has just struck me that it would be a good thing if Henry's brother Stephen went on holiday to Austria this summer. You see, I've known these boys all my life. Their father was my husband's friend. Henry was brought up to worship his brother Stephen. Stupidly, my husband always thought. Stephen was older, and much more of a success – to his mother's way of thinking, anyway.'

Bel caught her meaning. 'You mean that Stephen could persuade Henry?'

'Persuade Henry and bring Phœbe home. You see, Bel, she's terribly young. And perhaps a little reckless. She won't want to have her second baby so far away, I do assure you.'

'And David will be delighted to give Stephen the time off and what money he needs. After all, Phœbe is David's sister. I'll make a point of seeing Stephen whenever I get home.'

Bel expressed appreciation. But now that it looked as though she might have her way, she was filled, perversely, with misgiving and a sense of guilt. She knew how angry her mother would be with this. Perhaps, after all, Mrs. Barrowfield's counsel was right. Should not they all forbear from interfering? Had her emotions, her tenacious love for this sister of Arthur's who had once done so much for herself, betrayed her reason?

But, after all, what did it come to? A child brought safely into the world among its own kind. Some months of separation for the young couple, at the most. A triumphant Phœbe returning to rejoin her husband with their baby. And yet Bel knew she would not, when next she found herself at Monteith Row, admit just what part she had taken in this affair. She hoped Mrs. Dermott might arrange it so that it would look as though it had been settled between Henry and his brother Stephen.

The men were joining them now, and Grace and Margaret were appearing.

Bel's eyes met David's, and she threw him a smile. But if the smile was elegant, it was likewise artificial. She was not so sure now that she liked David as much as usual. Mrs. Dermott had said that David was delighted about Wil Butter. Now she was quite certain he would be delighted to send Stephen Hayburn to Austria.

Bel decided that she liked men who were not always so easily made delighted.

V

Now Phœbe seemed to be all by herself in a swing-boat in the People's Prater, clinging to its sides for dear life, as it swung up in-finitely high, then crashed back with a sickening shudder, amid the roar of the people who had gathered round to look at her. Why didn't it stop? Why couldn't she get out? Why did it always tremble so shockingly when it reached the bottom of the swing? As though at any moment it would fall to pieces and kill her? And why did the people always roar each time it fell back? She must get out at once!

But where was Henry? Why wasn't he here with her? Oh, there he was, standing among

the roaring crowd, looking up expressionless, as though she did not belong to him!
She would give him a good scolding for this
when they let her out! Didn't he know that
she was going to have a child? His child?
That all this horrible swinging was the worst
thing possible for her now?

But who was it that was pushing her like a
madman? She must try to turn round and
shout to him to stop it at once! She could
hear him howl with laughter every time he
swung her! Yes! Just as she thought. Stephen
– Henry's brother. Stephen's behaviour was
amiable and good up there with them in the
little house in the forest. They had spent
several gay weeks together. But now, in the
Prater, he looked like a maniac, a demon, as
he hurled himself laughing against this
dreadful swing!

Again there was a crash and a shudder as
the swing descended. If the people would
only stop roaring, she might make herself
heard. Oh, there was Bel, pushing her way
determinedly through the middle of them,
trying to get to her! Bel would stop Stephen's
mad behaviour! Force him to see reason!
Make him understand that she was going to
have a child; that she must be careful, just
now. Bel was always self-possessed. Always
knew exactly what to do. Even now she
looked calm, almost complacent. But wasn't
she too complacent? Didn't Bel, even, grasp

the danger of this mad joke?

Now she was swinging down to the ground again. The swing was shuddering dreadfully. This time it would certainly fall to pieces! And what a roar the people were making! But all the same she must shout. Bel *must* be made to hear her!

'Bel! Bel! Stop him! Stephen must stop!'

'It's all right, Mrs. Hayburn, I'm here beside you. Just keep calm. The captain says we'll be in the Firth of Forth in about an hour. Then we'll be in sheltered water.'

Was she coming back to consciousness? Had she been dreaming? Or drugged by that silly student who was the only doctor on board ship? Or had fever made her delirious? Now, at any rate, she was in her senses again, and knew she was on her way from Hamburg to Leith. Coming home into Bel's care to have her baby. And who was this beside her now? Of course, the stewardess.

Once more a wave struck the side of the little steamer, causing it to rear, shudder and fall back again like a stricken animal. Spray struck the glass of her port-hole, like a handful of sharp pebbles; then the wave rose against it, filling her cabin with green darkness. Her tortured body could feel the engines chugging, vibrating, then racing as the propeller left the water. As the ship rolled back she could hear the water rushing from the deck above her, the roaring of the wind; and now her port-hole showed a disk of grey sky once more.

Must she be sick again? Must she rack her exhausted, pregnant body yet more?

'I'm sorry, stewardess.'

'It's all right, Mrs. Hayburn. Don't mind about me. Is that better? Wait a moment. Now lie back and rest. A drink of water?'

'Thank you. Did the captain say an hour?'

'Yes, Mrs. Hayburn. Just about an hour.'

In an hour this heaving torment would have ceased; this racking sickness would have stopped adding itself to the fevered chill, or worse, she had so foolishly given herself, sitting with Stephen, lightly clad, much too late, in the garden of a Hamburg restaurant. The day had been hot. They had dragged round the sights. She had stupidly overtired herself. Merely to sit on and on in the cool night air had been delicious.

But now she was paying for her folly. Her throat was on fire. There was a cannon-ball in her head. Her limbs ached with fever, and there was other, more ominous pain. If only the storm would stop! But in an hour. Just about an hour, the captain had said.

But she smiled gamely as another wave struck them, and said: 'Stormy.'

'Yes. It's one of the worst late August storms I've known, Mrs. Hayburn. I've been on this trip a good many years.'

But the pale girl had closed her eyes again,

and consciousness seemed once more to have receded.

Sometime over an hour later Stephen Hayburn crawled from his cabin. The steamer was still swinging back and forth, but this was heaven to the last two days. He knocked gently on Phœbe's door.

'Mr. Hayburn?'

'Yes; how is my sister-in-law?'

For answer the student doctor opened Phœbe's door, closed it behind him, and stood supporting himself against the hand-rail in the passage. Was there sweat upon his brow because he too had been sick? Or was it the condition of the patient he had just left?

'How is she, Doctor?'

'Oh, she'll be all right. It's just this storm, and the other things coming together.' He was still callow. His reassurances did not yet have quite the professional ring.

It was dark now as Phœbe came back again – dark, except for the light of the candle in its hanging socket. She opened her eyes and lay looking at the white-painted boards of the ceiling reflecting the dim yellow light. Her sleeping-bunk was quite miraculously still. Now and then on the deck above her there were footsteps. The port-hole must be open a little, for at intervals a light breeze made the flame flicker, and there were dockland smells of tar, smoke and seaweed.

Far-off shouts came across the water, and the horn of some distant vessel on the move.

She closed her eyes again. How strangely still it was! She could hear the water of the dock lapping gently against the iron sides of the boat. Now she could rest. If only this shivering would leave her; this rawness all the way down her throat. She would try to fall asleep; perhaps she might wake up better.

But now she caught a faint perfume in the cabin. What was it? Why was it so familiar? Of course. It reminded her of the soap they used at home in Grosvenor Terrace. She had forgotten. Viennese soap smelt quite differently. The stewardess must use this soap, too.

And the stewardess was good. She was still sitting, holding her hand. By way of thanks, Phœbe pressed her hand in return.

But the hand was soft. It was not any more the workworn hand of a ship's stewardess. And why was her own hand now being lifted up and pressed to someone's lips? Phœbe raised her head and looked down. In the candlelight she could see a familiar, fair head bending over her; a fair head that was bowed in an agony of love and contrition.

Chapter Sixteen

It was warm work toiling uphill on his 'Kangaroo'. Even now, in this first week of September, as Henry headed towards the little house in Ober Döbling, the air was still and sultry. He pedalled laboriously. His long, loose body sweated profusely. When he got in he would take off his clothes and stand under the spray he had arranged for himself in a corner of the garden. That would be cool and pleasant. And after his outdoor meal he would sit on for a little, inhaling the evening breath of the forest and the scent of wet earth, as his old landlord, Herr Weigel, moved about in the dusk, watering his garden.

But he must not linger long. He was resolved that all his time should be taken up with work while Phœbe was away. He had let himself get behind with things. It had been too pleasant up here this summer. Every night, almost, they had sat outside talking.

Now Henry was puffing along a dusty, suburban boulevard. Children on the pavement called to each other. They had come to look for this long-legged foreigner, mounted so strangely on two revolving wheels; for at this time the new 'safety' bicycle was a novelty. Some of the bolder ran alongside, shouting. Young women sewing and gossiping together, as they sat on public benches beneath dusty chestnut-trees, looked up and smiled as he passed them by. But Henry was used to all this – so well used that he did not even notice.

No. There was much for him to do. There was no need for the loneliness he shrank away from. Phœbe and Stephen had been gone almost a week and he had managed very well. He had kept himself occupied with his books and his drawing-board.

He was passing villas now – villas separated from the street by high railings, hanging with dusty bougainvillea and parched rambler roses. Beyond, in their gardens, beneath umbrella-shaped trees, housewives were sitting at little metal tables set on the white gravel, occupying themselves with embroidery. In some gardens the evening meal had been laid out and was already in progress.

This being alone, this letting Phœbe go home with Stephen, was, after all, the right thing for him to do, surely. Was it not for the sake of their child?

It had flattered Henry's simplicity that Stephen had come out here to them. He had always looked up to Stephen, envied him his easy manners, his knowledge of the

world. His coming had been a pleasant surprise, and his companionship just what
Phœbe had needed during these summer
days of waiting.

And Stephen, primed with David's money
and Mrs. Dermott's arguments, had set
them thinking. After all, their child's welfare
must come before all else. If the chances of
its arriving safely into the world were better
at home, then home, as they both at last
came to see, Phœbe must be sent. Now that
Stephen would be able to take her with him,
Henry had felt he must let her go.

Their Viennese friends had been bewildered. The disappointment of Stephanie
Hirsch knew no bounds. That she should not
be near Phœbe at the coming of the child,
had been a blow to this gentle-hearted
woman who had so much time and affection
to throw away. She had begged her nephew
Max to intervene. But it was all of no avail.
And so Stephanie, and even the elder Fräulein Hirsch, had come with tears and roses to
the Nordbahnhof to see Stephen and Phœbe
go.

Now Henry had jumped from his bicycle,
and was pushing it uphill. The way was
steep and dusty. But for an occasional wine-
garden, where heady, year-old wine was on
sale, he was now quite in the country. To his
left and right stretched the wine-lands. The
clusters of grapes looked ripe already, as

they hung in the evening sunshine, gold-green and matt blue, drinking in the last of the warm rays that slanted down upon them over the western forest. Their blue-sprayed leaves were limp with the long day or heat.

Now he had mounted again. In a short time he would be home. He pushed on with determination. Perhaps tonight there would be a letter. He had received an electric telegram saying Phœbe had arrived in Scotland. It had merely given that information; nothing more. But this evening there might be a letter giving him the details of her journey.

Now he had turned off the main road, and was walking once more, up towards the little house. The Saint Bernard dog had spied him, and was stirring up the dust with his great, soft paws as he gambolled down to meet him. Old Weigel was working among his tomato plants. As he pushed his 'Kangaroo' through the gate, the old man heard Henry. He shouted an evening greeting, and told him that letters had come.

II

Two hours later Henry was still in the garden, sitting motionless, staring before him. They had brought out his supper to him. Later they had taken it away again.

The old couple took counsel with each

other. Something had happened to him. He had received bad news. They were afraid to ask him. But something must be done.

It was getting dark. Old Weigel lit a candle, set it inside its glass funnel and carried it out into the garden.

Was Herr Hayburn quite well?

Henry's eyes wandered up to his face and he nodded.

Was Herr Hayburn's letter from the gracious lady?

The eyes that looked up at him were wild. 'My wife is very ill. The child was born dead.'

The old man winced. He stood by the little garden table unable to speak.

A cool breeze blew down from the woods. It brought with it a scent of pine resin. Here and there, down in the village, lights had begun to twinkle. In the distance there was the sound of a woman's laughter.

Herr Weigel came to Henry, laid a hand for a moment on his shoulder, then took his old, fat and sympathetic body into the house. There was nothing he could do in the face of this. Nothing he could say.

Some little time later the Weigels looked out once more into the garden. It had become quite dark. They could see him still bent forward, his arms resting on the checked table-cloth, his strained face caught in the circle of light. In one hand were the folded letters.

The great dog ranging in the garden came and brushed against Henry, bringing him back to life a little. So there was to be no child. And Phœbe was dangerously ill. No child. Even with all his young anticipation, he had not fully known how much he had looked to having this child.

But Phœbe? Supposing there was to be no Phœbe either?

He didn't know. He wasn't the kind of man who could manage himself, who could command his stunned feelings.

Now there might be no Phœbe.

His landlady came from the house. She had a glass of cognac in her hand. She sat down at the table beside him.

'Take that, Herr Hayburn.'

He took it from her and swallowed it obediently.

The good woman was encouraged. 'It's getting cold, Herr Hayburn; come inside.' She led Henry into her kitchen. 'I'll make you some coffee. You've eaten nothing.' He came with her, obediently, like a boy.

Now he was sitting warming himself by the stove and drinking the coffee she had given him.

'*Na?* Herr Hayburn? Better?'

He nodded. She was a motherly woman, this, with the kindliness of peasant Austria.

He began talking, his year-old German stumbling here and there. His wife had caught a severe chill, bringing on high fever. Following on that, she had crossed the North Sea in an August gale. She had been very sick. They had taken her straight to hospital in Edinburgh where her baby was stillborn and where she, herself, now lay in danger.

It seemed to give him relief to tell them; to loosen the tension.

The old man tried to encourage him. The gracious lady would be well soon. She was young. Many young people had lost a first child. Their married life was only beginning. Would it not be better now that Herr Hayburn should go and lie down?

Henry went. Their wooden bedroom was still redolent of Phœbe. Of her clothes; of scent Stephen had bought her; of herself. There were one or two odd belongings she had left behind. Some ribbon. A handkerchief. Some books.

He sat down on his bed and re-read his letters. One from Arthur Moorhouse. One from Mrs. Barrowfield. Arthur's was a formal letter, stiff, sympathetic and put together with difficulty. Henry must believe Arthur when he wrote that Bel had acted out of her great affection for Phœbe. Bel and he were deeply sorry. Bel was refusing to leave Phœbe's side.

Mrs. Barrowfield had taken upon herself to write to Henry, too. Her letter was full of an old woman's love, and – if Henry's wit could have read beyond the restraint she had imposed upon herself – rage, at what had happened. She, too, had come to Edinburgh. And while the doctor had assured her that Phœbe would recover, she thought it would be wise for Henry to come home.

III

It was four o'clock in the afternoon some weeks later. Vienna lay drowsing beneath a late September sun that was bland and golden. Fashionable streets were beginning to give signs of life. Show windows had begun to display the novelties of the early winter.

In the many public gardens there were riots in the flower-beds. Trees and shrubbery were beginning to take on the brilliant reds and yellows of the autumn. The City was shaking itself free from the dust and heat of the summer.

Next week the Emperor Franz Joseph would have returned from his hunting-box at Ischl; the Crown Prince Rudolf from boar-hunting in Moravia; and it was believed that the Empress Elizabeth, who was somewhere on the Adriatic, would be returning to the capital shortly.

The autumn season was beginning. Everywhere friends met friends. Where had they been? In the Tyrol? In the Carpathians? On the Baltic coast? In Carlsbad or Gastein? At all events, it was splendid to see everybody again, and to look to the excitements, artistic, musical, and social, that their City had in store for them.

Maximilian Hirsch came down the Kärntnerstrasse humming to himself. A pleasant lunch-party, the weather and Vienna were having their effects upon him. For a moment he stopped before a flower shop to look at its triumphant display of colour. He meditated for a time as to whether he should commit himself, just at present, by bestowing these dark red roses in a certain quarter. But he decided with a chuckle, which interrupted but did not stop his humming, that, much as these wonderful flowers were crying out to be sent somewhere, it would be better, perhaps, just at the moment, if he avoided new complications. Having made up his mind thus momentously, he continued humming on his way.

Suddenly he became aware that he was being hailed from a carriage.

'Max! Max!'

'Aunt Steffi!'

'You bad boy. Were you trying to walk past me?'

'Of course not!' It was nice to be called a boy at fifty.

'Jump in beside me. I want to talk to you.'

'Do you want to scold me for something?' He stepped up into the carriage, and put her hand to his lips.

'Not this afternoon, Maxerl, although you look as if you needed it. Next time, perhaps. No. I want to ask you about that poor child.'

'Who? The little Hayburn?'

'Yes. Have you got an hour to spare?'

'No. But I shall spare it.'

'That's a good boy. I'll drive you across to the Krieau, and you can give me a cup of chocolate.'

'But with great pleasure! Oh! One moment! What about the silk stockings you were going to buy?'

'I wasn't going to buy any silk stockings. I won't tell you what I was going to buy.'

'I'm quite sure it was silk stockings. Never mind. I'll buy a pair, and send them to you.'

'Please, Johann. To the Creamery in the Krieau. Oh, I dare say you'll buy the silk stockings. But you won't send them to any-one so old and ugly as your Aunt Steffi.'

The old coachman drove off laughing. The young Herr Maximilian had so much fun about him! He always had the effect of mak-ing his old ladies quite witty.

Maximilian was pleased with this encoun-ter. It suited his mood. It was just right to go driving on this golden autumn afternoon with a fond and flattering woman, who, being old and a relative, did not make any claims upon him, other than those of family affection. 'Tell me,' Stephanie began presently, 'has her husband come back?'

'Oh yes. Two or three days ago.'

'He might have come to see me, Maxi. He knows I love his wife.'

'He has been very busy. Actually, it was very difficult to let him go. But of course, I had to.'

'Of course. And what did he say?'

'She has been very ill, but now she is out of danger.'

'Thank God!'

Maximilian turned and smiled at the facile tears in his aunt's eyes, as, ranging from one side of the Ring to the other, they seemed to be seeking solace, at one moment in the Stadtpark, at another in the high buildings that faced it. 'Was the child she lost a boy or a girl?'

'A boy.'

'What a tragedy!' The loss of a male child was, of course, more serious.

'Yes.' Maximilian said nothing more for a time. He sat back comfortably in the sunshine, letting himself be lulled by the motion of the carriage.

'Poor young people!' Stephanie said after a time, wiping her eyes with a handkerchief. Then, by way of taking comfort to herself, she added: 'But there will be more children and they will forget.'

'The young Hayburn told me there will be no more children.'

She hesitated for a moment, then asked: 'Maxi, do you mean he is afraid for her to have them?'

'No, not that. They told him it would be very unlikely.'

Stephanie did not ask anything more for a time. Her misted eyes looked about them unseeing as they made their way down the Praterstrasse. She loved this odd, foreign young woman.

Oh, if they had taken her advice, and the little Hayburn had remained here in Vienna, where there were the best doctors in the world! Why had her relatives forced her to go home to that cold land, where no one knew anything! And that sister-in-law! She must be hard and possessive, as she had heard so many Lutheran women could be!

Now they had passed the Prater Stern and were in that part of the Haupt Allee which lay on the way to the Krieau. The memory of the May Corso and Henry's comically gloomy face brought her back.

'What about Herr Hayburn?' she asked.

'He's very unhappy. He's stupid with unhappiness.'

'Poor boy!'

For reply, her nephew Max shrugged, casting his eyes around at the very considerable press of fashionable traffic about them, and the high, yellowing chestnut-trees.

'Is he still in the little house in the forest?' she asked.

A smile played round Maximilian's mouth. He was certain that what he was going to say next would make her very angry. 'No,' he said, 'he has gone back to the apartments in the Favoriten. He says he can work there.'

Much to Maximilian's surprise, Stephanie did not explode. She merely turned round and looked at him with interest. 'Tell me, Maxi,' she said, 'there's a young girl there – a music student – isn't there? I seem to remember the little Hayburn telling me. Do you think he has – a friendship?'

Again he shrugged, and threw his eyes upwards. 'Who knows? These British people are so strange! One can guess nothing!'

Chapter Seventeen

On the first of October, 1880, Baillie George McNairn died. The news found Bel at the breakfast table after everyone else had gone out. She sat wearily, leaning on her elbows, swallowing tea and staring before her out of the window. Sarah had come to her with a note, and Bel had directed her to tell the messenger she would come down to Albany Place this morning.

Bel poured herself yet another cup and leant forward pondering. Sophia, who had written her the note she had just received, was with Mary, so there was no need for her to go to Albany Place at once.

George's end had been expected for some days now. Bel's grief was not deep. But she was sorry for Mary, that her husband should be taken from her at so early an age as forty-five; she was sorry for Mary's children; she was sorry for Arthur, upon whose shoulders the worries of Mary's affairs would certainly fall; and she was a little sorry for herself.

Bel went on swallowing and staring in front of her, putting off the moment when something must be done. Whatever happened, she reflected, whatever blunders she might make, it was always herself and Arthur to whom the family turned.

She thought of Phœbe. That had been her great blunder this autumn. Those weeks in an Edinburgh hospital when she had scarcely left Phœbe's side. It had been so exhausting, and she, Bel, had felt so repentant. When Henry Hayburn had come, she had wept and blamed herself to him. But Henry had been stony and bewildered. He had not shown her whether he forgave her or not.

Yet it was herself, Bel, who sat yearning by Henry's wife through the days her life was in danger; herself whom Phœbe had wanted. And, knowing that the young couple's purse could be none too long, it was her husband, Arthur, who had defrayed the expenses of Henry's journey from and back to Vienna.

And yet, when at last Phœbe was out of danger, and she, Bel, had come back to Glasgow, she discovered that Henry had been to see her mother, and unburdened his outraged heart in Monteith Row. The old lady was now waiting, armed and ready with accusation and reproof, for Bel's long-suffering self.

Bel had not, of course, intended to tell Mrs. Barrowfield of the Duntrafford conspiracy. The old woman, knowing her daughter, had got it out of her. And thereafter Bel had to stand naked and ashamed before her mother's fury, forced to account for her actions towards a young woman about whom she need never have bothered, on whom she need never have expended any affection whatever.

Well, she supposed she and Arthur would always go on being like that. Always taking responsibility, and often receiving blame for the responsibility they took. Always being asked for help and advice, and often having their help and advice called interference.

Bel sighed, set down her cup and prepared

for action. Thank goodness Phœbe was now safely in the Duntrafford Dower House, whither her convalescence had now allowed her to travel. Margaret had been insistent that she should come to her at the earliest moment possible; that she would find health in her native countryside more quickly than elsewhere. Bel, occupied with Mary, had relinquished her grasp of the beloved invalid.

But what was there to do now?

Mary's boys – Georgie and Jackie Mc-Nairn – were staying here in Grosvenor Terrace at present. Only half an hour ago she had packed them off to their school at the same time she had seen young Arthur off to his. She had better call for them, she supposed, and take them down to Albany Place.

She would need the carriage for that. Indeed, the carriage would be needed all day. To fetch Arthur and David. To take clothes to be dyed black, and to take herself to buy not unbecoming mourning. To take Arthur – it would, of course, be Arthur – to make the funeral arrangements. To do endless errands.

While she waited for it to come, Bel wrote to Grace at Aucheneame, who had in her charge the little twin girls, Anne and Polly. Bel offered to see to their clothes. George McNairn's daughters, who were not yet quite six, must appear at his funeral in all the black correctness of Victorian mourning.

II

A strange, unfamiliar Mungo stood at the door of Duntrafford Dower House looking about him at the rich autumn beauty of this quiet, sunless morning. His sturdy body was clad in the formality of a black frock-coat. On his head was a tall hat, and in one hand he carried black kid-gloves. The merest onlooker would have known that this was not a dress to which he was accustomed. It was the day of George McNairn's funeral, and in a moment he and his wife Margaret must leave for the City.

His other hand was given to his fifteen-month-old son, Charles Mungo Ruanthorpe-Moorhouse, a person of much importance, in spite of his childish petticoats and his still inarticulate tongue.

He was not a beautiful baby. As yet, there were none of the Moorhouse good looks about him. His little snub face and popping eyes gave him a strong resemblance to his grandfather, old Sir Charles – a resemblance which became quite remarkable when the baby laughed, as he was now doing at a yellowhammer that had alighted for an instant on the gravel of the drive only a few yards in front of him. As he pointed and looked into his father's face, Mungo was seized – not for the first time – with an odd feeling that, somehow, he was bending to hold the hand of a strange, miniature Sir Charles, with little dark curls and a pink face.

'That's a yella yite, son,' he said, giving the yellowhammer its Scotch name.

In reply, the baby laughed louder, and the bird flew away.

Mungo turned to find Phœbe standing beside him. 'Hullo. What are you doing out of yer bed at this time of day?'

'It's after ten.'

'Well, that's early for you. Has Margaret allowed ye?'

'I didn't ask her.' Phœbe bent down and put her arms about the baby.

'Now, Phœbe, don't try to lift up that bairn. He's ower heavy for ye.' Mungo spoke sternly.

'It's all right. I won't.'

Mungo watched his sister as she supported Charlie's steps across the gravel of the drive in the direction of a wicker chair that had been placed for her on the lawn beyond.

'Will ye be quite warm?'

'Of course. It's stuffy this morning. When do you go?'

'In two or three minutes.'

He looked across at Phœbe. His countryman's eye did not approve of the thinness that gave her body too much elegance nor of her pale face with the dark rings about her eyes. But in spite of these, or indeed because of them, Mungo – at most times slow to notice – did not fail to remark the unreal, almost ethereal quality that suffering and a great disappointment had given his sister. She looked fragile and lovely as she sat there bending over the little boy.

Too fragile. For a moment Mungo felt misgivings. But immediately he reminded himself that once before, as a child, Phœbe had suffered a great shock and that her country stamina had stood by her.

Now his wife had appeared.

'Hullo, Mungo. Where's the trap? If it doesn't come now, we'll miss the train.'

'I think I hear it.'

'Oh, hullo, Phœbe. I didn't know you were down. Are you all right over there? They've been told what to give you for lunch. And don't let that child worry you. Call Mrs. Crawford and hand him over the moment you get tired.'

Now a groom had come with the pony-trap. Margaret crossed to her son, gave him a purposeful kiss, patted Phœbe, then took herself, her black finery and her husband into it.

'See you at dinner,' she called as the pony trotted out of sight.

III

Now her nephew was quiet in her lap, pulling a spray of Michaelmas daisies to pieces.

'Don't, Charlie. Don't put them in your mouth.'

It was comforting to sit here on this warm, sunless morning, pressing this little creature against her. And Margaret was good. Her kind brusqueness suited Phœbe. She didn't nag or insist. And yet her attentions did not falter. Phœbe was glad she had come here almost directly from hospital.

She had received a letter from Stephanie Hirsch this morning – a foreign letter full of bad English, love and regret. Had it been from anyone other than Stephanie, she would have despised its sentimentality. But Phœbe was learning. She had begun to realise that even the sentimental, even those who expressed themselves too easily and too much, could feel as deeply as the stern and the reticent.

Stephanie had seen little of Henry. She thought it was a pity that he had gone back to the Quellengasse. But Phœbe did not think so. Her husband was a lonely, vague sort of creature. Frau Klem, she knew, would look after him.

She lay back in her chair thinking of Henry. The two days he had spent with her in Edinburgh had been a wordless misery. Neither of them had Stephanie Hirsch's ease in expressing their feelings. She had been glad when Henry had gone away again.

But she must get well and go back to him. Now that she only had Henry, would always only have Henry, the thought of him seldom left her.

As she sat thinking of him, tears of weakness sprang to Phœbe's eyes. But at once contempt sprang after them. These were not Phœbe Hayburn's tears. They were the maudlin tears of a foolish invalid.

She became aware that she was pressing the child so tightly to her that he was kicking to be set down. 'Poor Charlie! Was I squeezing the life out of you?'

Mrs. Crawford appeared at the door with something she must take.

'Oh, Mrs. Crawford, is it time for that already?'

Phœbe swallowed what she was given, handed over the child to his nurse and went inside to write letters to her husband and Stephanie.

IV

Today Sophia's chatter helped rather than hindered. And it was unceasing.

'Now, Mary, I don't think you feel well enough to come downstairs to the service. You've been wonderfully brave, dear; but remember, it has been a long strain for you. Well, if you feel you ought, there's no more to be said. I'll sit beside you.

'Oh, Bel dear, there you are! Are you all here? Only the two Arthurs and yourself? Yes, of course. The other children are too small. Still, I thought, maybe Isabel– But what about Phœbe? No. Of course. She's at Duntrafford.

'Don't bother about that, Mary. I'll do it.

'Good morning, Margaret. We were just talking about Phœbe. How is she, poor child? Well, of course. When you think what she has just come through. And how is that wonderful son of yours? The image of his grandfather? Fancy!

'Oh, Grace dear, there you are! Yes. Poor Mary! It's terrible, isn't it? Oh, of course, yes. I was just saying that to William this morning. We must all make sacrifices according to our ability, to help Mary through. It was very kind of you to keep Anne and Polly. Hullo, dears! How are you? How nice you look in your new dresses! Your Auntie Bel *did* get neat ones for you, didn't she?

David! Come and kiss your old sister! You're not too grand for that, are you? How's little Robert? Wil says he's just terrified of you in the office. You're so great and important!

'Oh, here you are, William, and the children! William, have you got the black gloves I bought for you? What do you say's coming down, Margy? Wait a minute. I think I have a pin. There, that's better. Remind me to sew it. Now, children, go and kiss your Aunt Mary and say how sorry you are.

'Oh, Arthur, are you coming back here to read George's will? Yes, I thought you would. Well, of course we'll help as much as we can. But remember, William is a poor man! He hasn't got what you and Mungo and David have. Isn't that so, William?'

William Butter said nothing.

'Oh, here's the minister! Now are you sure you feel quite up to the service, Mary dear? Very well. But I'll sit with you at the end of the front row, so that we can just slip out if it is too trying. Georgie, Jackie, you're the chief mourners. You had better sit with Anne and Polly in the front row, too. That's right.'

And so, in Mary's darkened dining-room, the service was read over the remains of her husband. And when that had come to an end, Baillie George McNairn was followed by the men of the family to his last resting-place.

283

Later in the afternoon, Mary's brothers, together with William Butter, sat round the dining-table while George's lawyer read his will.

Only the tongue of flattery could possibly have called George McNairn clever. And he had died at the early age of forty-five. But, after his kind, he had been shrewd and acquisitive. His affairs were in good order. In the time that was given him he had been able to save a sum which, if it seemed small now, to David's and Mungo's magnificence, would provide for his widow the necessary upkeep of the house in Albany Place.

There was, then, Arthur said, looking round the table, only the education of the children to be considered. Georgie was fifteen and would soon be earning. But Jackie was twelve. And there were the little twin girls, whose education had not yet begun. But girls did not need much education. They had only to grow up, stay at home, learn to dust and find husbands.

What, then, Arthur asked, was everybody prepared to do? For his part, he would see to all the immediate payments, thus saving Mary embarrassment in her first distress. And thereafter he was ready to take his full share.

Mungo said Arthur had better find out exactly how things worked out as they went along, and promised he would not see Mary and her children stuck.

David pointed to the fact that times were bad, and that his mother-in-law still drew a very substantial income from Dermott Ships, in addition to Grace and himself. But, yes, certainly they could count upon him putting his hand into his pocket for Mary and her children when necessity arose.

If anybody had been looking at William Butter, they would perhaps have noticed that the colour in such parts of his face as happened not to be covered with black hair had deepened a little at these declarations of _____ his lips had parted for a moment as though he _____ king himself to some kind of articulate utterance. But as no one *was* looking at him, his lips closed again, his colour receded once more, and William did not feel himself called upon to make any more definite gesture.

When they joined the women upstairs for tea, Sophia was still voluble. 'Oh, there you are, boys,' she said, presiding at the tea-table in place of the afflicted Mary. 'Now you must tell me how you like your tea. I *should* know, but I keep forgetting. And I've just been saying to Mary how she had nothing in the world to worry about, Arthur. You and William are really just on her doorstep, ready to help at any minute, and Mungo and David are not really so very much further away.'

Bel turned from the window where she had been standing, cup in hand. 'There's McCrimmon with the carriage, Arthur.'

As the horses trotted westward, Bel's curiosity overcame her. 'How did things go downstairs, Arthur?' It was difficult to ask questions with their small, sharp-eared son sitting opposite, but she could not help herself.

In reply Arthur grunted.

'I suppose you've offered to pay everything and take the responsibility?'

Again Arthur grunted. But his grunt contained a note of assent.

Bel sighed, looked out of the window and said: 'I suppose you and I are like that. We just can't help it.'

The eyes of Arthur the Second remained deceptively innocent. But what he had heard had done him no harm.

V

It was the first week in December. Bel sat looking at Phœbe as they drank tea together before a blazing fire in the drawing-room of Grosvenor Terrace. Phœbe was recovering – but slowly. Her disastrous journey had occurred at the end of August, but still, even now, there were the marks of her ordeal upon her.

Phœbe folded a letter she had been re-reading, put it back in her workbox and took up her cup of tea. Her eyes met Bel's.

'How is Henry, dear? You never give me any news.'

'Oh, Henry's all right, I suppose.'

'You suppose? Doesn't he write to you regularly?'

'Not regularly. But he writes.'

Bel laughed.

'That letter I was reading wasn't from Henry, if that's what you mean. It was from _____ in London. I met her at the Mission _____ there at the end of _____.'

'Who is she, Phœbe?'

'A governess. She wants me to travel back with her.'

'You can only do that if you're well enough.'

'I'll be all right.'

'But is she quite a nice person, Phœbe?'

'She's at least sixty.'

Bel gave a satisfied 'Oh.' Age and niceness went, apparently, together.

'I was hoping Henry would come home for you.'

'He's very busy.'

'Still.' Bel looked at the fog outside the window for a minute, then turned her eyes to the fire.

'I've been thinking,' she began. 'Arthur says things are getting better. Wouldn't it be a good thing for Henry to try to get something here at home? Surely with all the experience he's had–'

'But how can he? He's too far away to look for anything.'

'Arthur would help. And look at David. He knows everybody now. You don't want to stay in Vienna all your life, do you?'

Phœbe considered this for a time, then said: 'I don't know.' For a moment her thoughts carried her back to the Imperial City. She had known rapture there. Her eyes had been taught to see, her senses given a new awareness. Whatever her outward seeming, she was a different young woman from the one who had gone there less than a year ago. Now, once more, they were standing, she and Henry together, in the cool magic of an early May morning. They were in their nightdresses by the window in the Quellengasse. Over there in the mist, the Prater. And there the Arsenal. And there the Karlskirche. And further off the spire of Saint Stephen's. There had been nothing more to ask of life that morning. The universe was bursting into bloom.

Deliberately, Phœbe drew out the dagger of grief and disappointment that was stabbing her. She examined it calmly. She was even a little proud that she could find strength now

288

to perform this trick.

Bel wondered why she was biting her lip. 'Don't bother about these things now, dear,' she said. 'Only, I thought it would be nice to have you both at home.'

Phœbe paid no attention. She put back the dagger. Things must go on.

Yes, there was Henry. So long as they were together it didn't much matter where they were. She would write to this woman, in London and tell her she would travel back to Austria in her company.

Chapter Eighteen

Frau Klem was at her wits' end with Herr Hayburn this autumn. She had not meant to have a lodger in the Quellengasse now that Pepi was at home again and contributing something to the household from odd work in the theatres. But on his return from Scotland the young man had come, told her of his misfortunes and begged her to let him have his old room once more.

The good woman had been moved and flattered. Moved by his loss. Flattered that he should look to her and hers for comfort. She did her best for him. She saw that he was fed; that he was kept warm; that his clothes were looked to. There was little else she could do. But, together with her daughter, she held many a conference about him.

Pepi grew hot at Phœbe's treatment of Henry. Frau Hayburn had been a fool to go back to Scotland to have her child; and now, having lost it, to leave him all alone like this. It would serve her right if Henry–

No. Pepi must not talk like that. You had only to look at Herr Hayburn with his wife to know that there was only one woman in the world for him. And these Scottish people were very strict, Frau Klem had heard; as strict as – well, any decent persons ought to be. But she noticed a toss of Pepi's head, and wondered if, after all, life in the theatre was good for a young girl. Besides, Pepi must remember what poor Frau Hayburn had been through.

But Pepi did not seem to be much touched by the thought of poor Frau Hayburn.

After these discussions Frau Klem would end with a sigh and go back to her housework; while Pepi went back to her singing practice, taking her scales as high and as loud as she could, until her simple mother was driven to wonder if these slate-pencil sounds could really have anything to do with music.

But in the first weeks he had come back to her, Herr Hayburn seemed a poor creature enough. Frau Klem had seen him one day by chance in the Favoritenstrasse. As he passed her by, his eyes had the same look of suffering witlessness that she had seen in the eyes of the oxen as they were driven down this same street on their way to the slaughter-house. But presently, as better news of Phœbe came, things turned more bearable for Henry. He was glad now that his homing instinct had brought him back to the Quellengasse. These people were kind. They helped him to keep going. To take a hold of himself.

Once more he allowed himself to become one of themselves, as he had done in his first months in Vienna. On Sundays they went together on little jaunts. Often Henry stood treat in some suburban wine-garden, where, in the splendour of the dying Austrian autumn, they ate their *Schnitzel* and drank the year-old wine.

He began to take long walks. Often Pepi Klem would go with him, chirping along by his side, talking good-naturedly of anything that might distract him. Henry readily fell into the habit of having her with him. Soon he was paying no more heed to her than he would to his brother Stephen. She asked him to talk English. They began to call these walks her English lessons.

October, November. Still Phœbe's letters did not say when she would be with him. What was wrong? She had assured him she was recovering. Very well, then. It was impossible for him to go back to Scotland to fetch her, but her coming could be arranged. He had written about her coming, many times, and she had replied that she would come soon. Why, then, didn't she do it?

He was a man now. Fully awake. He longed to hold his wife once more in his arms. This thought, indeed, had become an obsession that blinded him, in part, to what his wife had suffered. He began to nurse a grievance. He began to forget she must be given time.

In the second week of December he wrote, telling her yet again of his loneliness, and begging her to return to him. Phœbe replied with a letter that was gay and teasing. Sending him all her love, telling him nothing definite, wishing him a Merry Christmas, and saying she would see him soon.

From her letter he did not guess that she planned to surprise him.

II

It was twelve o'clock on the last day of the year. Henry crossed from his office in the Neubau, making for his usual mid-day eating-house in the passage off the Herrengasse.

Vienna lay under snow. It had been swept

up into great heaps on either side of the Ring. A silver sun had broken through, and its glitter upon the snow, in the Volksgarten, on the Burg Platz, on the palace roofs, threw back reflections that forced Henry to contract his eyes to mere slits.

But presently he was in his little restaurant, bidding his usual vague good-day, and waiting to have his meal set before him. Except for himself the room was almost empty. It contained Christmas decorations, but few customers. The *habitués*, it seemed, were elsewhere. Most of them were not at work today, and thus they had not sought their usual eating-place. Henry, too, was finished now.

'Der Mister' seemed out of spirits, the rotund proprietor said to his wife; out of spirits, and downright bad-tempered. They watched him as he sat, slumped in his chair, tugging his beard and staring at the glowing ribs of the tiled oven, the door of which had been left open. The good woman gave it as her opinion that he looked ill.

Henry had been living in daily expectation of news telling of Phœbe's return. She had not written for a fortnight. Yet since Christmas he had got a letter from Mrs. Barrowfield saying she had seen her, and that she looked very well. He could not understand it. With the prospect of nothing to do, either this afternoon or tomorrow, bitter loneliness had fallen upon Henry like a beast of prey. The Klems, he had been told, would be little at home. Pepi was not in work just at present, and able to go visiting with her parents.

There were many things he might have done, acquaintances he might have seen. Even the ladies in the Paulanergasse would have been glad to see him, for his wife's sake. But in these last weeks Henry had clung to the routine of his work. He had tried to think of little else. It had been his lifebelt. Now, for the next days, there would be no work for him to do.

As the old man brought him his soup, he asked if the gracious gentleman felt well? Henry said he did. His host said that it was very cold, but sunny. Henry admitted that this was so. The old man asked what the gracious gentleman did on Sylvester Day in England. The gracious gentleman snapped ungraciously that he didn't know, as he did not come from England. Defeated, the old man retired.

Shortly he came back, however, professionally cheerful, with Henry's meat, fried potatoes – and a bottle of wine, which he begged Henry to drink with his own and his wife's compliments. It gave them pleasure, the good man said, to make a present of this bottle of Hungarian red wine to one who patronised their modest house so regularly.

Henry unbent a little. The determined friendliness of the couple had penetrated. He thanked the man and, remembering some kind of manners, bade him bring two more glasses. His host and hostess must drink with him to the New Year. The man did as he was told. His wife came from behind, wiping her hands on her apron, and beaming. The glass of wine warmed Henry.

He was inventing yet another toast, and filling up their glasses once again, when Pepi Klem came in. Coming from the dazzling sunshine, for a moment she could see nothing in the dim gaslight. He had seen her in this place only once before. That had been last spring, when she had just returned to Vienna. In his desperate, mock heartiness, Henry called to her:

'Hullo, Pepi! Come and drink to the New Year.'

She gave a little start, then smiled in recognition. 'Oh! I didn't know you still came here. I expected to find some friends.'

Another glass was brought and another toast drunk. The couple were pleased to see that so bright a companion had come to chase away 'der Mister's' glumness.

The old man laid a place for her, smiling; taking it for granted that this was Henry's girl for whom he had been waiting, impatient and angry.

Henry's loneliness responded to Pepi at

once. Here was someone he knew who was gay and friendly. For the time, at least, he need not be miserable. He bade her choose her lunch, and ordered another bottle of wine.

Now it was pleasant in the little warm restaurant. Pepi talked nonsense, hummed snatches of songs and laughed at nothing. He watched her; half smiling, half bewildered. But she was cheerful and feminine, and her presence soothed him.

She asked him if he were working this afternoon and what he intended to do. He told her he was not working and had no plans.

She said nothing to this – merely went on humming dreamily. One or two others came in; along with them two students, friends of Pepi's. But they only nodded in recognition, and crossed to their own table.

Henry asked her if she did not want to join them. She smiled vaguely and said that the wine had made her sleepy. He said that he felt sleepy, too. They could hear, somewhere, a church clock strike two.

'I didn't know it was so late,' she said, looking round her.

'It doesn't matter to me. I've nothing to do.'

'Neither have I.' Suddenly she sat up and looked at him. 'Herr Hayburn! Shall we go for a sleigh-drive in the woods? It would be

wonderful today! We can drink coffee somewhere.'

Henry was surprised to find himself assen-
ting.

III

They had hired a horse-sleigh in the
suburbs, and were speeding out towards the
Vienna Woods.

Now, as Henry sat thickly wrapped beside
his companion, he took the trouble, British
fashion, to assure himself that this was just
the thing his health and spirits needed. That
a run in the sharp winter air would clear his
head, disperse the cobwebs and render him
fit to begin the work of the New Year.

His companion saw that he was cheerful,
that he was pleased to find himself with her.

Their way took them up through Dobling
and in the direction of Weidlingbach. It was
some time before Henry realised they were
coming out in the direction of the house
that he and Phœbe had rented last summer.
They passed the end of the path that led up
to it. Now, in the snow, everything seemed
unfamiliarly familiar.

Memory forced itself upon him. The still
evenings in the garden up there. The roses
and the pine-trees. Their hopes. Stephen's
companionship. Phœbe's last descent

through these trees, when at last they were persuaded it was right for her to go. The evening he had received the news.

Seeing his solemnity, Pepi spoke. 'You lived up here in the summer, didn't you?'

'Yes.'

'Where?'

'Oh, quite near here.'

But she wanted him to stay in the present, to be merry and think of herself.

'Oh, look! Isn't it beautiful!'

The snow was just right for a sleigh-drive. It was dry, powdery and not deep enough to make running difficult. There was no wind to blow it into drifts. The sun had been bright as they started out, but now it was obscured by clouds hanging so low that it looked as though they might run into them as the road climbed higher. The meadows, lit by the grey winter light, lay flat, white and monotonous around them. Now in the woods the pine-trees stood motionless, each branch bearing its heavy burden. On other trees, too, the frailest twigs were rimed with powder.

Everywhere they turned there was beauty, peace and mystery. Even the hoof-claps of their horse were muffled as he drew them on and upward, his breathing changing to little clouds that floated past them. For a time the only sounds came from the sleigh-bells.

The valley was narrowing. The road was taking them up one side of it. Down there was the stream. Now they could catch, here and there, the bickering of such water as still ran over the black stones and under frail bridges of ice. Yet further up, where the rock had been cut to make the road, dropping water had formed grottos of icicles.

Presently they were on the top and almost in the clouds. It was becoming misty. They could only see the nearer trees, the road, and the huddled back of the driver's sheepskin coat, as he sat in front of them, cracking his whip and calling to his horse. Their universe of whiteness had turned suddenly clammy – menacing and unfriendly.

Under the rug, Pepi came closer to Henry, grasping his hand as though in fear.

Presently they had passed the top and were dropping down. The sleigh was running easily, the bells playing a different tune. Now the mist had parted and they could see the snow-covered roofs of a village beneath them.

Pepi gave a little cry of pleasure. She called to the driver. Down there was a room where they could drink coffee. The man replied that he could do with it.

The inn parlour was warm and friendly with its decorated Christmas tree; the innkeeper welcoming. Today he had expected no one. The young man, he saw, was foreign.

But he knew better than to ask about a couple who had so plainly escaped beyond the frontiers of convention. It was natural with young people. Who was he that he should blame them?

Henry drank his coffee morosely. In the sleigh, the touch of Pepi's hand, the nearness of her, had brought a sudden excitement. Longings had risen within him – longings that clouded his reason. Now Pepi's voice as she talked to the inn-keeper moved him strangely and brought him near to despair. What was it she was talking of? He did not know.

The man had left them alone. He poured himself fresh coffee and threw it, scalding, down his throat. Now he was ready. He must get out. Out of here. He reached for his coat.

'But what's wrong?' She asked.

He turned at the door, dazed. He spoke hoarsely. 'It's time we were getting back.'

'But why? I haven't finished yet.'

'I'll go out and speak to the driver.'

'The driver? I sent him away. I thought it would be nice to wait here for supper and go back in the moonlight. Didn't you hear me talking about it just now? You must have been far away! When you said nothing, I thought it was all right. The innkeeper said there was someone here who could take us.'

He looked down at her, beaten.

She came to him. 'My dear, are you sure you feel all right? Has anything happened?' She took the lapels of his jacket in her hands.

He caught her to him.

It was the next afternoon when Henry returned with Pepi to Vienna.

IV

'And your dear husband will be at the station to meet you?' The elderly English woman with whom Phœbe had travelled from London smiled across the carriage at her with a prim, tired smile. The carriage was stuffy. Neither of them had slept much.

'No, he won't. I'm giving him a surprise. That's why I planned to arrive on New Year's Day. I knew I would catch him in his rooms.'

'When did you leave Vienna?'

'August.'

'He will be surprised!'

Mrs. Hayburn had lost a child, her companion gathered. Poor little thing! And she was so young! But now she was going back to her husband, to her youth, to all the intoxication of this city that held so many foreigners in its thrall.

The older woman envied her. To be coming back to a steady, British husband, and, at the same time, to the gaiety of Vienna, was a thing any woman might envy. Phœbe's companion sighed, as she straightened her veil and buttoned her mended gloves.

Like so many other governesses, French and English, she had come at first to Vienna for a year, merely to gain experience. Now, after more than thirty, the Imperial City still held her. She could not leave it for longer than a few weeks at a time. In common with others of her kind, she had spent her days moving from one noble family to another, educating daughters, helping worldly mothers to sell them to the highest bidders in the Empire's glittering marriage market; a mine of gossip about the intrigues and scandals that raged perpetually in Austro-Hungarian society.

Phœbe looked from the window. The train had almost passed through the mountains to the west of Vienna. In a short time they would be in the Westbahnhof.

On hills and forests the snow lay thickly. The sky was grey and leaden. Now the suburbs were beginning – the familiar villas and gardens of Vienna, taking their New Year's morning rest under the blanket of whiteness. There were few people to be seen. Everywhere there was peace and stillness. Now the City itself. The train was slowing down. Now the rush and confusion that went with the arrival of the morning express from Western Europe.

Her heart was beating as a *Komfortable* took her towards the Klems'. She could see Henry already. He would be newly awake and dishevelled, his eyes staring like a boy's. She laughed at the thought of him.

Her excitement mounted as the *Komfort-able* entered the Quellengasse. She had no eyes to notice that some of the buildings, half-finished in the spring, were now complete and occupied. And here was the Klems', and there was the old house-porter, beaming broadly and ready to help her with her luggage.

And had the gracious lady brought the gracious gentleman with her?

What did he mean?

Merely that he thought that he was not upstairs. He could not, of course, be sure.

Phœbe laughed. He must be there. Where else could he be?

The Klems' outer door on the staircase was still closed.

Phœbe rang with determination, once, twice, many times. At last she heard Herr Klem himself grumbling behind it. Now he was standing, leonine, unkempt and angry, in his shirt and trousers. But at the sight of her his colour mounted and his face took on a grin of confused welcome. How was she? Had she just come? And what had she done with Herr Hayburn?

He led her into Henry's room. It was as she

303

would have expected. His books and papers were scattered on his worktable. A suit of clothes, folded no doubt by Frau Klem, lay upon a chair. Her own photograph stood by his bedside along with one of his mother. His other belongings were everywhere.

But the bed had not been slept in. Phœbe turned.

'Where *is* my husband Herr Klem? He must have gone somewhere.'

The man shook his head uncertainly. He asked if Herr Hayburn had known the gracious lady was coming this morning.

'No. It was a surprise. But Henry *must* have said where he was going.'

Herr Klem shrugged. He knew nothing of it. Perhaps his wife—

And now Frau Klem, flustered and untidy, came to add her greeting. She was genuinely pleased to see Phœbe. She would bring her hot water and make coffee at once. And was the gracious lady quite well and glad to be back? It was a pity Herr Hayburn was not at home to greet her.

This time Phœbe's eyes filled with anger. 'But *where* is he?' Couldn't the woman stop gabbling and tell her where he was?

At once Frau Klem was humble. Didn't the gracious lady herself know? She had taken that for granted.

'How can I? I've only just come from Scotland.'

'He must be with friends.'

'What friends?'

'*Na?* The gracious lady must know Herr Hayburn's friends.'

They stood bewildered for some moments longer, then Frau Klem went to make coffee, followed by her husband. He shut the kitchen door behind him.

Together they agreed that this was very unlike Herr Hayburn. But really, if his wife wanted her husband to confine his escapades to such times as she was not arriving back in Vienna, it would be much better if she told him when to expect her.

'Perhaps Pepi knows,' Herr Klem suggested.

'Go and see if she is there. I didn't hear her come in last night.'

But Pepi's room was empty, too.

'I don't think that child should be going so much to Lisa Fischer's,' Pepi's mother went on, preparing breakfast. 'Oh, I know Pepi's an artiste, too, now. But I don't think mixing with Lisa's friends is doing her any good.'

Chapter Nineteen

Henry's transparent honesty would neither allow of apology nor concealment. He had sinned against his wife. And at once he hastened to admit the enormity of his sin. Let Phœbe do what she liked with him! Leave him! Divorce him! Anything! No punishment could be bad enough!

His conscience, consumed for a time in a flame of madness, sprang up once again, sharp and more vigorous from its roots, sprouting thorns to torment him. Thorns of tradition; of background; of the rigid code by which he and his kind lived.

Now they were having it out in their room in the Quellengasse. It is difficult to tell which of them suffered more.

Shocked and bewildered, Phœbe sat watching her husband pacing up and down; dishevelled, broken and ashamed. In any other circumstance the sight of his unhappiness would have melted her. If ever Henry was a lame duck, he was a lame duck now – lamed by his own hot folly.

But this folly had been committed against herself, against their own past intimacies, against her own body, so nearly broken by the disastrous, stillborn birth of his child. Her young, burning pride could find no forgiveness.

Flushed, expressionless and silent, she watched him, as he went back and forth, blurting out his misery, his loneliness, his weakness. She could not answer him, throw him a crumb of comfort. Had she not suffered, too? Had not she made that dreadful journey home? Been ill? Suffered these weary months of convalescence?

Had it been to amuse herself? Did he imagine she *liked* losing his baby?

At the thought of her child, Phœbe felt the tears fighting to come. But she dug her fingernails into the palms of her hands and bit her cheek until she could taste blood in her mouth. Her eyes followed him, dry and hard, as he moved about the room. She could not forgive him.

They were living in a foreign land, she knew, where such things were looked upon differently. But this had nothing whatsoever to do with herself and Henry; nothing whatever to do with their own strict ways. That they had learnt to live among the people here, to understand and like them, to find toleration, even, could not condone Henry's behaviour.

But what was she to do?

Henry was asking her. She must, she supposed, find an answer.

'The first thing we must do, Henry,' she said, speaking evenly, and with no show of emotion, 'is to get out of here.'

Henry clutched at the word 'we'.

'Then you've made up your mind to stay?'

Phœbe did not reply to this at once. Stay with him? What else?

Go home to Bel lamenting that she had insisted upon marrying a waster? No. That was a thing she could never bring herself to do! Her mother's Highland pride flamed up white within her. She would rather go down to the Franzjosefskai and pitch herself into the Danube Canal!

As yet she had no idea of her feelings – no idea if she loved or hated her husband. But one thing she did know. She must fight out her battle here in Vienna alone. Alone and apart. Free from leering gossip, from over-eager sympathy. The family at home must know nothing until, at least, her decisions were taken.

'I've made up my mind to stay in Vienna in the meantime. I don't suppose you're any more anxious than I am that this should reach home. But I am leaving this house at once. You can come with me. I haven't unpacked. We can go back to our old hotel, and take two bedrooms. One for you and one for me.'

II

'Well, Maxi?'

Maximilian bent over his aunt's hand and raised it to his lips; then, this salutation being too formal, he kissed her on both cheeks.

'How are you?'

'Very well, my dear. But your Aunt Helene is in bed. Nothing. A little cold.'

'I'll see her before I go.'

'Yes. You must.'

Stephanie rang for coffee and led her nephew to a seat. 'We haven't seen you since Christmas Day, and that was only for ten minutes. And now it's the middle of February.'

'I've been very busy.'

'Amusing yourself, Maxerl?'

'Working, Aunt Steffi.'

'*Na?* A little of both, perhaps?' Maximilian looked about his aunt's pleasant old-fashioned room. The February sun was casting pale, slanting rays through the double windows with their draped lace curtains, catching silver dust-particles, and throwing patterns of light on the floor. The room was warm from the stove, and heavy with the scent of spring flowers.

'It's nice here,' he said.

'Then why don't you come oftener?'

Maximilian did not reply to this. He had got up and was wandering about, looking at familiar pictures and photographs. Aunts and uncles. His own parents. Suddenly he stopped and held up a filigree frame.

'Hullo! This is new.'

'Which, Maxi?'

'This photograph of the little Hayburn.'

Stephanie laughed. 'You take a great interest in the little Hayburn, don't you?'

'Of course. An uncle's interest, my dearest aunt.'

'I'm glad. Do you know, Max, I believe you only come to see me when you want to talk about the little Hayburn!'

Maximilian was still examining Phœbe's photograph. 'I say!' He exclaimed. 'She's very smart, isn't she?'

'Yes. I sent her to a place in the Kohlmarkt.'

'I was sure her clothes were Viennese!' He continued to admire Phœbe. Her close-fitting jacket. Her slim waist. Her modish bonnet. And the expression of her face had a new elegance, somehow. A little harder, perhaps. A little more sophisticated. But it pleased his sense of style. He looked up. 'That young woman could almost be called a raving beauty. "Mister Henry" had better look after her.'

'They've just taken a small flat quite near here,' Stephanie said after a moment.

'The Hayburn told me. Much more sensible.'

Stephanie signed to the servant, who had come in with the tray, that she would pour coffee herself. She did not want him in the room.

'Maxerl,' she asked as she gave her nephew his cup, 'has anything gone wrong between these children?'

Maximilian sat down. He shrugged. 'I took them to "Lohengrin" at the Opera a few weeks ago. It's the only time I've seen her since she came back.' He thought for a moment, then added: 'She seemed a little more artificial; a little older; a little more – what shall I say? – remote. It's easy to understand – losing her child.'

In turn, Stephanie took her cup and sat down beside him. 'Do you think the Hayburns are still in love with each other? It was a marriage of love, you know.'

Maximilian considered. 'I should say he is. I don't know about her.'

'What do you mean, Max?'

'Well, that night at the Opera he behaved as if he were her servant. Holding things for her. Running for this and that. Watching her expression to see if what he said pleased her. I wanted to laugh. And if you could see him in the factory! He's getting more and more bad-tempered!'

'What do you think it means?'

Again Maximilian shrugged. 'Who can tell? The English are strange animals. But it seems to me the Scotch are stranger!'

They sat silent for a time, drinking coffee and following the train of their thoughts. At length Stephanie turned to her nephew.

'Do you know what I think, Maxi? I think the poor child is trying to grow a shell.'

Her nephew smiled. That was nothing new in Vienna.

III

Yes, Phœbe was growing a shell. A shell of elegance. A shell of fine manners. A shell of social interests. Things that might have been good in themselves, if all else had been well with her; but now they were anodynes for her sharp unhappiness.

Henry, ashamed and obsequious, allowed her to do what she liked. In the rented flat in the Wieden she had taken to receiving such of the English and American colony as she chose to invite – wealthy students mostly, and one or two Viennese. She learnt to chatter of music, of the theatres, of the doings at Court.

Her husband watched her, troubled. This was not Phœbe. Not the girl he had married. But he blamed himself, left her alone, and found his own anodyne in more and yet more work.

But daily, Phœbe found herself face to

face with her misery. Lying in the darkness of her lonely bedroom, she fought her battle, time and time again. Why had Henry done this to her? They were not of the same clay as those people here. They could not take things lightly.

But by degrees the mists of intolerance began to clear a little. She began to wonder about this patient, untidy, lost young man who left the flat early each morning and usually came back in time only to go to bed.

Towards the end of March, Henry, exhausted and ill with overwork, was at home for some days.

She nursed him with devotion, though she showed him no affection. When he thanked her, she turned his thanks aside with hard, impersonal brightness. But when he had gone back to work, the house seemed empty. And so, through this unhappy year, Phœbe and Henry blundered on. Contrition and distress on the one hand; pride and bitterness on the other.

A sharp old woman of their own kind – Mrs. Barrowfield, for instance – might have brought them back to reason, and a measure of happiness. But here, in their exile, there was no one. And the colourless letters they sent home gave no inkling of their distresses.

IV

And meantime Imperial Vienna continued on her brilliant way. More brilliant than ever; for in May the Emperor's son, the Crown Prince Rudolf, was to be married to the Princess Stephanie of Belgium.

By April, at many points in the Ring and at such other places as the royal processions would be seen to advantage, scaffoldings for seats were being placed. No trouble would be spared. That the Princess might not see the waters of the Wien river, muddy and full of factory refuse, as she crossed the Elizabeth Bridge coming from the Palace of Schönbrunn, the entire bridge was to be turned into a bower of flowers in which young girls would stand and throw rose-petals at her carriage. On a tribune opposite the Burgtor the mayor and dignitaries of Vienna would present addresses of welcome. The spire of Saint Stephen's itself was to be outlined during the nights of celebration with glass bulbs containing electric lights.

The month of April was cold and wet. The scaffoldings, undecorated, looked bare and forbidding. People kept telling Phœbe how wonderful they would look with all their garnishings. These things chimed, somehow, with Phœbe's mood of cynicism; with her feeling that all was vanity; that reality's scaffolding could never long be hidden.

At first she had thought of Pepi Klem merely as a wanton, who had set a cruel barrier between herself and Henry. But now, as time went on, she found herself possessed by an unnamed urge to see her. She had caught sight of her in January in the chorus of an operetta. Henry had not been there, and she was glad. But although her curiosity had sent her back to the same theatre, Phœbe had not seen Pepi again. What had become of her? Phœbe did not want to meet her face to face, but the desire to see her amounted to morbidity.

And meanwhile preparations for the Imperial marriage continued. The first of May, a Sunday, was wet and cold. The yearly Prater Corso fell flat. In the afternoon it rained, and there was little of the customary glitter. The Hirsch ladies, ever conventional, drove the length of the Haupt Allee but they did not invite the Hayburns to accompany them.

Now, however, the weather had changed, as though by Imperial command. There was warmth and brilliant sunshine. With luck, it would continue until the wedding-day, which was the tenth.

Vienna thrilled with interest at the news of each important arrival. Gossip and surmise flew. The Prince of Wales was here. He had been greeted on the platform by the Archdukes and by Sir Henry Elliot, the British Ambassador. The Belgian King and Queen were at Schönbrunn Palace holding their own temporary Court, and giving out that their daughter already felt more at home in Vienna than in Brussels. Prince and Princess William of Prussia had arrived in the royal train from Berlin. Regal and imperial blood was flowing to Vienna from all parts of Europe.

And humbler Vienna was kept carefully and properly informed. It must be entertained by the doings of the great. It heard that the Prince of Wales had dined with the Archduke Karl Ludwig. That two thousand five hundred of the Empire's aristocracy had been to a ball in the Imperial Palace, where the Emperor and the Empress had shown themselves particularly gracious.

And now, on the day before her wedding, the Princess Stephanie was to show herself to the people over whom one day, she would be Empress. Her future Emperor, the Crown Prince Rudolf, had, to increase his worthiness of her and to prepare himself for matrimony, just returned from a pilgrimage to the Holy Shrine in Jerusalem.

On a seat in one of the stands erected on the Ring, Phœbe sat with Henry, waiting for the Princess Stephanie's procession to pass her by.

She had been surprised when Henry, who

cared little for such things, had come to her with place tickets. But Henry had become like that. He thought, now, of things to please her.

She sat looking about her, while her husband sat woodenly beside her. The Ring was dense with people, most of them carrying bunches of lily-of-the-valley, for this, it had been said, was the favourite flower of the Princess.

Now there was no longer any bare scaffolding. There was bunting everywhere. The black and yellow of the Empire. The yellow, red and blue of Belgium. The white and blue of Bavaria; as a compliment to the Empress. Where there was no bunting, there were festoons and garlands.

Now the Princess Stephanie was coming. There was shouting in the distance that could be heard above the pealing of church bells and the firing of artillery. Down there on the pavement below them, people were struggling for a better view; darting out, only to be pushed back by the soldiers cordoning the street.

Suddenly, as the procession was nearing them, Phœbe saw a young woman dart forward, trip and stumble, laughing into the arms of a gendarme, who roughly ordered her back. It was Pepi Klem. To show her composure, Pepi made him some reply and did not return to the pavement until the man had commanded her yet more harshly. Then she walked unhurriedly back, giving Phœbe time to look at her.

Now the splendour of the Austro-Spanish Habsburgs was passing Phœbe by. Red trumpeters mounted on black horses. Court servants in seventeenth-century uniforms. Horse-guard. Foot-guard. Carriages with the suite of the Princess drawn by black thoroughbreds harnessed in gold. More soldiery. And now the fair young Princess with her mother in a carriage drawn by milk-white stallions of the Imperial stud, their heads nodding with ostrich plumes, the postillions in mediæval white and gold. Bells rang. Guns fired. People shouted. Flowers were thrown.

But Phœbe had no eyes for a Habsburg exhibition. She had seen that Pepi Klem was going to have a child.

V

Somewhere about midsummer Henry received this letter from Mrs. Barrowfield:

'DEAR HENRY,

'It vexes me sore that it should have come to this. You may well be miserable! If you are, as you say, repenting in sorrow, it is no more than you should be doing. I am glad to hear the Lord has given you that much grace, anyway.

'Your letter says that "sheer desperation" is making you tell me everything. Well, my dear boy, maybe you might have done a worse thing than write and tell Granny Barrowfield. She has always been fond of you and your wife, and would do anything to help the both of you. And I may just tell you, that two or three minutes – since just before she went to look for her ink-bottle – she was down on her knees asking her Maker to put some common sense into her old head, so that, with His help, she would maybe write and give you some of His Divine Guidance.

'You are not a bad young man, Henry. You never have been, and never will be. There is nothing vicious in the build of you. You are just a great big innocent. But, if I know you at all, your blood runs twice as quick as most young men's, and your feelings are strong. It may be hard for an old woman of seventy-six to judge the strength of a young man's temptation. But what is wrong is wrong.

'All the same, I never thought it was right, the way they took Phœbe away from you last August. It was against nature and against common sense. When Bel told me what she and Mrs. Dermott and Lady Ruanthorpe had done, I could have taken a stick to the three of them. I could never abide the Dermott woman anyway, and I dare say the other old cat is worse.

'I was very, very sorry for you at the time, dear Henry. I nearly came out to see you. But at seventy-five, and me not used with the travelling, how could I do it? And mind you, I think these three women – and I am sorry to say my own daughter was one of them – sinned against you, just about as much as you sinned yourself. Only their sin is not listed in the Ten Commandments, so maybe it is harder to put a label on it, and not so awkward for their consciences. But you can take it from me, that conscience or no conscience, Bel heard all about it from her mother!

'I doubt you will just have to put up with what you call Phœbe's hardness. And if you think she has got harder since this woman is to have your bairn, surely you can see the reason for that, too? As your wife, Phœbe can only see the whole thing as a terrible affront. (By the way, how do you know this bairn will be yours? If the besom is anybody's girl, then it may be anybody's bairn. Be sure to write about this. Don't forget.)

'I wish I could give you more comfort, Henry. But remember this: Phœbe's blood runs quick, just the way yours does, and if you give her time, I think things will get better. She would not be staying on with you if there was no love for you left in her.

Have patience, ask help on your knees, Henry, and brighter days will dawn!

'I hear from Arthur that he can get you the offer of a good job here at home. But he will be writing to you himself, I dare say. That would be far the best for you both.

'This has been a long letter for an old woman to write. I hope the Lord has made me put down everything I should. But anyway, now I must stop. As you ask, I am sending it to your office.

'Yours lovingly,
             'ISABELLA BARROWFIELD.'

Chapter Twenty

The Volksgarten was quite still this morning – still and autumnal. From the Franzensring outside, the traffic sounded far-off and muted. When, some minutes ago, the clocks of the City had announced the hour of eleven, their peal had come to Frau Klem, sitting here in the garden, with the unreality of those strange bells said to come to the ears of becalmed sailors from belfries long since sunk beneath the sea.

The children near her went about their games quietly; throwing dead leaves into the pond and watching them thoughtfully, as they floated on the glassy surface; or hiding from each other noiselessly and without enthusiasm behind the pillars of the Theseus temple, while governesses and nursemaids sewed and gossiped in whispers on the seats around.

Frau Klem sighed, looked into the face of her sleeping grandson, adjusted the shabby shawl that was wrapped about him, decided that her seat was hard, and wished that Pepi would come back to fetch them.

She must have been gone almost two hours now. Surely they must have reached a decision about her by this time. The letter from the Director had said half-past nine. But theatres were go-as-you-please places, she had always heard. Still, Pepi was only seeking student work in the chorus to earn some now very necessary money, and her voice was true and strong.

A trio of tiny children passed. They were richly dressed in little velvet coats, and attended by a nurse in Bohemian peasant costume. The children of some nobleman, perhaps. Frau Klem stroked back a wisp of untidy fair hair, and her eyes followed them until they had passed from sight among the shrubbery. A pang of jealousy and regret caused her to hold the bundle in her arms yet closer.

No. She had never expected to have grandchildren so rich and well tended as those three. And yet, if Pepi had married a respectable burgher – like, say, Willi Pommer – it would have been the delight of her heart to make and contrive small clothes for them, and lead them out – a proud grandmother – before the world.

Not that she did not love this child; but its coming had been unfortunate, look at it as you would. Oh, she had been assured that Pepi would be a great singer, that she would one day earn enough money for all of them and bring up her son to be a gentleman; that you had to make all kinds of allowances for people as highly gifted as Pepi's teacher declared her to be. And, of course, young people were highly inflammable.

But Frau Klem did not like it. She liked things straight and settled. Herr Hayburn had been very good. He had been to see his son, and had been helpful. But he was a stern, remote young man; and he couldn't be Pepi's husband. And say what you would, a husband and a ring on the right finger was better than a weekly allowance. Even for a young woman who was going to be a great opera star.

The little creature in her arms was awake now. He was looking up at her with wide, dazed eyes.

As though she blamed herself for these thoughts, Frau Klem gave rein to her instincts. She kissed him; she talked nonsense to him; told him he was the sweetest baby in Vienna and that she would not change him for all the other children in the Volksgarten, however grand they might be.

For a moment, one or two elegant nurses raised their eyes to look at the rather shabby woman fussing with the untidy infant over there on that seat by herself.

But she was sorry that Pepi had needed to look for work so soon after the baby's coming. Whatever the doctor had told her, it couldn't be good, either for herself or for the child. Still, if she got this work in the new season of operetta at the Ring Theatre – as the Comic Opera House was coming to be called – she would be able to pay for her lessons, and help with other expenses, too. It had been nice of her cousin Lisa to put in a word for her. More people were coming into the garden now. A young man with a roll of music in his hand passed near her. She wondered if he had been to have his voice tried, too. A staid old gentleman in a black frock-coat, a grey cravat with a pearl pin, and whiskers cut like the Emperor's. One or two women of fashion.

Suddenly a modish young woman emerged briskly from a side alley. She was almost standing over Frau Klem before they recognised each other.

Colour flooded to the roots of the elder woman's hair. It was Frau Hayburn. Frau

Klem smiled stupidly.

For reply, Phœbe responded with the coldest of nods, turned her back and walked on quickly up the gardens.

Frau Klem watched her as she went. The encounter had been uncomfortable. Frau Klem's heart was beating. But poor Frau Hayburn! You could hardly blame her, when you remembered she had lost her own child!

Now she saw that Phœbe's steps had slackened. That she had stopped. That she was coming back. Now again she stood before her.

'I'm sorry, Frau Klem. I was rude to you just now. I apologise.'

How beautiful, how elegant Frau Hayburn had become since last she had seen her in January! Elegant, and strangely bright, like a diamond.

Frau Klem was friendly and humble. 'Please, Frau Hayburn. But I understand!'

Phœbe said nothing to this. But she did not move. The woman could see that she had lost colour; that her strange, dark blue eyes were ranging about the gardens as though they were seeking help.

For a moment Frau Klem wondered if she were going to faint. But now the blood had come back hot into her face, and she was looking down at the child.

Her voice, as she spoke, was low and controlled. 'Is that your daughter's child?'

'But, yes. You see, Frau Hayburn–'

'My husband's child?'

For reply, and finding no words, the grandmother uncovered the child's face. As she held him up for Phœbe to see, he opened his eyes once more and looked about him.

She wondered at Frau Hayburn's quick, low cry. She did not guess that a familiar twitch of the tiny mouth, a hovering frown about the dazed, scarcely focused eyes, had almost torn the heart out of her.

'I must go now.'

Frau Hayburn turned and went away without another word.

II

December the seventh.

Henry Hayburn sat at the back of a box in the Ring Theatre taking no part in the conversation.

Some time ago Maximilian Hirsch had come to him saying that he had, by good fortune, been allotted a box for the first performance of Offenbach's 'Tales of Hoffmann', and would Herr and Frau Hayburn care to join his party? The presentation of this, the only serious opera the dead German-Parisian composer had written, was being awaited with excitement in Vienna. Maximilian was sure Frau Hayburn would be interested.

Henry had accepted. Not because he wanted to go in the least. But because he thought it might please Phœbe. This was a rule with him now. Helpless, he was forever seeking to make amends.

He looked at Phœbe. She was sitting in the front of the box, talking with the other young woman of the party. Together, they were discussing the many well-known people who were appearing at this important premiere, pointing them out to each other, as they came in. An Archduke, one or two ambassadors, stars from other theatres, a society beauty.

Phœbe was brilliant – lovely. And quite detached now from himself. It was as though she had encased herself in sophistication that he might not come near her. He did not know, any more, what Phœbe was thinking. They occupied the same house; ate meals at the same table. But they had fallen into a dull politeness, the one towards the other. Sympathy, emotion, between them was, it seemed, dead.

Maximilian turned to say a word to Henry, to draw him into the conversation he was having with the husband of Phœbe's friend. But as he did so applause broke in the theatre. The conductor had come in, and was taking up his baton. Herr Hirsch turned back to listen to the opening music of the new opera.

There was little overture, apparently, for almost at once the curtain had risen on Luther's wine-cellar in Nuremberg, lit only by beams of moonlight, while the voices of the Spirits of Good Cheer could be heard singing their opening chorus behind the scenes.

Henry was glad to be left alone. Let them sit listening to this tomfoolery, and leave him in peace!

Now the innkeeper had come in, carrying a lamp. Obediently the light on the stage jumped up to reinforce the effect of brightness. The engineer in Henry was puzzled. How could so many gas-burners jump into flame at once? But he was forgetting. He remembered having read that the new Director had installed a system of electric contacts near each gas-jet. By merely switching on the current of electricity and the flow of gas at the same time, immediate and full illumination would result. It was ingenious and interesting. But they had better take care. People, these days, were rushing into all kinds of new uses for electricity without taking enough thought.

Now the prologue was over. People whispered that Herr Ferenczy was singing this new part well. There was applause while the curtain descended slowly on Hoffmann, as he began to tell of his unhappy loves. Presently it had risen on the first of the Tales.

Henry watched the traffic of the stage without bothering to take it in. The chorus of Spalanzani's guests were coming in to hear the song sung by Olympia, the wonderful mechanical doll.

Suddenly his eyes were caught by a little, plump lady of the chorus. Her paint, patches and high marquise wig merely underlined her identity. It was Pepi Klem. Sweat broke upon him. He looked at Phœbe. Had she, too, seen Pepi? Would she think he had brought her here, knowing, yet caring nothing?

But the fixed, charming smile remained on Phœbe's face. Now the human doll had been brought from its cabinet. Spalanzani's guests passed down before it, one after another, to admire its finery. Now for a moment Pepi was right in the front of the stage. Phœbe could not miss her.

But Phœbe's expression did not change.

This was horrible to him, this iron control! It was well that she did nothing now. But when once they were home again, he knew she would smile, say what a pleasant evening it had been, bid him a bright goodnight, and go off to her own room.

Doing what he conceived to be his duty, he visited his child regularly. He had learnt from Frau Klem that Phœbe had seen the child in the Volksgarten. That it had upset her. But not by the flicker of an eyelid had Phœbe betrayed any of this to himself.

And he loved Phœbe. He always would love Phœbe, he supposed. Yet this coldness would kill him! In her heart she would blame his callousness for bringing her here tonight. But he hadn't known. Pepi had said something about work again, but he had, typically, taken little notice.

Down on the stage the doll was singing her elaborate, high-pitched song. Sitting among Spalanzani's guests, Pepi was simulating an elaborate, coquettish interest.

Crude rage took hold of Henry – crude rage and revulsion. That young woman was a slut! She should be at home. What right had she to flaunt herself thus brazenly, with a child little more than two months old? He was glad that soon he would shake the dust of this terrible strumpet city from beneath his feet!

But now, in the flash of his rage, a dark place was illuminated. *Would* he be glad to leave Vienna? What of the child he would leave behind him in the Quellengasse? He knew now that his son had entangled his affections.

His desperate eyes again sought his wife. The fixed smile was still upon her lips.

A great bitterness flooded Henry – bitterness and dark bewilderment. The doll had finished her song. He could see Pepi down there on the stage clapping in mock applause.

He must get out of here! Out, to walk by himself and think. Real applause had broken in the auditorium at Fräulein Jiona's singing of the doll's music. Under cover of the noise he opened the door of the box, signed to Maximilian and went. Outside, rudderless and distracted, he fought himself back to some kind of composure, striding up and down the empty foyer.

When he reappeared in the box at the end of the act, Phœbe hoped, with every show of elegant concern, that there was nothing wrong with Henry.

III

December the eighth.

It was after half-past six. Pepi Klem sat in her corner of the chorus gazing into the mirror and trying to decide just where, on her cheek, she should place the dab of black paint, which from the auditorium would look like a beauty spot. At last she decided upon the top of her cheekbone, just a little beneath the corner of her right eye, took up her paint-stick, made the spot and sat back to examine the effect.

All about her in the large room was light, laughter, noise and comedy, half-dressed women. This was no hack, ageing chorus. The Director, Herr Jauner, had been determined to have everything and every-one of the best – soloists, chorus, orchestra. The posthumous masterpiece of Offenbach must be rendered with all the care and reverence due to it, and in accordance with the traditions of this, the most musical of cities. In February the dead composer's work had been acclaimed in Paris. Now in December it must be still more acclaimed in Vienna.

Several of the girls were clearing their throats, singing snatches. Pepi did the same, hoping that those nearby would note the fineness of her voice. But as nobody showed any interest, she stopped, gave her pert little face an additional dusting of rice-powder, and decided that she was enjoying herself.

She was grateful to her cousin, Lisa, for getting her this work. It had come very soon after the birth of her baby. But work with this management was a chance not to miss, and she needed money. If she made a some-what plump little guest in Spalanzani's house and Giuletta's palace, the chorus-master had been pleased with her voice, and she would soon regain the slimness of twenty-one. Besides, her mother helped with the child, and a neighbour, a good woman who had borne a child at much the same time as herself, had been glad, for a consideration, to undertake the nursing of it.

Last night, on the part of the dressing-table assigned to her, she had placed photographs of her father and mother. The other girls had photographs. She must give herself the importance of having photographs, too. Now, tonight, she remembered she had another. She took it from her bag and wedged it between the glass and the frame of the mirror. It was of herself, holding the baby – a thin little card, of which she had only one copy, done cheaply and inexpertly in the Favoriten. The baby was not very clear – he had not stayed quite still – but it wasn't bad of herself, she thought, as she looked at it now.

'Whose child is that?' the girl next to her was asking.

'My child.'

'How sweet!' The girl smiled. Experience had taught her not to ask too many questions.

But time was getting on. A call came for the ladies of the chorus to go down. Pepi stood up and gathered her loose dressing-wrap about her. As a Spirit of Good Cheer, she had only to stand behind the scenes and sing. When that was over, there was ample time to come back up here and finish dressing for the first of Hoffmann's Tales.

She found the large stage milling with people. Discipline in the Ring Theatre was not as strict as might be. This presentation, it was said, took more than two hundred, and most of them seemed to be here – men and women of the chorus, dancers, soloists, carpenters, scene-shifters, men in charge of the lighting.

She pushed her way through them to the front of the stage and the closed curtain. To Pepi, as to any other stage-struck girl, this great wall of cloth, which would presently rise and disappear out of sight, was the very essence of excitement, of romance.

Another girl was examining the audience through a peep-hole. Pepi touched her arm. 'Please, will you allow me for a moment? I want to find my mother and father.'

Yes! There they were, high up, right in front on the fourth gallery.

She had wanted them to come last night, but the first night demands of the more influential had made that impossible. Besides, today was a Roman Catholic holiday, and her mother and father had been able to join the newly formed queue just after four o'clock. Pepi herself had left the Quellengasse long after they had. She had waved to them pompously as she passed them outside just before six.

At the peep-hole she laughed affectionately at her blonde, untidy mother hanging over the brass rail, scanning the auditorium beneath her with the excitement of a young girl. Her father was sitting back in a typical attitude, running his hand through his fair mane, looking cross and impatient for the performance to begin.

Still at the peep-hole Pepi became aware of a hissing of gas. For a moment she did not bother to turn round. They were testing the lighting apparatus. They had done so last night.

But now there was an excited shout! She turned round.

By the new mechanism, the gas had been turned on, but the electric contacts had not lighted all the jets. Gas was streaming everywhere and rising to the hanging scenery above. All at once a darting flame set one of the side-pieces alight.

The mob on the stage turned and ran, Pepi with them. But because of her distance from the entrance, most of the people on the stage were before her. She could hear a girl screaming as she fell and was bruised by the others on the stone stair leading down from the stage to the street. She would wait for a moment and keep calm. The men would control the fire presently.

Suddenly she remembered she had foolishly left some money in her bag. She must take time to rush up to her dressing-room – it was only a step or two – seize her bag and bring it out to safety.

Now she found herself standing, panting,

before her mirror.

Two other girls were there – fetching their valuables, too, perhaps.

She took her bag and turned to go.

Suddenly the lights went out.

Down on the stage no one was at his post, and hysteria vied with folly. An excited scene-shifter drew the burning side-pieces up above the stage to where the other scenery was hanging, and worse – to where escaping gas kept collecting. The gas exploded; the scenery caught fire and began to fall down upon the stage. No one opened the cocks of the safety water-tank above. No one lowered the iron curtain. The cloth curtain was blown outwards, revealing the blazing stage to the waiting audience, who had, as yet, suspected nothing.

There was panic and a rush to escape. But the same hand that had turned off the gas in Pepi's dressing-room had turned it off on the stairs and in the passages. Only from the stage, which was supplied from a private gasometer on the roof, did gas continue to pour itself into the theatre, asphyxiating many more people than were burnt.

Folly piled itself still higher. Cloakroom attendants had the keys of emergency doors in their pockets. It was nobody's business to call the fire brigade. When the firemen came at last, they fought their way to the floor of the theatre, only to have their lamps extinguished by roaring draughts and their lungs choked by gas and dense smoke.

But folly was not yet finished. In spite of the choking smoke, the firemen called out to ask if anyone were still in the theatre. There was no reply. They came out to say that everyone was safe, and took to removing furniture from reception-rooms and records from the office.

Yet hardly any from the third and fourth galleries had been able to leave the theatre! The one or two who had fought their way to safety gave this terrible news! When the firemen returned at last to the help of the upper galleries, the narrow staircases were so much blocked with the crushed and the suffocated, that by the time these were removed, the galleries were collapsing into the inferno beneath.

The windows of the chorus-room were few and high. They were shuttered against the December weather. Neither light nor air could come to the three girls that way. There was black darkness – black darkness, an increasing smell of smoke and, above all, the stupefying, giddy smell of gas.

They called to each other, groping until their hands touched: then they clung together. Pepi could feel the others shuddering, sobbing with terror and coughing convulsively.

She must try to keep her head. 'We must

feel our way round the wall until we find the door,' she said, as firmly as her voice would let her.

They advanced until they touched a wall, then began to feel their way along it. They went slowly. The hands they felt with trembled.

But the sickening smell of gas, combined with the acrid smell of smoke, made Pepi's head spin. Now she needed all her resolution to keep upon her feet.

'Here's the door!' Her voice did not seem to belong to her. It came from far away. Unreal. She had felt like this once at the dentist's. Bells rang in her ears. She seemed to feel herself fling the door open.

No! That made it much worse!

This smoke and gas! But was it, after all, a real door? Or was she–? If only this smoke and gas–! And was she on her knees–? Or was she imagining that, too?

Her baby's face seemed to be suspended above her, expanding and contracting like a reflection on glassy water.

The Hayburn. But the Hayburn couldn't help her here!

Her mother. Her mother could help her. If only her mother, leaning up there on the rail of the gallery, would– Oh, this smoke! She must keep her eyes tight shut. And this coughing! So bad for her voice, too! How could they expect her to sing if–? Yes, her mother could–

But Pepi Klem no longer thought what her mother could do.

The little moth had flown into the flame.

IV

Phœbe had waited in the night once before – when, as a child of fourteen, a fierce instinct had held her until she could snatch to safety the little boy she loved. Reason had fallen away from her then. It had fallen away from her now. Once again she was nothing but an instinct; but this time an instinct blinded by hurt pride.

Bareheaded and dishevelled, she thrust her way through the surging crowd, pushing back and forth among them; dodging policemen, soldiers and firemen; jostled, shouted at, insulted – caring for none of them, in this red world of flame, smoke and embers.

What did she seek? An escape from her own jealous sufferings? Appeasement for the heart Henry had come so near to breaking?

But why was she seeking these things here?

Or was she standing, primitively, crudely paying unholy homage to the gods of this dreadful holocaust?

It was only when she found herself before the burning theatre that this strange madness came upon her. She had been waiting for Henry to return for his meal in their rooms in the Wieden. He was late, as he so often was these days. He had much to hand over, he said, before he returned to Scotland. But tonight he might be hanging back. The sight of the Klem girl on the stage last night must have increased his embarrassment.

Then the house-porter's wife had come up, fat and breathless, to tell Phœbe that the Ring Theatre was burning; that you could see the glow in the sky. Phœbe threw on her fur jacket, took up her gloves and went out to look.

Everything around lay ominously quiet. Silver snow and moonlight. Somewhere a clock struck half-past seven.

Yes. Just over there to the left of the Karlskirche there was a red glare in the sky. And was that a distant shouting? Phœbe made her way into the Wiedner Hauptstrasse to get a better view.

Here she found excited people streaming towards the Opernring. She followed with them. As she passed the Opera House she saw the audience in their finery leaving hurriedly, or standing on the steps distractedly seeking *Fiakers*. The performance had been stopped. As she cut behind the Opera and thence along the Herrengasse, all the sky in front of her glowed red and angry. Her heart beat in her throat. Now she was in the

Schottengasse. And now in the Schotten-ring among the mob before the theatre itself.

It was after eight. But she had taken no account of time or exertion. She stood, panting. The flaming theatre lit up the Schottenring as though it were broad day.

About her the agonised citizens of this emotional city were standing, weeping aloud, imploring one another to do something. Some of them, as was obvious from their holiday clothes, had been in the theatre – people in poorer circumstances, most of them, who had gone early to cheap seats. This young girl cried that she had left her mother behind. She had hoped to return with help. This man – a wife and two half-grown children. This woman – her lame husband. If the firemen would only run their ladders up to that window there – she was sure it was that window – her husband had said he would wait. Oh, why didn't they do it! The woman tried to tear her way through the crowd, fighting like a wild cat.

A burst of sparks shot upwards from the roof. A gust of wind caught them and blew them towards the crowd. Police and soldiers shouted at the people to stand back. They paid little heed, brushing hot cinders from their clothes. Flames blazed up now – blue gas-flames.

Phœbe moved again, struggling forward;

341

her Highland eyes wide open, gleaming and possessed.

They were suffering, these people around her. But she had suffered, too! Suffered when she lost her child! They were suffering and lamenting, for those who were suffering still more in that monstrous, burning trap.

She was plunged in an ocean of suffering. Tossed hither and thither in buffeting waves of suffering. It filled her with a sullen exaltation.

Another burst of sparks drove the crowd back for a moment. The licking fire roared and crackled. Again Phœbe thrust her way forward. What was that wild screaming. People at upper windows shrieking for help? They were suffering, too! She had suffered when she learned that Henry had been unfaithful to her; had touched, as she thought, the bottom of the pit. But when she had seen the Klem girl at the crown Prince's wedding celebrations–! No. It had been too much!

What was that man doing? Going to jump into the stretched canvas the soldiers were holding? Now there was a string of them, jumping one after the other, like sheep through a gap. Why couldn't the fools wait? They would be killed if they jumped down, one on top of the other! No wonder firemen were shouting at them to stop! That was right! Play the hose on them and stop them!

Was that woman crazy – out of her senses? Was she actually going to hurl her child down without waiting for the men to spread the cloth for it? Oh–! A groan had gone up from the crowd in front. Good thing she could not see! Even in this black exaltation she could not have borne it.

No, she, Phœbe, had not had *her* child. But if she had, she would never have pitched it from a window! She would have pitched herself first! And that child she had seen in the gardens? What of it?

But what–? Had the crazed mother thrown herself from the window after her child? But she was quite right. She wouldn't mind losing it now.

Phœbe did not know that she was shuddering; that her eyes were mad and staring.

These people should stop gesticulating and howling at the windows! It wouldn't do them any good! The firemen were getting people from the building as fast as they could. Those at the windows might still have a chance. Though how the heat didn't finish them off, she couldn't understand. Even out here in front it was hot!

But the howling at the windows was stopping. The white faces were disappearing – falling away – and in their place red, cruel squares of fire! The fire must be coming to the front now. Driven by the heat, policemen, soldiers, firemen, crowd were falling back.

Why didn't these people about her stop this senseless moaning? This senseless wringing of the hands? Queer to think she had been in there with Henry last night! What if they–? But she would have kept her head and done something. Or perhaps not. And her suffering would be finished and done with.

But she must move from here. The heat was unbearable.

Suddenly there was the sound of an explosion. An eruption of flames to the sky. Now a crash. Myriad sparks rose with them. A man shouted that the gasometer which fed the stage had exploded and fallen, taking the roof of the theatre with it. People stumbled back in terror. Phœbe with them.

V

Why didn't she leave all this? Why didn't she go home? Hadn't she had enough?

But now, for the first time, having reached the edge of the crowd again, she saw the Sanitary corps at work. Laying down the bodies they had brought out. Piling them on carts that would take their shocking loads to the General Hospital to await identification. Some of the bodies were burnt past recognition. Others – by far the most – untouched by the flames, were dead of gas-poisoning or suffocation from the smoke.

Why was she staring at them? What was she seeking? These horrid shapes were no concern of hers.

A young woman was sobbing beside her – searching among the dead as the soldiers set them down. Phœbe turned to look at her. She saw she was half-dressed; that her teeth were chattering with cold. But why was her colour so absurdly bright? Phœbe looked more closely. Her face was painted. Of course; she must be one of the singers.

'You'll get pneumonia,' Phœbe said sharply.

The girl continued to sob. Her brother and sister had been in the fourth gallery.

'You should go home. If they're safe, they're safe. And if not, you can't help by standing here getting your death of cold. Look. Take this and put it on. My dress is thick.' Phœbe took off her fur jacket and forced the girl to wear it.

The girl stopped sobbing. 'A foreigner?'

'Yes.' What could it possibly matter to the girl what she was?

Suddenly a new, quivering urgency was shaking Phœbe. 'You're one of the singers, aren't you?'

'In the chorus.'

'Are you all safe?'

'Most of us. But one or two–'

'Did you know Josephine Klem? – Pepi Klem?'

The girl looked up without at once replying. The paint upon her face did not conceal her strange expression. 'Did the gracious lady know Pepi Klem?'

'Is Pepi Klem safe, Fräulein?'

The girl looked away in distress. Why did this foreign woman speak so sharply. What did the tone of her voice mean? Why was her look so crazed?

'Tell me if you know anything of Pepi Klem.'

The girl raised a hand and pointed. 'They brought her out, just before the explosion. I was looking for my brother and sister. She's lying over there.'

Phœbe turned and ran. Now she knew why she had come! She would see the body of this woman before they carted it away. The body of this harlot who had taken Henry from her. She stumbled forward, her eyes staring, her lips parted.

Yes. Here was another cart. And here the bodies waiting to be loaded.

'Get out of the way, please! Haven't you been told already to keep back?'

Firemen, soldiers, men of the Sanitary Corps were working, perspiring, smoke-black and grim. And hardened, it would seem, to the awful bundles they must carry.

Phœbe stopped with a cry, as though some hand had struck her! Pepi Klem was lying at her feet!

She stepped backwards. Her eyes looked stupidly about her. The night spun round. The street – the crowd – the sparks – the roaring, burning building.

Were her senses slipping? Was she going to faint? What was happening?

No. She was still here – still in this world of terror. And the woman she detested was lying at her feet.

Detested?

She looked again at Pepi Klem. In the brilliant fire-light she saw that Pepi's eyes were closed as though in sleep, that Pepi, too, was painted. She had not been put down roughly; she lay easily – round-faced and artificial – pert and childish. A beauty spot was set high up on her cheek. Her thin wrap had fallen back, exposing her neck, circled by a ribbon of velvet. Her full bosom was pushed high by the lacing of her corsets.

Pepi Klem. Or a little rococo archduchess peacefully asleep among the laurels of Schönbrunn?

Phœbe stood over her, shaken and appalled. Appalled that she herself had had it in her to nurse so great a hatred against this silly, pretty child! And now Pepi Klem was dead! She could never trouble her any more!

Shame took hold of Phœbe – shame and a storm of weeping. This wilful girl who had so many times despised the tears of others stood now, heedless of the tragic rabble, crying out her heart, in abandonment and wild hysteria.

How long she stood thus, Phœbe did not know. But now a hand was laid upon her shoulder. 'This body must go to the General Hospital. You can identify it there.'

The men had gone with Pepi. Phœbe pushed herself free of the crowd, hoping to find some kind of cab to take her home. Why should she wait here any longer in this place of burning death?

Had she not found the release she had been seeking?

VI

A little later Phœbe jumped from a *Komfortable*.

No, Herr Hayburn was not at home, the house-porter told her. Yes, he had been to the fire, but he had come back some time ago and gone away again. He had asked where the gracious lady was, and left the key for her. She had run out, leaving it on her dressing-table. But wasn't the gracious lady very cold? Hadn't she gone out in her fur jacket?

Phœbe said she must get some money to pay the driver, and went upstairs. In the sitting-room she struck a match, lit the gas and looked about her. The evening meal had not been touched.

A shiver ran through her. Yes, she was cold, she supposed, and hungry. And certainly she was very tired.

But what must she do now? Where was Henry? She could not stay here, quiet and alone. The excitement of the night, the tumult in her senses, would not allow it, tiredness or no. She must find her husband. But where? If only her throbbing head would let her think! She could think of nothing but the raging fire and the face of Pepi Klem.

Pepi Klem. Now she knew.

Impatiently, Phœbe tore off a piece of dry bread and stuffed it into her mouth. She poured herself a glass of wine and took it with her to her bedroom to drink while she found warm clothes. In a few moments she was downstairs, placating the *Komfortable* driver, who was grumbling at being kept from his trade on such a profitable night.

But why was this foreign woman jumping into his *Komfortable* again? Was she going back to the fire?

'To the Quellengasse, please.'

'The Quellengasse in the Favoriten?' Why should he drag out to a suburb, when trade was so brisk in town? He shrugged his regrets. 'Impossible.'

'Double fare.'

The man hesitated, for a moment. Then he

shook his head. 'Not tonight. The gracious lady must see that my horse–'

'Treble fare.'

The man slammed the door and jumped up.

The familiar staircase in the Quellengasse was alight tonight, as was, indeed, every staircase in Vienna. Women with whom she had often passed the time of day were hanging, chattering and anxious, at the entrance. They ran forward.

'Is that the little Klem? Oh – the gracious lady!'

They fell back disappointed.

Phœbe jumped out. 'Can you tell me if Herr Hayburn is here?' They looked at each other doubtfully, then one of them, seeming to decide that on such a night nothing should be concealed, said, 'Yes.'

Phœbe paid the driver and turned back to them. 'Are the Herr and Frau Klem upstairs?'

They chattered round her like tragic magpies.

The gracious lady could not know, of course!

The Klems were in the theatre tonight!

To see Pepi!

They were going to the fourth gallery!

No one was saved from the fourth gallery, except one or two who jumped!

They had gone early, and would be

trapped near the front!

The fourth gallery had crashed some time after nine o'clock! Where were they, if they were safe? Frau Klem would certainly have come back to the child.

But Pepi? Why hadn't Pepi come? All the singers and stagehands had escaped, they had heard.

Phœbe looked at them blankly. She would not waste time giving the news now.

The Klems' door was opened by a woman with a child of her own in her arms. Again the quick look of hope, followed by disappointment.

'Where is Herr Hayburn?'

The woman, who knew Phœbe by sight, tried to look bewildered. But her distress allowed her to dissemble no better than the women downstairs.

'Please. Where is he?'

'In there.'

VII

He was sitting in a chair, his back to her, bending forward, as once before she had seen him bending forward in her brother David's room. This time he held a bundle in his arms.

She was afraid, for the child's sake, to startle him. She crossed the room and stood,

351

looking down upon them. Lame ducks.

He did not raise his head. He thought it was the woman she had just seen.

'Henry!'

He looked up quickly. But her voice held tones he had not heard for many months.

'Phœbe!'

'My love!' She went to him, pushed back his hair and kissed his brow.

Now she stood beside him, gripping his shoulder to steady herself. But she must tell him somehow.

'Henry, I saw the baby's mother tonight.'

He did not answer at once.

As she waited, she saw from a window that no one had bothered to shutter, how the sky, far away to the left, was alight with evil smouldering red. She felt him move uneasily.

'When? If she's safe, then why–'

'She isn't safe, Henry. The poor child won't see her baby any more.'

'Dead?'

'Dead.'

She took her hand from his shoulder and moved towards the window.

He looked up once again. 'But what am I to do? The child's grandmother must have been killed, too!'

She turned.

'Henry!' Her tone was accusing.

He looked away again, distraught and shiftless.

But Phœbe had dropped on her knees in front of him and was taking the child into her arms.

Chapter Twenty-One

On Saturday, December 24th, 1881, the family, being Scotch, held their Christmas dinners.

Mrs. Robert Dermott's, given in her house in Hamilton Drive, was truly astonishing. And the most astonishing thing about it was that the chief guests should be Sir Charles and Lady Ruanthorpe, who were, astonishingly, staying with her.

The news that this formidable couple had accepted Mrs. Dermott's invitation, and were coming to Glasgow, had shaken Bel a little. Would she, too, now be expected to invite them? Bel was far from unenterprising, but the thought of having the strong-minded baronet and his lady to stay at Grosvenor Terrace alarmed her. Their daughter, Margaret, had, at first, been bad enough. In the secret places of her heart, Bel found comfort in the thought that Sir Charles was old, delicate and might soon – although she dare not admit this hope even to herself – be dead. Besides, she was receiving him, along with the others, in Grosvenor Terrace tonight after dinner. Perhaps that could be counted as gesture enough.

Now, in the presence of her guests, Mrs. Dermott's ample hospitality, quite unlike Bel's, was in no way clouded by foolish fears or murderous hopes. Indeed, she regarded having induced her new friends, the Ruanthorpes, to leave Ayrshire for the Christmas weekend as a triumph of friendly persuasion.

She looked down her lavish dinner-table, very much as she was used to looking down her committee tables, beaming goodwill and practical, strong-minded encouragement; conveying somehow to her incongruous guests that she expected them all to enjoy themselves, get on with each other, and see life – for the time being at least – from the same angle as herself.

And the party *was* incongruous. In addition to Sir Charles and Lady Ruanthorpe, all the four Butters were there; David and Grace, of course; Mungo and Margaret; and, to make even numbers, Stephen Hayburn. But Mrs. Dermott's firm gentility was holding everything together splendidly.

Sophia's tongue, halted a little by the presence of the laird and his lady, and also by the fact that she was eating the dinner of her life, was really not too hard to keep in check. The Davids, the Mungos and Stephen

Hayburn could be depended upon to take their share of rational conversation. William Butter could be counted upon to say nothing whatever. That was why she had put him between his own daughter and Grace. And Wil and Margy were nice young things, whose bright, adolescent intelligences counselled good behaviour when occasion demanded.

Old Sir Charles upon her right hand and firmly under her eye, an eye which saw that he should lack in nothing – found himself doing very well. The dinner was good, his hostess had got hold of some quite reasonable wine, and really everything was very jolly. All that was lacking was a pretty woman to look at. Mrs. David on his other side wasn't bad; still, he had always found her a bit colourless. But they were driving across to Arthur Moorhouse's for an hour or so after dinner – somebody's sentimental idea that the whole family should be united tonight – and there he would see Mrs. Arthur herself, who was always damned handsome. And Phœbe Hayburn, he had heard, was just back from Vienna, in which city, unless she were more of a fool than he took her to be, she would have found a dressmaker with the wit effectively to underline her odd, but definite beauty.

'So there's to be quite a number at Arthur Moorhouse's tonight?' he said addressing no one in particular; attempting, a little consciously, perhaps, to be genial. Further down the table his daughter, Margaret, caught the tone of his voice. She knew it for the one her father used at servants'-hall and tenants' entertainments.

Grace answered him. 'Oh yes, Sir Charles. You'll see Phœbe and Henry just home from Vienna. And Bel and Arthur themselves, of course. And Mary McNairn and her two boys. Her twin girls will be in bed, I expect. A great family reunion, really. Mary didn't want to come. But Bel insisted. She couldn't bear the idea of Mary being left alone. So like Bel! She's the kindest person I know!'

Sir Charles grunted, not an ungenial grunt, then returned in silence to his turkey. He did not know about Mrs. Arthur's kindness, but he knew she could look deuced smart.

'Mamma.' Margy's fifteen-year-old modesty was addressing her mother further down the table.

'What is it, dear?'

'Can I see Aunt Phœbe's baby, tonight?'

'I don't know. You'll have to ask her.'

'I can at least go up and see him sleeping.' Margy gave herself up to an exquisite anticipation.

Craning her neck round an epergne, stuck with maidenhair fern and hothouse carnations from Aucheneame, Sophia caught her daughter's eye, smiled upon her with foolish indulgence and shook her head.

Margy had become, as only adolescent girlhood could, maniacal about this Austrian child. Her life was made up of the moments she was with him, and the barren stretches of time which must elapse until she should be with him once again.

No one else took up the theme of this orphan baby, whose parents had been burned in that dreadful theatre fire. Innocently, Margy had laid a constraint upon the tongues of these doting parents and grandparents – the constraint of primitive jealousy.

Babies of Moorhouse blood came into the world red and unattractive. Good looks might come later. But for many months they continued ugly and uncomfortably like young birds. At three months the Austrian foundling was perfect. He had none of this Northern lack of finish. In spite of early upheavals, in spite of change in home, nurse and diet, the new Robert Hayburn was thriving like a mushroom. He bore now no noticeable resemblance to his father. His small limbs were rounding out to a dimpled perfection, that caused those aunts of his adoption, who came to see him bathed, to force such rapture as common politeness demanded from throats that were become dry with envy. When he was a little older, there would be nothing left for him but to sprout dove's wings, shoulder a rope of roses, and help the *amorini* and the dolphins to draw the fluted barge-shell of the Venus Aphrodite across the painted waves.

As they put on their wraps to go across to Bel's, Sophia, released from the constraint of the dinner-table and Sir Charles's presence, expressed herself to Grace.

'Of course, in a way, I think Phœbe and Henry were awfully good, Grace dear, to adopt this little boy. Especially as he has lost both his parents in that dreadful fire. Do you know, I missed reading about it properly. Wasn't it annoying? My silly maid has used that morning's newspaper to crumb fish on, and the bit got soaked with egg! And then, of course, with Phœbe losing her own baby and everything– But, as William was just saying this morning, you never know what kind of wild blood, these adopted children have in their veins. It's a terrible risk! And foreign blood too! And I think, in a way, it was foolish of them to give him Henry's father's name. They should have kept his own, if they knew it. But, then, I dare say it was too diffi-cult to pronounce. Oh, Grace dear, don't think I'm being unsympathetic! He's a lovely wee thing! Margy's crazy about him! But I just hope he'll grow up to be a good and righteous man, and be a credit to us all!'

Grace hastened to say that she had no doubt the Hayburn foundling would grow up without flaw. But the jealousy that troubled Sophia had not left even Grace's gentle heart untouched. As she descended to the carriage she found herself seeking comfort in the fact that her own baby – disappointingly plain at almost a year old – had nothing but good, West of Scotland blood in his veins.

II

It was not a large gathering, by Grosvenor Terrace standards. Bel and Arthur, with Arthur the Second, who was now ten. Mary and her two sons. Phœbe, Henry and old Mrs. Barrowfield. But it had been homely and pleasant, and when the time came for tea to be set out and Mrs. Dermott and her party to arrive, there was no one who did not regret their coming a little. Bel and her guests felt they could have been very happy left to themselves.

But now here they were, filling the room with noise and fussing. Kissing, shaking hands, giving and receiving greetings. Admiring Bel's decorations, asking how each other did, welcoming Phœbe and Henry home. Insulting already overloaded stomachs with currant bun, and behaving in all things with a Christmas spirit.

Mrs. Barrowfield had found refuge in a

corner. She sat with Mary, unobtrusive and apart, drinking tea and looking on. She had no wish to be nearer the formidable Lady Ruanthorpe, who sat holding court by the fire. Still less did she want to be near Mrs. Dermott, whom, for reasons known only to herself, Mrs. Barrowfield detested. Yet, illogically, she was pleased with her own daughter, that she could move among these grand people with so much calm assurance. Tonight Bel's fairness profited from the simplicity of black satin.

Called now to Lady Ruanthorpe's side, Henry and Phœbe were crossing the floor. Mrs. Barrowfield watched them with affection. She felt a link with them. She was the only one here, or indeed anywhere, who knew their story. Henry looked tired and older. Tonight he seemed aloof; a little arrogant; as though he didn't care whether the Moorhouse clan liked him or not. Which, when she came to think, was probably true. But his maturity suited him. He would now, at last, develop, Mrs. Barrowfield hoped fondly, into that paragon of paragons, a successful businessman.

Phœbe was elegant in a dress of unrelieved white. She had bought it in the Kohlmarkt. She looked beautiful, the old woman thought; although there were signs of strain in her face. And a suggestion of that look she had once had as a child, after she had brought young Arthur from the slums. It seemed, almost, as though Phœbe were seeing things that others could not see.

But Mrs. Barrowfield was pleased with her. She had, after all, refused to quit Henry, and thus, once more, their ship was safe in open water.

For a moment Bel's crowded drawing-room swam before Bel's mother's eyes.

Now she heard Phœbe's voice. 'Bel, Lady Ruanthorpe wants me to bring down Robert. Do you think I ought?'

Margy Butter was running forward. 'Oh, Aunt Phœbe, let me come, too!'

Bel gave her consent.

III

The child had been inspected and admired. And now, for a moment, they were isolated, all three of them, under the gaselier in Bel's drawing-room. Phœbe, Henry and the child in Phœbe's arms.

The new Robert Hayburn had been sleepy, but now he opened his eyes wide and looked about him; as though he, in his turn, were inspecting this strange race of Northerners, with their bland self-satisfaction, their benign importance-seeking, their innocent, provincial shrewdness.

The ghost of a gay little smile passed

across the baby's face – the mere suggestion of a smile; but it was enough to cause Sir Charles to put his hands behind his back, bend forward, scrutinise the infant, and remark: 'If you ask me, you won't have your sorrows to seek with that young man!'

And then, his eyes catching the bright lights above him, the child stretched up one of the small, rosy starfish that served him for hands, and, being a son of Vienna, seemed to be trying to reach their glitter.

Sophia came forward. 'Oh, Phœbe dear! I was just saying to Grace tonight, how *good* we all think it is of you and Henry to take this wee man! And we all think–'

With one of those quick gestures that bewildered even her nearest and most beloved, Phœbe turned, the child still in her arms, and left the room.

On the landing, behind the closed door, she halted. What was it that had stung her? Did she sense Sophia's insincerity? Had she become intolerant of family judgments?

Good?

Was it because they persisted in measuring goodness and badness with their own smug yardstick? Phœbe now had learnt that there were things that would not let themselves be gauged by cautious Moorhouse standards.

As for this child of Henry's: she had followed her instinct. That was all. And the family could think what they liked about it!

Find out what they liked!

But after a time the flame died down within her. Had she been unjust? Or was she still a little overwrought? She stood now, remembering things that would not let her be.

A young woman lying dead at her feet, lit by the light of a savage fire. The tolling of bells, and a great city bowed in mourning. A Mass said in a suburban chapel for the souls of a departed family, a family that was kind and simple, according to its own, too easy ways. The Mass attended by two young strangers, who knelt in humility, knowing nothing of its ritual.

The same strangers standing by a graveside – the graveside of her child's mother.

These memories were near, and as yet she could hardly bear them. Later on, perhaps, their outlines would be softened.

But why was she standing here? She looked at the child in her arms. His eyes again were heavy.

Phœbe mounted the stairs, laid him in his cot and turned the gas low. For a time she lingered. Presently she bent forward to assure herself that he was settling to sleep. Then, leaving the room quietly, she went back to join the others in Bel's drawing-room downstairs.

The publishers hope that this book has given you enjoyable reading. Large Print Books are especially designed to be as easy to see and hold as possible. If you wish a complete list of our books please ask at your local library or write directly to:

Magna Large Print Books
Magna House, Long Preston,
Skipton, North Yorkshire.
BD23 4ND

This Large Print Book, for people
who cannot read normal print,
is published under the auspices of

THE ULVERSCROFT FOUNDATION